CHOSEN

A Paranormal, Sci-Fi, Dystopian Novel

Book One
of the Chosen Series

By A. BERNETTE

CHOSEN by A. Bernette

Paperback: ISBN-13: 978-0692743607, ISBN-10: 069274360X
Amazon.com: ASIN - B01H7TAQXW

DEDICATION

In loving appreciation and gratitude to KC, CE, KC, RW.

Thank you.

ACKNOWLEDGEMENTS

I would like to acknowledge my mother who has always been my cheerleader. I would like to thank my husband for his confidence, support, and beta reading through this process. A special thanks to C.E. and K.C.

I would like to acknowledge and thank every person who has read my works and who will read them.

Thank you to those of you who supported me as beta readers and error finders.

I would also like to give a special thanks to the editor who swept in like an angel and helped give this book wings – M

Common Terms Used in Series

ARC: Antarctic Research Center
EAT: Eastern Allegiance Time
Lubles: Form of currency
SEP Agents/Officers: Security, Enforcement, and Protection Agents or Officers
PDU: Personal Disposal Units
ROC Room: Research, Observation, and Control Room
RePM or RePM Division: Relocation and Population Management Division
Southern Allegiance: South America
Northern Allegiance: North America
Northern Liberty: Europe
Southern Liberty: Africa
Eastern Way: Asia and India
New South City: Atlanta, Georgia

CHAPTER ONE
Crossroads

Location: Unnamed
Time: Unmeasured

"WE ARE AT a crossroads. If something drastic doesn't happen and happen soon, we will not be able to continue," Kean said moving slowly across the space in front of Yin, San, and Cho.

"What we need to win this battle has yet to be retrieved and the Chosen don't seem completely up to the task. Everything is happening to ensure that things are right when we finally get there. If they don't get to the end, all we have done up until now is a waste," he warned his three Earth Council members.

They were absent sensation in the empty space of nothingness. No heat, no cold, and no discomfort. It simply was, without justification or explanation. There was no depth or parameters by which to perceive any measure of space or time. This is where they existed, in their refuge from what was once their home, but was no more.

If they wanted to have a life outside of the void, it would have to be Earth or they would be forced to wait, possibly thousands of years longer. Yin, San, and Cho sat uncomfortably in this void, under the studious gaze of Master Councilman Kean who was scrupulously estimating every possibility.

Kean had been selected to oversee the midlife projects including those on planet XM-471, also known as Earth. Before they'd come into the space that has no name he already knew what they would communicate to him and he'd forbidden them to speak it into the vibratory force.

His almond shaped amber eyes with golden flecks reminded his team of a lion, strong and fierce when needed. Dark grey hair crowned his head where much darker hair had finally given way, but he still had the vigor of his youth. He considered each member of his team one by one, gathering their thoughts as if picking them out of a muddled soup.

Their thoughts, ideas, and solutions on the problem they faced were all jumbled, floating about in one large kettle set on high heat. It was the problem they'd been trying to solve since they had initially been sent to XM-471.

That was before the humans even began truly measuring time themselves or even had the concept of it. It was when Kean and his kind had lost something critical to remaining viable on planet XM-471. He now second guessed the Council's decision to do the program as they had done it.

Success required such a specific combination available only from their people, the humans, and something that had only been possible in the last human generation. But that was a decision already made, and now the four of them, along with the rest of their surviving people, had to live with it.

"I am unimpressed with the prognosis, with what has happened to date, and even with the prospects for the plan as it stands. Time and again I've seen the senseless slaughter of innocents. The metallic taste of blood is still etched in my memory from where it seeped into grassy battlefields, forever staining the land like a curse. I have watched the burning carcasses tied on stakes. Those charred bodies that once contained the screams that wracked their dying bodies," Kean shook his head, but the memories never left. What he'd seen was unforgettable and it was the reason he was nearly out of hope for XM-471.

But he continued, for the benefit of those looking to him to lead them to their final home and for the three before him who hadn't been involved in the mission as long as he had. "I've heard the sound of body clapping against body as they rolled down dirt embankments into shallow, unmarked, mass graves. We all know too well how the scent of rotting flesh could fill the air for miles." He let the image hang on the emptiness of the space, allowing their silence fill the void.

If he let himself think about it he could still smell the scent of death around him. He'd witnessed the sorrow and mourning of those left behind, searching for a token or a memento among the dead and decaying bodies before covering them or burning them. In those moments he'd wept with them.

Kean spoke again, this time without the drama of reminding them of the wretchedness he'd seen in humanity.

"They've had chances to change, chances to prove they could be good stewards of the planet and nurture it, together. But over and over I've had to conclude that this species is too immature and stubborn. It could be many more millennia before they will be mature enough to participate as an ally or hold a place as a member of the Master Council of the Unseens," Kean said with a shake of his head.

"They are making progress – at least now," Cho spoke up hesitantly.

"Unfortunately, we don't have millennia. We cannot continue living in the void, borrowing temporary homes of our allies as our population dwindles to nothing. Now - it has to be now," Kean said before his thoughts passed beyond that moment.

Looking in on XM-471 now, with its beautiful greens and blues, it floated like a beautiful giant ball - brilliant and bright. It once held so much promise. He wished he was wrong but he was sure he had been right in his assessment. They needed the current plan to be successful. Otherwise, if the human species was successful in making their home planet uninhabitable, the subject XM-471 would be no more.

Earth, as it was called, would be classified as no longer viable as a possible home until the planet healed and allowed new life to begin again. Until then, it would be among the ranks of the other young fading stars that were stuck in an endless rotation, waiting to sustain life.

Kean reflected on his rocky tenure and the number of other young systems he'd studied and tried valiantly to guide, only to see them lay waste to themselves. None had made it even as far as Earth.

When Earth made a major shift towards industrialization nearly two hundred fifty years before, Yin had been assigned to the Earth Council. She was the youngest and newest member of the Council. She still held onto the hope that the Chosen eight and their Keepers, a group they'd been designing and cultivating for generations, could find success where others had failed. Yin believed that with the eight and the aid of the Loyalists, Earth could be saved from itself.

Yin looked out the side of her eye at her fellow Council members, San and Cho. They were all reluctant to look directly into the golden eyes of Master Councilman Kean. They could feel his disappointment crawl along their nearly non-existent skin and then slip through underneath, where it would linger.

Failure would be devastating, leaving them and their fellow beings caught in the void while a search continued for a new home. They were the last chance for Earth, the final Council group that would be assigned to the planet. If they could not save Earth, the planet would be abandoned as unsalvageable and the allies would move on.

CHAPTER TWO
Serum

University of Southern Allegiance in Santoria, Southern Allegiance
Year 2149

DR. CLAUDIA LIMA prepared the last dose for the final pair of the Chosen. Within the month she would head to Antarctica to administer the specially formulated serum during the thirty-ninth week of pregnancy, as she'd done for the others. It had taken her nearly twenty years of research to come up with a combination that met the Council's requirements after the failed initial experiment.

The Chosen had to have the vibrational energy of the continents infused into their DNA along with the proper levels of testosterone to accompany the initially approved serum, that she'd adapted later for their needs.

At the time, the request had sent her reeling, at a loss for how to do what was asked. However, as years passed and she progressed in her research she'd found the solution, as she had eventually done with the unique use of quartz. The Council had given her the idea but she still had to make it a reality.

Years of research and trial and error had led her to identify a key crystal that naturally formed on each continent. She'd broken them down to their chemical elements and integrated them into the serum. The children would forever hold the vibration of their birth continent and together, the vibrations of the earth.

It was a breakthrough that had taken longer than the Council had hoped but the solution came quickly once the science and technology became available. Despite having found the answer, the work and administration of the serum hadn't been without its setbacks. Dr. Lima was concerned with the shortcomings in the current program.

Ren had been the first, and after his injection and reaction, she'd been forced to revisit the delicate balance of all the chemicals and crystals used. He didn't have the benefit of the quartz crystal in his serum like the others. Alexis was her second charge and she'd only added a small amount of the quartz and green chrysoprase.

Looking back she probably could have added more but she didn't want to have a repeat of the violent reaction experienced during Ren's birth. Not even Kim knew how close she'd come to dying during the seizure she'd had after he was born.

She'd given one last push and the serum that flowed through both of them caused the seizure that rendered her unconscious and unresponsive while Ren fought more than any newborn should have to. When Kim woke a few minutes later, Ren was still crying but she had no memory of anything after the last push. She took him to nurse, never knowing how close she'd come to death.

Marco's had been uneventful and his mother had agreed to it for health purposes. She'd served during the wave of the flu that was going around at the time and saw the lives it claimed. If a shot during pregnancy could protect her son, she would do it. Dr. Lima smiled at the memory of Teresa before her thoughts turned to the one mother who hadn't made it. She quickly pushed that memory aside. The child had survived and was still thriving, healthier than most who came through the line of Descendants.

There were still the last two children and she needed to remain focused on the present. She shook her head and filled the vials with serum, placing them delicately into her small silver box lined with soft thick foam. She placed the box inside of a black portfolio size briefcase, which she then placed into her medical bag.

She'd done what the Council had asked and as she was committed to do as a Loyalist. They all had to do their part for the mission to be a success. She'd given her entire career to designing the formula and identifying the parents who would bear the children chosen to heal the world of its corruption and abuse. After this, she would be nearly done and could perhaps find more time for her real job at the university.

Her private lab was funded by an unnamed group of other Loyalists and held the serums administered to the prior six infants. The first ones were already toddlers. After the twins were born, her last job connected to the administration would be to clear the data from the systems so the children could not be found or identified later. As she wrote her daily report, she let herself play with the idea of being done with this phase of her life.

The research she'd begun as a doctoral student of twenty-five had taken her to nearly forty-five years old and brought her in contact with amazing people, including the three Keepers under her guidance. Sometimes, she thought it funny that she'd been chosen to be their guide even though she wasn't that much older than any of them.

She considered her daydream of being done despite knowing the Council wanted more from her after this. She was still only in her forties. She still had plenty of time to live.

CHAPTER THREE
Birth

Antarctic Research Center
Year 2149

ZURA WHIPPED HER chair around, almost causing herself to fall out. "*What the hell?!*" A few of the individual twists escaped the black hair she'd neatly tucked into a bun that morning. What she'd seen was a flash of bright gold, like a small burst of brilliant sunlight, coming from behind. It had caught her eye, startling her. The room seemed brighter now as the walls pushed out ever so slightly from whatever energetic force she'd just seen and felt.

She couldn't imagine what the source of the disturbance might be. Something else was in there despite the fact that she had been alone in the research and observation center until that moment. Johan was leading the engineers and not many people wanted to risk interrupting her these days, unless they had a good reason.

Zura scanned the room briefly before her eyes were drawn to the spot. She could see it – the thing that initially appeared as a flash of gold. Steadying herself to stand up from her seat and she placed her weight on her swollen feet and ankles. Upon closer inspection, it was actually a glowing, pulsing ball of golden light. She'd heard of these strange energetic anomalies before, these orbs, but had never seen one herself. They came in the form of a sphere - pure energy. The only thing that they could carry was pure energy and vibration. This light carried sound, a message for her.

She waddled quickly across the floor, not wanting it to disappear. As she reached for the light the orb sensed Zura's energy approaching, and began to vibrate, releasing the message.

"The two are one, daughter and son. Protect and nurture them in their gifts and abilities. They are special and unique, but do not fear, their purpose will be clear. You are all here to help save the world."

As the words ended, the ball of light immediately vanished into thin air, not a trace of its glow remaining. Zura stretched her fingers out to touch where it had been. She could feel intense energy in her fingertips and warmth went through her hands. The vibration and heat continued to burrow into her hands and up her arms, sending shivers through her body.

The intensity of the pulsations grew stronger and centered around her abdomen before giving her a tingling sensation and disappearing. Then the remaining energy in the air was gone, evaporating as the light had. Zura reached down and felt her stomach. She stood there as time stood still, cradling her womb and the twins she carried inside of her. Fear and shock continued to resonate through her body as she grappled with trying to understand what she'd seen, heard, and felt.

The beeping sound from her watch brought Zura back from her daze. She stopped the beeping and swayed towards her chair. It was Johan but he would have to wait. She plopped back into her seat with a thud and tried to quickly jot down what she'd just heard. It had all happened so fast, but she'd gotten the idea. After scribbling down the message she checked to see if the recording system had picked up the strange occurrence.

At the same time, she wondered what it meant, whether to get Johan and tell him, and if he would believe her even if she did. Silently she watched the playback. The sound had gone out completely but she could still see the flash of energy.

What she'd seen as a bright golden ball showed up like a bright orb on the screen, looking like something was wrong with the video quality, but that was all. It wasn't anything identifiable or provable. It wouldn't hold up to Johan's scientific inquiry. She would have to keep it to herself.

Two Months Later

"AAAAAAAAAGGGGGHHHHHH!" AN EAR piercing scream escaped Zura's parched chapped lips. Sweat glistened on her forehead and tiny beads slowly followed the path to her neck. Curled tendrils formed across along her hairline from the moisture. After hours of labor her tears had all but run out and now she was just trying to hold on through the next painful contraction.

She stared up at the white blocked ceiling, looking for her focus spot. The tiny greyish colored blemish in the otherwise perfectly smooth white ceiling. Bright bulbs meant to aid the staff's sight gave Zura the feeling of an uncomfortable interrogation room.

As she searched for the elusive spot, she faded between being with everyone else in the room and zoning out. The only other thought running through her head repetitively was possibly killing Johan for his part in her present condition. He stood in the corner silently, rocking as if in shock, unsure of what to do and safely out of her reach.

She could smack him right now for shutting down while she endured the last of humanity's unjustifiable burdens. Zura felt like she might have been hallucinating as she looked over at him once again and he was still standing there. She hadn't just knocked him down along with that stupid look on his face like she'd imagined. The trick on her mind pissed her off even more.

As she screamed in the sanitized room attended by the staff doctor, a small private white aircraft slowly entered the strangely quiet hangar and stopped, hovering over the yellow plus sign painted on the grey cement floor. Mave, with her dark hair pulled into a high pony-tail, waited in the hangar for the craft, just inside of the small room to the side. She peered out of the tinted window as the door to the aircraft slowly lowered, dropping stairs to the floor.

When the stairs hit the floor, Dr. Claudia Lima jumped out carrying a bulky black case with a red medical sign. Mave had barely let them off the craft before yelling at them to hurry. She and the two doctors following her were all running behind Mave who'd come out of the office when Dr. Lima appeared in the doorway of the plane. She'd been waiting for more than thirty minutes.

She wasn't her usual patient self. Patience wasn't a luxury any of them could afford at that moment.

It was happening and if they didn't get there fast, there would be death on their hands. What they were about to do couldn't be proven to work successfully, not in humans at least. The official results had always been mixed, causing skepticism and abandonment.

What they were using wasn't part of any official program. It had never been officially tested or sanctioned and in fact, outside of a small circle, didn't exist. Still it was the only chance they had to give the improved treatment to the two children struggling to be born early.

Mave sprinted ahead of the group, her boots hitting the smooth concrete floor of the hangar, light and quick. Dr. Lima and the others struggled to keep up, their bags jostling beside them. They were soon at the entrance to the building where everything seemed to stand still, waiting for a miracle. Mave looked back to make sure she had everyone.

"Hurry! Only take what you need for the surgery!" she yelled behind her as she pressed her wrist against the scanner to open the door. The four were through, dropping their bags on the inside. They didn't need any extra weight slowing them down as they made it to the medical center. The door closed behind them trapping the freezing cold air in the hangar.

Mave rushed through a confusing labyrinth of intricate honeycomb style tunnels. Different pastel colors of each honeycomb section blurred together as they went from one honeycomb to the next through the connecting hallways. Dr. Lima and her team, lighter without their luggage, followed close as Mave barked at them to keep up. Sprinting ahead, Mave hoped it wasn't too late. As they got closer, another sharp scream pierced the tunnel they were in.

The stainless steel door with a single rectangular window slammed against the wall as Mave rushed into the birthing room. Soft meditative music meant to inspire a Zen-like state played uselessly through the speaker system. Zura lay on the water supported bed, her head thrown back into the plush down pillow. Her screams and cries sprayed like knives slicing through the intended peacefulness of the room, muting the music.

Zura could taste the beads of sweat that formed above her lip and seeped into the corners of her mouth. She'd only read of births like this happening before modern medicine. It was because of her stubbornness that she was living through what must have been the last original torture of womanhood.

"God damnit! What the hell took you so long? I am dying here. I am literally… dying… here!" Zura's eyes narrowed and then went wide again as she went through another contraction. After it passed, she had just enough time to spew venom at Mave and the other three as they slinked into the room behind her.

"Well, we are here now. So shut up and let us help," Mave said as she checked Zura's vitals on the screen and then felt Zura's full lumpy abdomen. The babies were restless. She listened for the heartbeats of the twins inside of her. They were struggling just as hard as Zura to be freed from the one world they'd known but they couldn't come out just yet.

"Claudia, your team needs to prep the serum and get it ready to inject. I'll pull up the view of the twins. Zura, just lay there as best as you can. Dr. Lima brought a local anesthetic with her. It'll help with some of the pain, but you'll still have to fight through it. I'm sorry," Mave said, squeezing Zura's hand.

Zura gripping the silicone wrapped support bars on either side of her, stared at the hand Mave held and the sky blue silicone beneath her hand. She then shot a look over at Johan and caught a glimpse of his terrified blue eyes looking back at her.

The team was working as fast as they could. What had felt like a spacious birthing room now felt cramped as the half dozen people moved around the equipment and bed. Mave gave Zura a small red pill and then sprayed Zura's stomach with the anesthetic. Tiny pinpricks stung all over her skin as it soaked in. Fifteen seconds later it turned to a dull sensation covering an eight inch diameter area on her abdomen.

"It takes three minutes for the combination to work. Then we can administer the serum," Dr. Lima said trying to reassure an anxious Zura.

She grabbed Zura's hand briefly before continuing to prep the double shot of serum. She'd done the procedure several times before, but never with twins.

Mave looked across the room at Johan. He was still in the same spot that Zura swore she'd kicked his behind in, twice. Leaning against the wall in the corner motionless but conscious, as if he'd been turned into petrified wood. His eyes were blank and his mouth partly open as he took in what felt like chaos. Zura couldn't see straight enough to notice him now.

"Get over here Johan. Hold your wife's hand and stop standing in the corner like you are a used up box of tissues. You aren't the one about to push out two frickin' babies, are you!?" Johan snapped out of his trance and rushed over to Zura's bedside. He took one of her hands and held it. At that moment her grip tightened around his, squeezing hard as she let out another blood curdling scream.

They were hoping for a miracle with this serum. It was officially designed for premature infants and it was meant to serve as an intrauterine immune system booster and metabolizer. The addition to the basic serum was controversial and some had disagreed that it was necessary or that it should even be used, given the potential risks.

However, Zura and Johan, being stuck in Antarctica, asked for it even with the risks. The benefits would give their twins the best chance for health and survival. That and Zura's faith that what Mave told her was going to be true had convinced them. The additional modification was added to the serum after it passed inspection.

The only people who knew about it were Zura, Johan, Mave and Dr. Claudia Lima. It was a special chemical that processed through the blood, attached to the bodies' natural antibodies, and was over time fully integrated into their genetic code. Over time it would restrict the host's DNA like a mutation. Whenever it learned how to fight an attacker it would alter the genetics for future use. It was an internal weapon against illness, disease, and degeneration.

The more recent testing on mice yielded very promising results after several modifications to levels of testosterone and the bonding process to the DNA. This was the last of the doses to be given. After the twins were born, the eight Chosen children would have received the serum. This time, unlike the generation before, it had to work.

The long-term effects couldn't be known yet and with only six other humans injected there wasn't much empirical evidence. What they had seen from the six who'd received it had been mostly positive, so far. It had only been a couple of years, but that was all the data they had to go on. It would have to be enough.

Zura looked at Mave, her face wrenched in pain and fear. She was second guessing their decision. She wrestled with whether they were doing the right thing, if it would even work, or if she was killing her babies with it. She began sobbing, with no tears and unable to speak, the pain of the contractions had stolen her voice. She'd put them in this situation and she had to ensure their survival in any way she could.

"We don't have much time. The serum only works when the babies are in the womb and have at least a few minutes for the serum to work through their system," Dr. Lima said.

"We are cutting this really close. These babies are already in position to come out." Mave looked at her watch and waited as a few more seconds went by.

The ideal situation would have been to wait until the babies were fully developed at thirty-nine weeks, but for Zura and the twins, the ideal wasn't an option. The twins were coming six weeks early. They could only hope that there would at least be those few minutes after the serum was injected for it to process in their bodies before they left the dark cramped safety of Zura's womb.

"Okay. Go now!" Mave yelled. It was finally time to begin administering the serum.

Dr. Lima and her team watched the infants on the monitor. They would inject the one closest to coming out with the serum first. Just as they were about to place the needle, they paused as Zura let out another scream. A few more of those and they would be out of time.

The cries of new life sounded through the halls as tears streamed down Zura and Johan's cheeks. The sound of Mave's long sigh was eclipsed by the twins. Dr. Lima smiled as she wiped her brow. They'd done it.

The screams given from Stella's strong lungs overtook the light whimpering of her brother Stephen. She reached for him instinctively as his eyes searched for her. He struggled with the overwhelming stress, lights, and being dragged by Stella into the strange place.

Both lying against Zura's chest, Stella found his hand and wrapped hers around it.

CHAPTER FOUR
Undercurrents

Rift Valley in Southern
Year: 2165

"DO YOU FEEL that?" Delia shouted out to her mother, Marie. She jumped up from where she sat against the white headboard of her extra-long twin bed. The headboard banged lightly against the wall, partly from her and partly from the tremor. She looked at her off-white walls. *Was that hairline crack there before?* The royal blue and white bedspread lay rumpled underneath her.

For the past hour, she'd been putting information into a small tablet she used to enter data at least once a month for the past six months. Still carrying it, she strode into the living room unable to ignore the persistent shaking.

"Of course I do. It's almost over," Marie said coming into the living room. Delia stood there looking out the window at the buildings surrounding theirs and thinking of all the people living around them. The old buildings made from stone and cement were now painted brilliant shades of purples, blues, greens, yellows, and clay reds dotted the city.

Direct sunlight rarely graced their unit because of the buildings that surrounded them that partially blocked it from view. Her neighborhood was filled with tall residences, apartments, and condos, all overflowing with people. The purple high-rise across the street from her had a finger wide crack that ran along the side. Although the crack had begun when the building settled naturally, she'd noticed it continue to spread over the ten plus years they'd lived there.

Her building was newer, with windows that stretched from her waist all the way to the aqua blue coffered ceilings, framed in eggshell white. From those windows near the top of the skyscraper, she had an enviable view of the city's aging but colorful skyline.

She was high enough to see the rooftops of most of the buildings around them. The hills in the distance were even visible from where she stood. She saw the same hills that hid the site of one of the larger pump holes, built years before, despite the overwhelming citizen protests that in the end hadn't mattered.

She loved the Rift Valley with the mountains and hills that greeted the rising sun and the colors that had made her home so attractive to millions of people. If she got up early she could go to the hills and look east to catch the sunrise. Dotted with trees, grass, and dirt they were filled with the beautiful green she loved. It was a luxury in the city to have the trees and grass anywhere in view.

"They're getting more frequent," Delia said to her mother who sat down on the orange sofa and turned on the news.

"I don't remember it being like this other years, at least not as long as we've lived here," Marie said.

"I was thinking the same thing," Delia said as she sat down next to Marie.

"Every time I look at the news coming in, they keep talking about these tremors and small quakes. They keep saying it's just the season," said Marie.

She scanned the channels until she found a woman in the media blue uniform and an artificial tan talking about the tremors before turning it over to the local newsperson. Marie waited expectantly to hear what was being reported for the city this time.

Marie was struggling to remain patient with all that was going on. Delia looked over at her as she pulled at her chin. She could feel her mother's worry and could tell her mother was thinking hard about something.

"I thought last year things were worse than normal, but this is even more than last year." Delia was trying to separate her mother's discomfort from her own.

"No, it's not normal. It's gotten worse and it's not getting better," Marie said looking out the window and back to the screen.

The local newswoman from the northern part of Southern Liberty appeared and started reporting on the tremors happening as being normal. A perfect white smile greeted the billion plus viewers before she began.

With practiced confidence she said, "Citizens of Southern Liberty, please know that there's nothing to worry about. According to some of our best scientists, this type of seemingly increased seismic activity happens every so often. Sometimes it takes a few generations, sometimes less, but don't be concerned about the small tremors. We have it on authority from those in the highest branches of government that all is well."

Her big brown eyes and long dark lashes batted at the camera as she smiled again. She turned to her cohost who then moved on to other news about productivity being down because of a forced shut down of some of the active emissions pumps, including one in Southern Liberty. Delia shook her head as the reporter spoke about how negatively it was already impacting the economy and the long-term impact on employment if it continued.

Marie snapped the news off, shaking her head back and forth in disbelief. She began pacing around the spacious kitchen and living room before stopping in the kitchen - she needed some tea. She pressed a button on the refrigerator before taking out her favorite ceramic mug with drawings of green creeping vines on it.

She rolled the cup in her palms waiting for the water to heat up. The lemon ginseng tea would help calm her for now. As Marie poured the hot water into her cup she felt the vibrations rolling beneath her feet again, just as Delia felt them under hers.

"I don't think we are going to get better answers, at least not from where we're supposed to look," said Marie as her eyes followed the small circles forming at the top of her tea as the tremor went through her to the water.

"What do you mean?" Delia asked, now curious about what her mother might not be telling her.

"You know exactly what I mean Delia. We hear what they are saying but what we really need to hear is what they aren't saying."

"Do you think we are going to have an earthquake like the ones they've had on the coasts of Southern Allegiance?" Delia asked with deep concern.

"I don't know, Delia. I keep thinking that the one we heard about may just be one of many others we haven't heard about. I just don't have a good feeling about what we are being told or about any of the information reported. It makes me wonder how many others haven't made the main news. What I do know is that we keep getting more tremors like the ones we are getting now and more of these small quakes. Eventually, it will lead to something bigger. It's just a matter of time. I just hope we aren't here when it happens," Marie said.

"Where would we go?" Delia wondered aloud. "We don't have family anywhere else."

"That's a good question," Marie said, letting her eyes fall back to the tea cup where the water had now settled. "I don't want you to worry about that right now." She placed the tea pod inside the mug avoiding Delia's questioning eyes.

Delia could feel her mother's discomfort. She wanted to ask the questions that sat at the tip of her tongue, pressing against the back of her lips, longing to be spoken but thought better of it. Something else was already weighing on her. Delia never wanted to be an extra burden or cause her more stress.

"How do we find out what's really going on?" Delia asked.

The moment the question came out another tremor, much stronger than the others shook their apartment. The cup of tea Marie had now placed on the table to steep shook, spilling over the sides, and Delia could hear something fall off the shelf somewhere at the back of their unit.

"Are we supposed to just sit here and wait for this to get worse?" Delia stood up and asked her mom. "I'm sorry Mom. I didn't mean it like that. They are evacuating us but still feeding us these lies? They keep reporting it like it's all separate and isolated. It's not just here. It's happening in other places too. Everywhere that's along a ridge or one of those tectonic plates is getting more of these. They may only register as between twos and fours on their Richter scale but still someone should be talking about it. No one is! I think they're full of bull," Delia said, her voice rising.

"Watch your tone, Delia," Marie said out of habit.

Delia shook her head. She wouldn't argue with her mom, but she couldn't be sorry about how she felt.

"I know it doesn't make much sense but I still need you to try and respect that we are under the World Consensus. We will know the things we need to know, the things that are important, when the time is right. In the meantime, there may be other things you can figure out. I can't answer it for you. At the same time, I don't want you stirring anything up or asking the wrong people questions. You understand that Delia? You can't afford to be considered disloyal," Marie said, grabbing her arms to make sure she understood.

"Okay. I got it - as always," Delia said backing away, trying not to show any more of her resentment at the whole situation.

"Delia, one more thing. Whatever happens, no matter what happens, keep asking questions. Keep searching for the truth. It is there. It's not always popular to go after it, but look around you and you will find out the truth."

Delia grabbed the door handle. "It seems pretty pointless asking questions, Mom, when no one is willing to give you an answer."

"I love you Delia," Marie called out as Delia pulled the door open.

She walked out the door, tempted to slam it but instead closing it softly, her tablet still in her hand.

***

LYN HEARD THE familiar 'knock knock knock' on the door and knew immediately who it was. Delia stood just outside the sterile looking white door marked with the silver numbers 32-11 in script. She leaned against the silvery metal frame with a look of frustration written all over her face, waiting for Lyn.

"Hey Lyn, what do you think about all those tremors we just had?" Delia asked as soon as she saw Lyn's face around the edge of the cracked door. Delia sauntered in and sat down on the simple wood-framed sofa.

"I don't know. It's more than we had back home," Lyn said, moving away from the door.

"They seem to be coming a lot. I nearly fell on that last one. Of course, I was standing on one leg," Ms. C chimed in with a shrug.

Ms. C and Lyn had been in the living room practicing their Tai Chi. Their large unit was inspired by their other home in the Eastern Way. What had been traditional art from the Orient lay in Feng Shui inspired groupings and patterns around the few small tables.

A large bust of a man who'd been called Buddha sat in the corner of the living room near a plant that had clearly been well cultivated and loved. Ms. C had brought it with them from the Eastern Way. She'd gotten bold and even painted a large yin yang symbol on the wall opposite the door. She called it her inspirational centerpiece.

Ms. C and Lyn had just relocated from the Eastern Way Region a year earlier. Lyn's father was an executive at one of the larger corporations manufacturing recyclable clothing and had been relocated to expand the business in the Southern Liberty Region. He divided his time between the Eastern Way and Southern Liberty. He was back in their home region now and Lyn and Ms. C would be joining him there for the evacuation.

Lyn spoke softly to Delia, "It wasn't that bad though right? I mean you get these all the time here, right?" Lyn asked looking for reassurance.

"No, we didn't used to. You haven't been here long, but this is not normal," Delia paused. "And here we go again. It's like a slow but continuous ripple," she said.

"It is happening more often, and not just here," Ms. C said to Delia and Lyn.

"We're going out for a walk, Mom," Lyn said before walking towards the door.

"See you later, Ms. C," Delia said following Lyn out the door.

CHAPTER FIVE
Rumblings

DELIA AND LYN walked down the brightly lit hall towards the expanse of windows without speaking. Everything was white - from the doors to the marble lined walls and floors. Delia pressed the down button to call an elevator and as they waited there was still silence.

Floor by floor they rode down, the only sound being that of the elevator chiming as they reached each level. Surrounded by mirrored images of themselves in the twelve by twelve alternating marble and framed mirrors, Lyn could see Delia's curiosity. They exited into the lobby that buzzed with activity as people came and went, or simply sat in the white molded chairs and sofas that intersected at unusual angles on white and grey striped rugs.

The coffee bar was still busy with a line that wrapped around one side of the lobby. Every table had either white roses or white lilies in clear glass vases. The floral scent coming off the elevator always made Delia smile, and reminded Lyn of their garden back in the Eastern Way.

Once outside, Lyn and Delia walked down the sidewalk along the back of their building, and headed towards the park. Lyn was trying to keep up today with Delia's much longer strides, but didn't want to start a conversation about why Delia was in such a hurry, lest Delia return the question with a question. Their friendship was as good as it was because they both understood the need to give each other space and not push too far, both having things they'd rather leave unsaid.

It was comfortable for Lyn to walk with a friend without talking and yet still enjoy her company. Both of them being only children because they were first born girls in the family made the bond even stronger. The institution of the rule of only one child if the first born was a girl was made as a way to manage population growth.

The rationale that a female can only bear so many children and fewer males in the population would mean fewer possible partners to procreate. The law had only passed twenty years prior and after two years of lawsuits that failed due the World Consensus's support of the law, it went into effect

Although there was nothing that could be proven scientifically, many argued that nature fought back, and in the years after, there was an unusually high percentage of first born males, restoring balance. Additional lawsuits were brought forth in the years that followed, and a decade after the law was passed, the World Consensus ended enforcement.

It was never removed from the legal records, leaving the door open to restore it if they ever deemed it necessary. Delia and Lyn had been born during the years the law was enforced and by the time the law had been put on indefinite hold, most parents of female children had already gone through their fertility restriction treatments.

***

THE PARK WAS just a few blocks away and it was one of the few places with green grass and real trees. There were hand-carved benches from salvaged wood, playgrounds for the younger kids, and a massive swing set everyone could use.

However, it wasn't Delia's intention to go to the park, not just yet.

As they walked along the side of the building, the Security Enforcement and Protection Agents, whom everyone called SEP Agents, followed them briefly with their eyes. They recognized the girls from their regular walks in the neighborhood.

"I want to check something out, Lyn," Delia said once they got around the corner and out of hearing range of the agents.

"What is it?"

"There is a spot I have been watching for the past six months and I want to show it to you. If you are up for it," said Delia, hoping Lyn would agree to come.

"Is it about the tremors and quakes?" Lyn asked.

"Yeah."

"Alright. Let's go and check it out," Lyn said with a smile.

They walked towards the neighborhood park, passing several families with young kids and couples. A young man had drawn an audience around him as he performed magic tricks to the oohs and ahs of the crowd. His black top hat and cape were his magician's adornment, and both had seen better days. The top hat had frayed from his fingers grabbing the rim so often. It also doubled as a tip jar which he passed around after every act, storing the lubles in a secret compartment.

An older man seeming to take a nap sat on a bench near the edge of the park - an apple in one hand around which his grip would tighten every time it was about to fall to the ground.

Lyn traced the path of a green balloon that floated towards the clouds as a little girl pointed at it and cried. Delia and Lyn continued walking, choosing a side street that backed up to a small man-made hill, which was a former dump site long since covered over with layers of dirt and grass.

The hill had a well-worn path in the dirt, beaten by the treads of those who used it as a shortcut to other parts of the city. Lyn and Delia followed the narrow path with low creeping roots, dried and dead. They could easily lose their footing if they didn't follow the narrow strip that had been worn over time. They climbed up to the top of the hill and back over, moving carefully as they leaned with the hill to keep from falling and sliding.

Once down the other side, Delia strode purposefully over to a round piece of metal. It was at least three and a half feet wide and flat, with orange rust around the two handles that were soldered to the top. On Delia's first trip, it was the rust that told her it had been there a while. Delia squatted beside the large cover, grabbed the handle on one side, and pushed against it. The large cover slowly slid out of the way, exposing what looked like a cement tube that quickly disappeared into the darkness of the earth.

"What is this?" Lyn asked.

"It's something I found one day last fall when I was out running. I'd been going up and down the hill, doing a few reps and when I stopped to rest up there on the top, I saw the metal cover and was curious, so I came down. This is what I found," said Delia, happy to finally show it to someone.

Lyn tapped the top of the metal circle with her foot and pulled it back, suddenly uncomfortable with the sensation. "Are you sure we should be over here Delia?"

"No, but we're here now." Delia ran her hand over the surface of the covering she'd handled several times before. "I am not one hundred percent sure, but my guess is that it's one of the emissions pump holes. Obviously someone made it and now it's not being used, and hasn't been for a while."

Around the circle was evidence that a structure of some sort had once stood nearby, but had been demolished. Loose stone and concrete were still scattered about, now partially covered by dirt, weeds, and grass.

The large factory in the area that made regional uniform emblems had closed a few years back, the business having been consolidated with other larger factories making emblems closer to the western coast. The emissions pump was no longer needed and the pipes that ran underground from the factory had been sealed and abandoned. The hole, however, had only been covered.

"Maybe it was abandoned because it was dangerous," Lyn said, stepping back another foot, but not able to get rid of the odd feeling.

"That might be true, but it is also interesting. Something real is going on and I think this hole is a clue. I checked it out the day I found it and noticed that when I came back after a few tremors the cracks in the cement looked worse. I couldn't be certain though, so when I came back the next time I brought something to measure them. I've been measuring them ever since. I have proof those cracks are getting bigger and I'm measuring again today," Delia said with a serious look in her face. Her mom and dad would probably tear into her if they knew what she was doing, but she had to find out.

Lyn stood near the gaping hole while Delia got down on her knees then her stomach. She leaned against the side to measure the size of the cracks along the walls in the hole. As she lay against the ground, a light rumbling started again. Lyn's eyes opened wide. She didn't know what was going on. Her body was tingling as the rumbling was happening. The rumbling in the ground ended and then the tingling in her body did too.

"That was strange," Lyn said, half to herself, half to Delia.

"Unfortunately, that's pretty normal. We are getting those rumblings all the time. What's strange is the smell that came out this hole when the rumbling was happening. It was horrible. Ugh," she said shaking her head, "and still is. The closest thing I can think of is the smell of rotten eggs and sewage. Bad combination. I've never smelled anything like it." Delia fanned her nose as she leaned back away from the source of the accosting odor. After a few moments she leaned back in, looked at the markings and entered them into her small tablet.

"Not that. I mean that too, but my body was tingling while it was rumbling. Probably nothing. Just strange."

"Or it's something," Delia said pausing to look at Lyn. "Maybe you are just…sensitive…"

Lyn shrugged, ignoring the question. There was something Lyn wasn't saying but Delia wasn't in the mood to question more than she already had. So far, she hadn't gotten any good answers from anyone today. Everyone seemed to only have half answers and those answers didn't feel right to her.

"Let me cover this back up and we can get out of here." Delia crouched down to a squat again and began pulling the metal plate back over the hole.

The earth shook again, this time much stronger. Lyn fell onto Delia who landed on the metal plate that wasn't quite covering the hole, banging her elbow on the edge. She let out a yelp before quickly closing her mouth to stop the gagging odor from entering and reaching her tongue.

Delia's upper body went into the hole and Lyn struggled to get up as the ground continued to shake. Delia was stuck between the edge of the hole and the plate now.

"Help me out of here before my nose burns off!" Delia yelled out to Lyn.

Lyn grabbed the handle on the edge of the metal plate and tried to pull it back. She wondered how Delia had made it look so easy. Squatting down like Delia had, she tried pulling again, this time getting it to move just a few inches. It was just barely enough for Delia to get her hand up for leverage.

"Thanks," Delia said with a push to the cover, effortlessly sealing the hole again. "Let's go."

"What do you think it means? With the cracks getting bigger and that horrible smell coming out?" Lyn asked Delia once they'd gotten back over the hill and were trekking back towards the park.

"Nothing good. I can't prove it but those cracks seem to get bigger with the tremors or quakes. And that smell only came out like that when the ground was rumbling. I doubt that is a coincidence," she said, her eyes narrowing in thought.

Delia and Lyn approached the park which the last tremor had shaken up as well. Now the benches, swings, and playground were nearly empty. The magician was gone and the kids too. Delia supposed those tremors must've jostled everyone out of their false sense of comfort and back into action. It was another reminder that they were evacuating and needed to get ready.

The nonchalant attitude towards the tremors and earthquakes characteristic of nearly everyone she saw or talked to surprised her. It was as if they'd suspended reality to continue believing the lie that this was normal and just a precaution. *How could they be so blind?*, Delia wondered. They'd managed to turn off their common sense to feel safe and maintain their false sense of security.

Delia and Lyn walked again in silence until they were in the middle of the park. The SEP Agents walked along the outer walls, scanning the center occasionally but not leaving their assigned beats to come in.

"My dad used to work for a small private company, as an environmental scientist, before it was bought by one of the UniCorps's companies," Delia shared with Lyn as soon as they were out of the range of the agents. "When they were bought out they were asked to do things that he wasn't comfortable with."

"Did he use to work with the pump holes?" Lyn asked curiously.

"He never told me what he was working on and still won't talk much about it, but I know that whenever he hears about these emissions pumps and the holes like what we just saw he gets mad. I mean cursing under his breath, storming out of the room mad. After about a year working under the new owners he quit and took a regular job where he couldn't be at risk of giving away secrets or being told he was possibly committing treason. He's retired now but I can't ask him about it. He flat out refuses to talk about any of this with me. Says it's better that way," Delia said in a hushed voice, checking the surrounding agents.

The SEP Agents' suits were so enhanced that she was never certain how much the agents might hear or if the park might have microphones planted around it.

Delia and Lyn stood up to leave the eerily empty park. Lyn's body was still tingling even though there was no shaking or tremor that anyone else seemed to feel.

CHAPTER SIX
Pressure

Capital City, Northern Liberty Region

REPRESENTATIVE GREGOR MAGIRO slammed the tablet down on his desk. He looked at the screen thankful he hadn't cracked another one. The small tablet had taken the brunt of his passion after skimming over the latest report from the emissions pumping field program while his assistant stood there waiting. His assistant was spared any further deluge.

"Leave."

His assistant turned and practically ran out of the room, just before Magiro was on his heels, slamming the door. It was becoming redundant. Each quarter, the reports and updates held the same news and it was never good news. He always read every report, every quarter, and eventually his electronic versions found their way into the deleted file.

This was his project and he would be damned if he watched it fail. He'd committed the past twenty years of his life to this one thing. As a businessman and politician, he had too much riding on it and couldn't let it fail. The reports told him it was failing though he didn't want it to be true. He'd drug his feet along with everyone else supporting a system that was good enough.

Gregor tapped his watch until he had Harold Fumar's contact information. Harold Fumar had been his contractor over the ground pumps for nearly a decade. The bastards were messing up his legacy. Harold Fumar's projection appeared in his room and Magiro immediately began talking.

"Harold, what the hell is this report? Is there a reason we can't monitor and catch these leaks sooner? Why the hell do I have to deal with another emissions pumping error? You are making me look bad Harold and I don't like to look bad. Fix it and fast!"

"If we can't make sure these pumps are secure we are going to have to deal with the public and you know UniCorps doesn't like that. Stocks will crap out and when stocks crap out that is bad for all of us Harold. You got that?! All of us. Yes, Harold, that means you too. I need an update ASAP of how you are going to fix this, Harold. That's all." He hung up while Harold still stood there without even opening his mouth.

The light on Magiro's watch blinked. It was Harold calling back after Magiro had ended the call so abruptly. Magiro's looked at the time before taking Harold's call. His next meeting, which he dreaded even more, was happening soon.

"Magiro, I think we got disconnected," Harold said smartly. "Look, I just need to make sure we are all on the same page. I'm getting two different messages. One from you and your team at the World Consensus, and one from UniCorps. I don't want to get in the middle of anything, but before you call yelling at me, maybe you both should get your priorities straight so you are both saying the same thing. That's all," Harold said curtly before ending the call the same way Magiro did.

Magiro pounded his desk and then thought of calling Dr. Zura Bello at the Antarctic Research Center. He changed his mind, realizing she wouldn't be able to make him feel any calmer about what was going on. In fact, she might send his blood pressure up even more. He'd wait for her report that would come at the end of their Summer. He hoped it wouldn't be like the others.

Magiro was frustrated. The promises he'd made and reputation he'd built as a younger representative of the World Consensus were at risk. His frustration at everything had grown over the years but he would not be made a fool.

A knock at the door brought him back from his thoughts as he picked up the tablet with the report again and sat it down at the oval conference table in his office. He put it in front of his seat, closest to the window.

"Come in," Magiro spoke up, sounding more confident than he actually felt at that moment.

The door opened with a bang, nearly hitting the wall behind it and a man whose head grazed the top of the door frame while his shoulders touched either side walked in. Behind him were five others, a mix of his contacts from the Science Division of World Consensus and the Science Division of UniCorps. The fifth person was a man from the Environmental and Ecological Preservation and Protection Agency (EEPP).

They were all usually pretty friendly or cordial at the least, having all at one time or another been employed by partner organizations of UniCorps. Today, there was already tension in the air. The large brash man who'd filled the doorway was now sitting down, right in Magiro's seat, at the far end of the glass oval table, nearest the window. He pushed the tablet in front of him to the side to make room for his own.

There was no mistake; he planned to be in charge of this meeting, even though Gregor Magiro had called it. Magiro calmly sat down next to The Stache. Mirkal Dempstead had been nicknamed 'The Stache' when he was much younger because of his thick bushy mustache, something very noticeable on an already very noticeable man. The Stache started to speak before the others even had a chance to sit.

"We cannot continue like this. If our numbers don't change, we are all going to be out of a job. Our stockholders, the people out there, the people I report to, the people you all report to, are demanding something be done to increase profits. We are bleeding from all the exploratory projects we are doing and all of the environmental requirements. If we don't start cutting expenses, people employed at our partner organizations and by the World Consensus are going to be out of work. All this environmental hullabaloo isn't going to amount to a hill of beans if no one can afford to eat, clothe themselves, or pay their rent."

"We are only in this position because no one ever wanted to sacrifice their precious lubles so that people would even have a planet that food could be grown on, where materials could be grown to make clothes, and where you could even live so paying your rent would even matter. You and your cronies' greed, as far back as the World Consensus has existed and even further back, is why we still haven't dug ourselves out of the environmental mess of the twentieth and twenty-first century. So why don't you and your ridiculous Stache and the rest of your spineless, mindless, suck the life out of the world zombies jump back into the holes you dug, cuz clearly that's where you came from!" Magiro blinked his eyes.

In his head Magiro had given The Stache a withering look and shot all this back at him. In reality, when it came to taking on UniCorps he had long ago learned that silence was key to political and economic survival and that some might think him spineless too, when it came to them.

"What do you propose we do?" Magiro asked instead of giving his tirade.

"Well to start with, our partner corporations haven't been able to produce at their target levels. They have been forced to withhold production even in the face of consumer demand. While this helps our short term prices because of supply and demand, we could be earning a great deal more in general and also give the people lower prices if we could just produce more. We have had a dozen pump holes for years and we've since doubled that and things are going fine. Why can't we operate all of them at full capacity? Heck, why can't we operate all of them? We've got some decommissioned just because of a little leak or gas coming back out. It happens but the pumps have been doing their job for almost twenty years, right Gregor?" The Stache looked at Gregor, awaiting his confirmation.

"Well, that's something we need to talk about," said Magiro sheepishly. He looked around the table hoping for support from the other representatives in the room, but was only met with silence.

"What do you mean? Never mind. The point is, nothing is going 'that' wrong and we have great minds already working on a long term solution, so why hold back our production? Manufacturing cannot stop. Besides, the current holes aren't even at capacity. Even if they were, we can just do what we did several years back and add a few more holes."

"Just add more holes?" Magiro asked skeptically.

"Sure. We have some of our partner corporations willing to personally support the funding of pump holes so they can grow their businesses. More holes would spread out the risk of any single pump hole. How about that? Yeah, how about that?" The Stache nodded his head and smiled triumphantly.

Magiro glanced over at Representative Litana Silver, his strongest ally when it came to this. She was silent as she listened to The Stache's argument. They were trying to do it again. They'd convinced the people and the Representatives that more pump holes were good for everyone and even the environment.

A temporary solution to deal with man-made pollutants had turned into a permanent one for many of the corporations and elected officials. They'd bought into the story, the same one The Stache repeated, in some variation, ad nauseam. *Everything was okay and there weren't very many problems.*

They'd managed to instill enough fear over changing to a long-term system that no resources had been committed to make a long-term system happen. Anyone working in those pump sites, and the town around them were also opposed to any ideas that might take away their jobs.

They had now convinced them that spreading the emissions and pollutants into more holes would prevent some areas having heavier use than others, thus making the risk and benefits of the program fairer for all people in the six producing regions. They promised that people could get more affordable products and businesses could make more money and hire more people.

Unfortunately, not much of that really happened. Except, of course, the businesses producing more and people buying more but the prices for what people paid barely budged more than a fraction of a luble. The corporations made out like bandits and Magiro had been forced to justify everything to the World Consensus and the constituents he represented.

"We should wait to see what the next quarterly report from the Antarctic Research Center says. We just got the last one in from our science division here this week and there were things in it that give me a great deal of concern. We are having trouble with leaks and seepage. They are small so they wouldn't necessarily be seen by someone monitoring at a high level but for the people who are actually working at these sites, they are seeing them and they are being reported more now than they were even just a few years ago. It's something we need to talk about." Magiro commanded.

"Haha Gregor! You worry about things you don't need to worry about. They told us years ago, a few leaks and a little seeping would be a normal thing to see. You remember, right? And they said as long as it is caught early and contained, it wouldn't do damage. You remember that too, now don't you Gregor? I was there. I listened." The Stache said smugly, smoothing his thick dark mustache.

Ignorant, thoughtless jerk, Magiro couldn't help but think. Mirkal Dempstead was one of those people that UniCorps paid to promote their interest, and it seemed there wasn't any maximum costs. Magiro wondered if he had a conscience hidden somewhere deep deep deep down inside. With his sheer size it could hide pretty deep down.

"Perhaps we should wait until the report to talk about what our options are for moving forward," Representative Silver, who sat opposite Magiro, finally spoke. Like him, Representative Silver was an elected representative and they would have to answer to millions of people, no matter what choice they made. Through many years and past mistakes, they'd both learned the hard way that it was better to wait and be right, than to rush into wrong. Silver didn't plan to have to justify another money driven move to her constituents like she and Magiro had done many times before. Not if a matter of weeks could yield better and more complete information.

"You two are acting like a pair of wussies! Ya' scared your little people are gonna get upset and not vote for you again? Well, how the hell do you think they'll feel when my people have to fire them because they can't make their bottom line? You wanna know how mad your people'll be then? Well, I can tell you one thing's for sure, they won't be blaming me!"

The Stache paused and picked up his tablet. "You call us back here when you've put together the rest of your sorry excuse for tanking the economy. The environment is going to be here. It'll work itself out. However, your job may not be." The Stache pushed his chair forcibly back and it smashed into the wall under the window. He smoothed his mustache again and marched out the door.

***

SILVER LEANED AGAINST the back of a chair and crossed her arms. She knew all too well how to play the politicians game, after giving thirty years to it, but when it came down to working, she was all business – and direct. These traits didn't endear her to many of her fellow representatives but it was something Gregor Magiro had learned to respect over the years. It was also something that got her respect from her constituents. They kept reelecting her, despite the money and votes that UniCorps' partner corporations and political funding pots would constantly throw up against her.

"Gregor, we need to talk," Silver said looking at the few who lingered as if waiting for something else.

"You all are excused. We'll give it another go after we get the report from the ARC in May." Magiro dismissed the others from his office.

They would be off for the coming two weeks as part of the more engaged schedule implemented by the World Consensus. It allowed for a four week on and two week off schedule with special adjustments made for major holidays.

Since going year round they had found themselves with more time to prepare meaningful legislation and actually review it. He'd been a part of the group that had pushed for the year round schedule when he was just a second year Representative. He, however, had selfishly chosen not to vote for the term limits on his position. This was his career and he wasn't going to self-sabotage it. That would be stupid.

Once the room was emptied and left to Magiro and Silver, they sat back down. Magiro pulled the report back up on his tablet and Silver pulled it up on her device. He always kept a paper copy until he was ready to recycle it. That was buried somewhere in a drawer at his desk. Magiro didn't trust that the information wouldn't disappear or change somehow with no record of what had really been there. It had happened before with a crucial part of the ARC program and was never recovered.

"Did you see this, Gregor?" Silver asked pointing to her projection of her device.

"Yes, I have Silver. It's not good. I'm afraid all of this may blow up in our faces if we don't do something. The one thing we cannot do is drill more pump holes," Magiro stated emphatically.

"I know. Still, the question isn't what can't we do. I want to understand what we CAN do? There is always a solution. Magiro, even though The Stache says people are working hard on a solution, I guarantee that if they really were, we'd have seen something by now. The Stache and UniCorps are lying. Point blank. We are going to be stuck holding the muddy stick trying to pull our way out of the muck, when everyone else has gone home to lie in their piles of money. I will not be the patsy, Gregor. You hear me? I will not. I have plans and this is not part of them." She was staring Magiro straight in the eyes.

"Silver, they aren't the only ones who can work on the solution. We need to be committing money to that side of the work too. Right now we have a lot of money tied up in monitoring, evaluation, the outer space discovery and exploration, ARC, and the pump holes themselves. The people won't want to put more money into this to solve a problem they don't even realize is a problem. BUT we can't tell them it IS a problem cuz then they'll all freak out. It's like the other thing. We know they are there but people will freak out, so we can't say anything." Magiro said waving his hand over his head and Silver nodded knowingly.

You know, when we ran for these offices decades ago we were young, naive. We foolishly thought that we could, just as one Representative, actually turn the course of a mammoth ship. We made promises to our constituents that things would get better and that we would continue to serve their interests. I personally promised to be honest and transparent and have done my best to keep those promises. Magiro, I don't want my life to be made into a lie. I don't think I could live with that. The only thing I have is what I leave behind. That is my legacy. How do I do what they are asking without erasing everything I have put into this career, every sacrifice made? You understand don't you, Gregor?" Silver asked as she began to walk back and forth in front of the window.

Gregor Magiro did understand. It was all he had thought about since The Stache visited him before the World Memorial Holiday. "Yes, Silver. I understand. I don't have the answer for how you're feeling right this minute since I am asking myself the same questions," he admitted.

Silver nodded, "Neither of us has the answer to that question. In the meantime, we need to get people working on a solution without having it funded by the World Consensus or UniCorps or scaring the people. Is there a super-rich uncle you've never told me about?" Silver teased.

"Not exactly, but I do have an idea. I know a retired scientist with a conscience. Are you willing to trust me a little?" Magiro asked.

CHAPTER SEVEN
Guests

STELLA JUMPED UP and down on the twin sized bed that lay to the side of the double window. She was busy losing herself while her roommate Alexis played music on her guitar. The sound of Alexis's strings floated through the air, carried by ribbons of color that surrounded Stella. Alexis couldn't see the color show, it was for Stella. With each jump off the bed that had seen enough college use, Stella tried to turn her body to get a different view of the campus outside their window.

Stella's parents signed her up for the extra science camp to help her make-up credits so she wouldn't have to retake her science class. That meant she was supposed to be studying and preparing for the end of camp presentations. Despite posing the best argument she could craft as to why she shouldn't have to go, she'd lost.

Unlike Stella, Alexis was getting extra college credit with the one week camp but neither could focus after the long day. Alexis had been the most normal person she'd come across there and on top of that she seemed to have it all. She was smart, drop dead gorgeous with raven hair and her eyes reminded Stella of the Antarctic Ocean when they first arrived each year.

Alexis had the boys on the campus drooling after her. She was confident on top of that. Stella didn't think she had an insecure cell in her body and wished she had just a little of the confidence that seemed as natural as breathing to Alexis. She was from Australia, another region that didn't get a new name and was now mostly dedicated to science and research.

Alexis had gotten into University a year early and was studying human sciences and technology, but that might as well have been a new language to Stella. It was the one area they realized they had very little common ground.

Even with that difference, Alexis was fun to hang with and could get them just about anything they wanted around campus. She had a way about her that people couldn't resist. Most people at least. Dr. Lima seemed immune to Alexis's charms but anyone else they'd come across so far was fair game.

Before her guilt stopped her, Stella had even thought of having Alexis try to get her something special from the campus gift shop that she'd seen the first day they'd gotten there. She would ask her mom for some extra money when she talked to Stephen. She'd been saving for something special and was rationing her lubles.

She and Stephen were on a short Spring break that was kept at the same time as most of the world during the first week of Spring, near the end of March. It was usually a couple of months before the Antarctic region became too cold and they left for home. That is, unless you never planned on leaving the artificial warmth of the ARC. Rather than doing a fun camp for art or music she was stuck in science camp, also known as school. She tried to comfort herself by reasoning that being there didn't mean she couldn't still have fun.

When camp was over Alexis would go back home to Australia where they weren't frozen in ice and she'd see real people who weren't buried in work, and even go to real school some days. She managed to make her time in Southern Allegiance fill two needs. Her father lived there with his new wife and he'd already come for her a couple nights and brought her back later in the evening. When camp ended and Stella went to Antarctica, Alexis would spend the weekend with her dad.

Stella could only imagine what it would be like to go to school all the time with other people. For her she only got the few weeks between leaving the ARC and the end of June and the months of August to November. Those were the months when school was in session and Antarctica was still in the dead of winter. The rest of the time would be spent on the ARC, learning virtually and through online classes or self-study.

She'd be heading home in less than two months and that alone made her smile. At least she would get to see other people for that last month or so at school and for her birthday party. It was better than spending it alone with Stephen.

As Stella jumped and tried to do kicks in the air, she noticed a growing crowd gathering outside in the square. She bounced slower trying to figure out what was happening. From where their room was, she couldn't see what was going on or hear anything.

She jumped off her bed. "Come on Alexis. Something's going on down there. Let's check it out."

Alexis stood up, looked out the window, and smiled. "Maybe it's a party. Let's go."

As they came out the door of the dormitory building they could hear the voice of Camp Director Dr. Lima. She was lecturing the group about something but they didn't know what. Confused, the girls slowly joined the crowd trying to get a better look and to hear what Dr. Lima was upset about this time.

Alexis, stood on her toes, and then came back down. "Nothing to see here really. Just some boys fighting. But that…now that is interesting."

Alexis pointed at a small group of men and women standing to the side, near a building, looking oddly stiff and out of place. They were staying in the shadows but backed away and out of sight as soon as they noticed Alexis looking at them.

"I wonder what that was about," Alexis said trying to see them better.

"Who knows? Probably nothing. Just seeing who the trouble makers are and adding to their files," said Stella.

"There isn't anything left to see here. You all need to go back to whatever it is you should be doing," Dr. Lima said, dismissing the crowd. As the crowd parted, Alexis began walking towards the building where the three had entered and disappeared.

Dr. Lima came up behind her. "Alexis. Alexis Murray-Cruz, right?" Alexis stopped and turned around with a smile. "Yes, and you are Camp Director Dr. Lima, right? Nice to meet you in person."

Dr. Lima was unimpressed. "Do you know why I stopped you?" she asked sternly.

"No, we were just heading to the pump," Alexis said convincingly.

"Yes, I'm sure. I certainly hope you, and that is, the two of you, have been studying and working on your projects. On Friday, you have your final presentation Alexis. And you have your demonstration of knowledge Stella. I will be there. I expect a great deal from you, Stella, being the daughter of renowned scientists." They stood waiting for her to say something else. "Good luck ladies. That's all." She walked off towards a group of kids who were standing by the doors where the woman and two men had vanished.

She shooed them away and waited by the door until they were gone before walking along the side of the building and out of sight.

"Now THAT was weird," Stella said, her eyebrows furrowing. Director Lima had intentionally stalled them so they wouldn't find the three who'd been standing by the doorway. Stella knew those three people were somehow important.

"Alexis, I'm curious. What do you think about a little snack? I don't have much but it should be enough for something small," Stella asked Alexis with a smile that pulled up just one side of her lips.

Alexis smiled back at the idea of investigating the strange three. "Yeah, the café is this way, right? I mean I still get confused on this big campus."

Stella and Alexis looked around to make sure Director Lima wasn't coming back from wherever she'd set off to. Then, they began walking towards the building where the three had escaped their view and snuck around to the corner of the building where the door the three had disappeared into beckoned them.

They tried to look inside the glass. The lights were off and it was too dark to see in with the sun already setting. Alexis tried the door and it opened. She turned to look at Stella, as if to say, "it must be okay, the door was open." Neither was sure where they were but both girls knew they couldn't stop now. Their curiosity pulled them in.

As they began walking along the wall, the light switched on. They could hear footsteps and several voices, including Dr. Lima's. Stunned, they hurried back out the door and across the campus courtyard to the pump; an old water pump that had been used during the water crisis of the late twenty-first century. It was a historic feature of the campus and a favorite hangout for the students.

The pump was connected to a system of caverns used to move water from underground sources. Once pumped it required being heated to boiling before drinking or cooking, but it served its purpose for nearly fifty years after what seemed like a double hit on the water. The first hit was a deadly bacteria that contaminated the water supply.

Before people realized the danger and could kill the bacteria, it had affected more than ten percent of the population at that time. Most who died already suffered from a weakened immune system. How the water became contaminated was never clear but it took scientists months to find a way to fight it and even longer to find a cure. By that time over a billion people had died. Every inhabited place was impacted. Anyone on the water system knew someone who'd become ill or died.

The low rainfall during that period meant the reservoir levels fell dangerously low and had to eventually be supplemented by the pump system. They had to dig deep to bring up the water that was left and at the same time planted over two million trees there and other forests were replanted as well. Even with that great effort, the area still couldn't compare to what they'd seen in photos from before the crisis. The pump was a reminder of the lesson society had learned, but it hadn't stopped society from figuring out other ways to destroy the planet.

Stella shook her head as she passed and thought about the work that kept her parents, Mave, Rupert, and now her brother so busy trying to, again, fix an issue destroying the planet. She wondered whether the old pumps still worked. Stella dropped back and walked slower, letting Alexis go ahead.

She stopped and picked up a pebble and dropped it in, listening to it rattle its way through the pipes until it stopped. She then took off after Alexis who stood talking with some other classmates at the end of the courtyard.

"Did you all see the woman and the two men standing near the building that, for some odd reason, is off limits to us?" Alexis said in a hushed voice as Stella walked up. "They were there when Director Lima was giving her little speech."

No one had noticed anything, having managed to tune out while Director Lima had been talking. Alexis rolled her eyes. She couldn't help but think that maybe that was why they were all there. They'd tuned out one too many times.

"You know what I think would be fun?" Alexis said with a sly smile to the group. "I think it would be fun to find out who those people are. I think it would be more than fun. I think it would be something important for us to do," she added. Alexis made sure to pause and look at each of the three she wanted to join her, in the eyes before moving to the next person.

"I think that it's for our own good to know what's going on." She then added, "I want to go into that building over there." Alexis pointed at the building with the lights still on at the other side of the courtyard. "I want to see what's in that building, because it would be good for me to know." Her eyes watched the group of four she was speaking to now. "It would be good for all of us to know."

She then simply said, "Come on. Let's go," and started walking towards the other side of the courtyard. Alexis gambled that she'd get at least two of them to join her. Any more than that would be a bonus.

Stella followed quickly and caught up to Alexis as she walked deliberately towards the building. Stella looked back at the others following them and whispered to Alexis, "What was that about? Why do you want to go back in there now?"

Alexis kept walking, not wanting to give the others a chance to clear their head and rethink their decision to go along. The truth was, she hadn't really thought about it, she just had to go back and do it at that moment.

Alexis opened the door to the building they'd just come out of a few minutes before. The lights were now off and it was quiet.

"Come on," Alexis whispered.

Soon she was tiptoeing along the side of the wall, trying to feel her way in the dark. Behind her someone bumped into a chair sending it screeching along the tile floor. They all stopped for a moment, anticipating Dr. Lima walking in and catching them, or someone else. Instead, nothing happened. They continued to the other side of the room undisturbed.

Once on the other side of the large room, they could see through the glass doors that led down a hall. The hall was dark except for the emergency lighting. Then Stella noticed a glow coming underneath one of the doors on the left. Alexis slowly pushed open the glass paned double doors leading to the hall and walked through as the others followed her silent steps.

The doors in the hall were all closed and none stood out more than any other. The small group continued to walk down the hall until they neared a door with voices talking from behind it. One of the voices was unmistakably Dr. Lima's. They also heard another woman and at least one male voice. The frosted window of the door made it impossible to see in as they stood against the wall trying to listen. Alexis put her finger to her lips to tell them to be quiet as she moved closer to the door. She lowered herself to her knees so her shadow wouldn't pass by the window.

"Yes, that is true. We have not been able to secure the eighth yet," Dr. Lima said sounding more timid than the others.'

"The eighth is the final piece and essential to the success of our mission," the voice of San said with concern.

"You told us you would be able to handle it. We are running out of time," Yin chided.

"I understand," Dr. Lima replied to the implied question. "But we have seven. We know who they are and where. The mission can still begin while we continue to work on the eighth. It is still possible for it to move forward to the end, if we don't have him."

"Yes, it can begin" Cho spoke, "but without the eighth we have to formulate an entirely new strategy with new people who haven't ever been prepped, who haven't been guided by their Keepers, who may not hold on to the Awakening should we even be able to facilitate it. Or, we have to take the other route and the Earth Council prefers not to go through that route."

"Yes, the eighth is mission critical" San chimed in, agreeing. "We risk generations of work and effort if we cannot bring the eighth in for the Awakening."

"I believe there is a bit of drama here. We all know that the Awakening would certainly help, but the eighth not being a part of it is not mission critical. Besides, there is always more than one solution. I know we will find a way and you won't have to take the other route. I for one…"Dr. Lima stopped speaking and she looked around for a moment. "Wait please," she whispered softly.

Dr. Lima walked towards the door, trying to keep her heels from clacking against the floor. She pulled the door open to an empty hallway. As she looked down the hallway, she saw one of the glass paned doors leading to the larger room close shut. She had an idea who it might have been. She closed the door to the room where the others looked at her curiously, and sat back down.

"What was it?" Yin asked. Dr. Lima hesitated telling her guests. She didn't want them to have any more concerns about the mission than they already had.

"I thought I heard something, but it was nothing." Dr. Lima looked at the three representatives, Yin, San, and Cho who'd come to see her. They were aware that she wasn't being fully truthful and suddenly Dr. Lima felt defensive. "There was nothing to see. Whoever it was had already gone," Dr. Lima added to her comment.

"It's not safe to talk here anymore. At least not now," Cho said nervously.

"The campus will be back to normal in just a couple of days. Let's talk again then. Same place, same time," Dr. Lima suggested.

Dr. Lima closed the door and turned off the lights. Her guests could see their way out. She walked back through the hall the way the students had gone and back through the same glass paned doors to the large room. Dr. Lima paused for a moment seeming to feel the room with her mind.

Someone had been in there. She'd felt their chi residue in the hall as well. It felt like the same energy she'd felt when talking with Alexis and Stella not long before. She didn't know how much they'd heard and was suddenly glad for the policy of no names and no specifics when meeting on this side. There couldn't be any more interruptions like that or any more delays in general.

She walked through the door leading back out to the campus courtyard and looked around before locking the building behind her. Alexis and Stella stood in the window of their darkened room looking out through the sheers at Dr. Lima as she hurried across the courtyard to her campus apartment.

CHAPTER EIGHT
The ARC

Antarctic Research Center

THE SMALL BAND on Stephen's wrist was beginning to wear at his patience with its silence, mocking him. He wondered if it was working properly and considered taking it off and checking its functions.

Unclasping it, he turned it over in his hand to inspect it. The technology he and nearly everyone else wore on their wrist told the time, made and received calls, messages, and other tele-transmissions, could connect to the international web of information and social networking for news, other televised programming, and was programmed to monitor the wearer's vital signs and link to the registration.

The device was commonly called a watch because it had been effectively designed to allow the World Consensus to watch over all registered citizens while providing the citizens with access to everything they needed to be active, productive, socially, and economically involved.

There was nothing wrong with it. *"Where is she?"* he pondered. Stephen paced nervously in his bedroom, stopping every so often in front of the double paned storm window. The interior steel shutters were magnetically held against the wall. He tapped it lightly, as he often did. It was secure.

He glanced out the window, as if suddenly she'd be there knocking at the pane telling him to hurry outside to see some intricate ice crystal formation or the colors painted on a passing cloud. The only thing he saw was snow and ice, packed down in most places. Patches of grey rocky ground peaked through where the ice and snow had long ago receded and hadn't come back yet.

Back within the confines of his orderly room he kept a consistent stride between his desk and the window. What he was really looking for eluded him, as he had yet to find it. It was his first Spring break without Stella. Now, after a few days he found himself missing her nonstop talking which could sometimes irritate him.

The door to his room squeaked lightly as he opened it to look down the hall. He already knew she wouldn't be there, but couldn't resist checking again. The idea of Stella possibly arriving without him knowing was senseless. Why would she come back before she was supposed to? Especially her, and to the ARC. No one came or went without planning, preparation, and someone knowing.

Without Stella the ARC felt more like a large sterile prison, where he was trapped and isolated. He'd spent every Summer of his life since he was five in this frozen tundra. It had always been no man's land. No one wanted it but every year he was here just the same for six months most years.

When they were young they only spent the few months that marked the Antarctic Summer on the ARC, but as they grew older Zura and Johan wanted them to spend more time there, on the ARC as a family. Now, just when it would start getting cold in Northern Allegiance, they would leave the mild winters of their home in New South City for what was arguably the coldest place in the world.

But Stella, she wasn't here with him and his heart literally ached. She hadn't sent him a message yet today and it was already 10:04 a.m. by her time. He kept looking at the wall expectantly. She always messaged him by 10:00 a.m..

"What's wrong? Where is she?" he wondered again aloud, as he checked the time on his watch for the one hundredth time and began tapping his fingers together.

Stephen passed the mirror and noticed his long grey jersey shirt not evenly tucked into his black cargo style pants. He fixed his clothing and smoothed his hair. He'd shot up over the past year and was finally taller than Stella. He was still thin and had not grown much muscle on his lean frame. He had hoped to add some weight and muscle while in Antarctica but not much had changed and their time on the ice was nearly up.

By May they needed to head back to Northern Allegiance where they could continue their research, taking files and samples with them. They'd set up their data reporting systems and then prepare to come back when the temperatures began to rise again to barely tolerable in Spring. Most of the other staff on the ARC wouldn't come until Summer had broken.

Before he could begin wondering anymore, he heard the ding and felt the vibration on his arm. It was Stella. *Finally.* She wanted to do a video call. *"Of course, it's Wednesday,"* Stephen thought to himself. She'd told him that on Wednesday she would call him during her morning break at camp which was in Southern Allegiance, once known as South America.

Stephen rubbed his head and clicked the button on the wall which projected her image into the empty space above his desk. There she was, smiling at him.

"Miss me much, little brother?" she asked. "I know you were pacing by the window and the wall. You need to relax, I think I was five minutes late," she teased him. She could see he was upset.

"Where were you? Why were you late? You promised you'd call right at your break? It's 10:07 a.m.!" he huffed at her impatiently.

Stella knew it bothered his sense of order and routine when things weren't like they were supposed to be or if they didn't go according to plan.

"I'm sorry Stephen. I had some problems with this new interface. I didn't mean for you to worry. How is it back there?"

Stephen hung his head and rolled his shoulders. He then glanced down at the closed notebook he had on his desk. A pencil sat beside it, line to line, its point sharp to the touch. Sometimes he liked the feel of paper and a pencil, even if it made no sense when you could get away with not writing anything at all.

Still upset but happy she was finally there, he tried to answer her question and thought to himself about the long three days since she left. He considered the fact that she only had to leave him because she refused to do her work when she was supposed to and was forced to go to camp.

He avoided looking up and letting her see his eyes. "I'm okay, I guess. We're very busy here. There's a lot to do - more than usual," he paused and the silence stretched on.

Their mom and dad were busy with their research. Stephen had gotten to a point where he could help them and he actually enjoyed it. However, it could become too much. They would go on for twelve to fourteen hours on a regular day, barely breaking to allow themselves to eat a real meal. He was lonely and he was tired but, most of all, he was concerned about what was happening.

"What's got you so busy?" Stella finally asked.

"Just some testing, data collection and data analysis. The usual, but not quite. We have to wrap up in the next couple weeks and there's just a lot. UniCorps and the World Consensus Science Branch will be coming sometime between next week and the following week. I'll tell you when you get back." Silence again stretched on as Stephen stared at her image and the fuchsia lipstick and matching hair band with fuchsia and other bright colors she wore.

She finally chimed in again mockingly, "And Stella, how is it going there? Oh, it's going great Stephen. Let me tell you! I've met some totally nine people here," she said before being interrupted.

"What's a nine person?"

Stella sighed dramatically, "You know nice. It's what they say here at the University, well the camp. Anyway, people from every region in the world. I'm the only one here that's ever been to Antarctica and the only person any of them know who was born in Antarctica. Of course, they wonder how that happened and I was happy to share the story of our crazy, persistent, stubborn parents. Oh, and there are all kinds of other people like me here Stephen.

"I'm happy for you Stella," he said in the second between her thoughts.

"Sometimes I forget the world isn't just scientists, engineers, and techies living with you, Mom, and Dad. Then add in Mave and Rupert and I'm surrounded. It's so refreshing, and, oh, what was that? What was that you just said?" Stella paused and looked as if she were straining to hear something spoken at barely a whisper, her head cocked to one side.

"I didn't say anything." Stephen said confused.

"What was it you just said in your head? What is it that you are worried about? It wasn't that there aren't enough scientists, but that was close, wasn't it?"

"I don't know what you're talking about," Stephen insisted, his eye twitching a bit, as it did when he was nervous or lying.

"Stephen, I know you and you know I know you like no one else knows you. What's going on?" Stephen put his head down. He couldn't let her see the worry on his face. She wouldn't be home for a few more days and he couldn't have her worried too.

He looked at the red brick wall behind her. She was outside, enjoying the warmth. Her hair was around her head like a halo with the sun accenting her curls. The scarf didn't even try to contain the hair, only accent it. He wasn't sure he wanted to talk about it with her out there. He didn't know who else might be around, listening and he understood that no one else could know, for now.

"It's nothing serious. I'll tell you when you get back." She didn't know how she put up with him for nearly sixteen years. He was infuriating at times. She shook her head and bit her lip.

"Stephen, you are frustrating the hell out of me…but I love you anyway. Can you tell mom that I need forty more lubles, please? I'm running low and I need my snacks and I want to get something from the gift shop. And remember, I want you to meet me at the hangar. It'd be nice if mom and dad or mom or dad also came but if they can't you better be there. Of course, I know you will." As she rubbed her sore forehead, she remembered the last thing she wanted to tell Stephen.

"And one more thing, stop banging your head against the wall. I've been waking up with headaches for the past two days. I know something is wrong because, as you know, I feel you! Okay, I gotta run. My break's almost over. Love you bro!"

And then, Stella was gone again, vanished into the thin of the air, just like that. He stared at the wall for a few more moments before sitting on his bed. He felt almost lost without her and he knew he was overreacting but there was literally no one else to talk to. The ARC staff were the only ones for miles on that desolate continent.

However, everyone else was constantly working as if their lives depended on it. Actually, all five of them were working like their lives depended on it. Sighing, he realized it was getting late and he needed to get to work too.

Stephen walked out of his room and pulled the door shut before heading down the hall in their family unit, past the pale yellow walls. He passed the main living area where there was rarely any real living done. The furniture rarely felt the warmth of a body and it wouldn't on that day either as he passed it, headed to the science center.

The science center was his favorite place on the ARC. It included a general workroom, lab, small room with control panels, and the research, observation, and control room, which held the conference table. Zura had nicknamed it her ROC room when Johan had designed it. If she weren't anywhere else, she'd be in there, working with her back to the door and her face towards the ocean.

Their house wasn't really a house. It was just one part of a large well-resourced science and research complex funded by grants from the World Consensus and private money from UniCorps. With that arrangement, there was always a delicate balance meeting everyone's needs while doing what was necessary scientifically.

The ARC was perched dangerously close to the icy waters with tunnels that led beneath the ice to the underwater lab and research center. Mave was at her crescent shaped glass desk sipping on an extra tall cup of coffee with real cream and turbinado sugar while underlining numbers on various reports.

When she'd agreed to come to the ARC she asked for the desk as the one thing she wanted for herself. She'd accepted nearly everything else that was provided standard, though she sometimes wished she'd asked for more. All those years ago, she hadn't considered just how much time she'd wind up spending there.

When the twins were around nine, the glass had to be replaced after an incident of them running into the lab. Stella had rolled one of the heavier chairs and slammed it into the desk causing it to crack across the top.

The crack had started small, but over time had grown to where Mave couldn't put pressure on it or even focus with it always staring back at her. The replacement took them nearly two months and during the wait they laid a piece of metal sheeting over the desk, which was more of an abomination to her senses than the broken glass.

Stephen stopped at the door. "Good morning, Aunt M." He never came into the work room if someone was there without some kind of announcement or greeting, as if in need of permission.

Mave turned around, saw Stephen, and smiled her big smile. "Well, good morning to my favorite boy in the world. Come on in."

Stephen didn't move for a moment, his face seemingly blank. He loved Mave. She always made him feel special, wanted, and needed. He couldn't remember a time when Mave wasn't around.

Stephen walked casually over to where Mave stood near the coffee machine, fumbling with a pouch of coffee and a large container sitting underneath the machine.

Despite the fact that they were not of the same blood, Mave was closer than any other family, outside of those on the ARC, and she had no children, nieces, or nephews. She found a quiet satisfaction in being called Aunt M.

"I spoke to Stella today. She's enjoying herself. She's met more people like her. She is the only person she's met there who has been to Antarctica." Stephen paused as he glanced around the room. "Where are mom and dad?"

"They are in the lab doing some testing. Do you need them?" she asked.

"Yes, I have to pass on messages from Stella and I need to help them today." he added.

"Oh, that's too bad. I was hoping you'd work with me today. I'm waiting on some test results but they'll be finished soon, and then there will be plenty of work to do." Mave stopped to check the time on the wall behind her and walked back to her desk. "Tell them I made more coffee."

"Okay. I will help you later if I finish up with them in time."

Stephen walked through a door, down winding steps to the small room with control panels measuring the temperatures, pressures, and oxygen levels. He slipped off his shoes, put little bootics on, and then he went into the small white decontamination chamber.

The fluorescent bulbs were engineered to kill bacteria that might be harmful in the lab. The small chamber had a second luminescent bacterial disinfectant that scanned the entire person and any objects being carried.

Once both doors were closed Stephen stretched his arms out and he waited for the three beeps that would tell him the scanning was about to begin. He closed his eyes, took a deep breath and held it, counting to ten in his head. *One. Two. Three. Four. Five. Six. Seven. Eight. Nine. Ten.*

Everyone told him he didn't need to hold his breath, but he couldn't help it. Three more beeps signaled that the scan was complete. Stephen exhaled and then pressed the button for the door leading into the sterile lab. This was Rupert's main domain when he wasn't in the larger science workroom with Mave. Windows at the top of the lab let light in from the ROC room.

Going through the lab he found his way to the door that opened into the ROC room. It was covered with windows on the outward facing side that started at two feet from the ground and rose to the ceiling. From here they had a full view of the ocean.

Along the bottom of the walls were three tunnels leading into the ocean for further observation and sample collection. His father had designed it that way to ensure they could continuously collect and monitor water samples, measure water vibrations, ocean floor vibrations, water levels, and monitor ocean life.

When it wasn't being used for work it was where Stephen and Stella had spent countless hours when they were young. The twins would sit and lay in the tunnels that led out into the ocean and watch the ocean life.

Both of his parents were in the room, focused, and barely noticed him enter. Johan leaned over his desk, looking at several reports spread out on paper, on tablets and even projected on the desk. His fingers kept tapping on the projection, going to different parts of the data he was studying. The data contained information on the changes within the past few months. His mom was intensely studying two reports while she paced nervously back and forth in front of the large windows.

"Mom?" Stephen said, getting her attention. Zura stopped looking at the paper in one hand and tablet in the other.

"Stephen? When you gave me that data yesterday what date did it come from?" she jumped right in.

"One week ago today, just like you asked. Did I do something wrong?" he asked with a look of self-doubt coming over his face.

"No. No. That's what I asked for. It just doesn't make much sense. The change between last week and the prior two months doesn't seem to be right. It's too big of a change." She put the reports down and nodded to Johan curiously. "What are you seeing over there Johan?"

His dad stood up slowly. He shook his head and wiped his thick brow. "Zura, I don't know what I'm seeing. Actually, I know what I'm seeing but I don't know if I believe it. I think we need to get Rupert and Mave in here."

"Wait, Mom. I spoke to Stella this morning and," he was cut off mid-sentence.

"What? You spoke to Stella and didn't come get us?" Zura shook her head as if to say, "teenagers".

"Yes, I spoke to Stella and she's doing fine. She needs forty lubles for snacks and a gift. Her aircraft arrives on Saturday morning at 9:16 a.m. sharp. I'll remind you again but she asked me to remind you now. She wants both of you to meet her at the hangar with me. If not both of you, then at least one of you."

"Forty lubles? After all we spent to send her to this camp; she needs forty more lubles for snacks and a gift! That girl." Zura took a few moments to open her banking application on her watch and entered her password to transfer money to her daughter. "Done. She can ask for money, but she can't pick up her hand and call me."

"Stephen, I'll go with you to meet her when she gets back. Your mom will have her hands completely full." Johan said cautiously glancing at his wife.

"Thanks Johan. You know you'll still be busy too but it'd be good if you could go with Stephen." Zura said turning back to the reports.

"I'll go get Rupert and Mave. Oh and Mave made some more coffee." Stephen quietly left the room.

He walked back through the decontamination chamber, the control room, and into the workroom where Mave was standing closely to Rupert talking in a hushed voice. Rupert stood with a smile on his face and the last of the coffee in his black mug that read *Solution Exists*.

"Hello Rupert," Stephen said. He always tried to be courteous and greet them when he saw them.

"Good morning, my man." Rupert responded with a nod, graciously sharing his smile with Stephen.

"They need both of you to look at some data. It seems to be bothering mom. I'll make another pot of coffee."

Rupert was the smartest man he knew when it came to looking at data and noticing details others missed. He was full of brains, having graduated second in his class to the woman he now stood beside. Even as smart as he was he managed to hold on to his relaxed and easy nature. His long locks were filled with salt and his beard was long. He would let it grow for weeks without trimming, especially during the cold months they spent here.

Rupert walked with a slight limp due to his right leg being a prosthetic. He'd lost it in an accident during a beach trip while in University soon after he turned eighteen. He'd been swimming out in the ocean, pushing past where the lifeguards said it was safe. A shark was swimming closer in than usual, searching for food and he'd gotten within striking distance. As his legs moved beneath the waves they must have looked like swimming fish to the hungry shark.

It had taken months for him to heal and walk again and that caused him to fall a year behind in school. Looking back, he realized that losing part of his leg and then that year eventually allowed him to meet Mave and led him to the ARC. He didn't forget to tease Mave that they would've both been number one in their classes if he hadn't had to make up that year. He would also joke that he'd given his right leg to meet her. The prosthetic barely seemed to slow him down.

Rupert's skin was like powdered cocoa but unlike his mother, he'd come from the beautiful islands off the northeast coast of the continent of Southern Allegiance. Zura had been born in Southern Liberty. Before the government of the World Consensus was formed, it had been called Africa.

Many of the old places had been renamed to loosen people's obsession with the divisions that had been associated with them, but since no one seemed too concerned with claiming the wasteland he was on, it remained as Antarctica.

And it was here, where no one wanted to be, that the questions that no one could ignore, would originate.

CHAPTER NINE
Questions

Antarctic Research Center

CURIOSITY FILLED RUPERT and Mave's eyes as they looked at each other.

"What do you think *this* meeting will be about?" Rupert asked Mave, already suspecting they both knew.

"More of the same probably. Of course Zura has the knack for seeing the bigger picture and the longer trends that we might have missed. Maybe she has something new for us."

"New would be good. Especially since we've been dealing with delivering them reports that no one likes for months and nothing has changed. I know they've invested billions of lubles into the infrastructure and the companies that maintain them but, at some point they have to hear reason, right?" Rupert asked Mave.

"You'd think that, but reason didn't stop them from using these emission pump holes to begin with. They pushed it through because we were in a pollution crisis and needed something quick."

"You're right. Anyone who tried to get real solid research done was considered a threat, disloyal, and discredited in some way or another," Rupert said, remembering some of his former colleagues.

"Now, they've got more reasons to keep doing what they are doing than to stop. At least, they have until now. I am hopeful it'll be different this time. I feel pretty good about Zura making the case," Mave said, nodding her head.

Zura had a keen eye and mind for seeing what was coming with just a few pieces of information. She must have passed that gift on to Stephen. His mind was almost like a computer when it came to patterns and probabilities. They were lucky to have him, even if he was just fifteen.

"I guess we better go then. She doesn't like to be kept waiting." Rupert said as the two made their way down the stairs and through the short tunnel to the control room.

They went through the same process as Stephen. Each removed their shoes, exchanging them for the white booties before taking turns in the chamber. Mave went first, taking the minute to collect her thoughts again before facing Zura.

When Rupert followed her, she knew he'd taken advantage of those quiet seconds as well. The two gave a knowing nod as they walked through the lab and into the ROC room. Rupert had barely exited the lab when Zura was showing a barely stacked pile of papers into their hands.

"Hey you two, take a look at this. I keep staring at it and it seems right but it just doesn't make sense. It doesn't seem to be possible. Tell me if you are seeing what I'm seeing." Zura projected the data that had held her captivated onto the center table and started walking around it in circles, as if she were on the hunt.

Mave glanced at Rupert and then said, "Zura, can we take it down just a half a notch. Let's sit and look at it. Remember, we haven't seen all the data together, only our pieces of the puzzle. It looks like you've put the puzzle together, so to speak. Give us a few minutes to look it over and then we can all talk about what we see. How's that sound?" she asked. Mave was always the voice of reason and calm.

"Good idea, Mave. Five minutes," Zura said as she got ready to tap a button on her wrist. "Start…now." Zura couldn't help but time it. She was particular that way.

Mave was the main reason Zura had made it through the first two years with the twins. It had been Mave and Zura's parents moving to Northern Allegiance for a few years to help that were her salvation. They told her when she was pregnant that they weren't going to miss their only grandchildren even if they were half way around the world.

However, it was Mave who kept Zura sane in the long cold months when she had to leave them in Northern Allegiance to come back to the ARC. She'd never felt she had enough time with them when they were young, but they still turned out to be good kids.

A few minutes later, Johan walked in holding a cup of coffee still steaming over the green brim. Stephen followed him, carrying a hot cup of coffee in each hand, delicately balancing them so that they didn't spill on him or on the clean floors of the ROC room. He didn't feel like getting on his knees to scrub the floors today, especially since he was so freshly clean.

"Sorry I'm late. I wanted to pull a few more data points from today before chiming in myself on this. Have you all had a chance to look at the reports Zura made?"

Johan's deep eyes moved between Mave and Rupert, before settling on Zura. She still lit up his world. He handed her the coffee he was holding, took one from Stephen, and sat beside her. Stephen, holding one last cup sat down in the last empty seat. With everyone being so preoccupied, they might not notice he was drinking coffee too.

Zura slid a report over to Stephen and took the data from Johan. She then began looking back and forth at the different reports. She stood up and restarted the data load into the center of the table through the holograph system that turned it into a three dimensional image. She knew where she wanted to start.

"Okay, let's go. Rupert, what are your thoughts?"

Rupert cleared his throat before beginning. "You see this data point here?" he asked pointing to what seemed like a random dot on the graph. "It seems like a minor anomaly at first, until you notice that it is repeated here, and here, and here, by proportion. So it becomes less of an anomaly but rather a periodic spike," he said as he slid his finger to move it along to what Johan had been studying.

"I think this goes along with Johan's findings. The spikes we see here are because the entire earth mantle is connected. What happens over here in the North and South Allegiances or over in the Eastern Way affects us down here."

"And," Mave added, "keep in mind they've been adding new drilling holes over the past decade where we'd previously had none. So rather than having these gases pumped into the ground in just a dozen areas, we are now up by nearly 100%, even with the three that are closed. No one is talking about long-term solutions."

"What I'm seeing," said Johan "is compressed gases being pushed into the surface and then expanding once they are below ground, pushing the earth apart underneath. It is literally destabilizing the layer that we live on and that the ocean sits on. It's, of course, worse where the holes have been drilled but, like Rupert said, it's affecting everywhere."

Zura nodded her head thoughtfully. She was restless and stood up to begin walking in circles again. It was what she'd suspected but needed to hear it from the people she trusted most. "So what can we do?" Zura asked. "And more importantly, how long do we have before these gases push against a tectonic plate or close enough to a volcano to erupt it?"

"It's already happening in some places. We've seen more volcanic activity even without full scale eruptions. There have been more tremors reported by the Science Institute and we've measured more here too, including on the ocean floor. The earthquake in Southern Allegiance was pretty bad, but that was just one of several incidents," Rupert answered.

"Based on the data collected over the past seventeen months, the probability of smaller events in the next six months however, is over .7 if conditions do not change." Stephen said in his nearly monotone voice.

"When did you work that out Stephen?" Johan asked.

"Last night, before bed. I hope you don't mind, mom. I borrowed copies of the reports," Stephen said to a smiling Zura.

"I don't mind at all. Thank you." She couldn't help but think, her son was a genius. Turning her attention back to the information projected and her teammates, Zura continued. "Based on that, what can we do to turn this around so that the conditions change and we avoid the next event in a series of events that will destabilize our world?"

Mave paused for a moment, running her hands through her long hair. She hadn't bothered to put it up that morning since she knew she'd just be around friends. She pushed her coffee mug back and leaned forward on the table.

"Zura, the first thing is to confirm what Stephen said. The second thing is to tell UniCorps and we need to tell our contacts at the World Consensus Science Division too," Mave continued to lean in, her eyes on Zura.

There was silence around the room, with the exception of Stephen's perfectly timed sipping of his coffee and subsequent gagging as he burnt his tongue. Zura looked at him and then decided to let it go. He'd been up working on this like the rest of them. He'd earned his grown up wake up. Stephen looked around the room at the faces of the people who had become of his family. He didn't get what the big deal was about telling their funders.

Quietly, his mother spoke, "And then what? We can't just go in and drop a bomb like this without having a practical and workable solution. I'm not ready to tell the science divisions of either UniCorps or the World Consensus. The World Consensus doesn't like bad news, never has. UniCorps doesn't like anything that may negatively affect their productivity or profits. Along with that, anything at all that might scare the public generally gets buried by everyone."

"We can't let this stuff happen and just be quiet about it. That isn't fair. It isn't right," Stephen said, disturbed at the suggestion.

"It's okay, Stephen. We'll tell them when the time is right. When we have answers for the questions. Right now, we don't have answers and we don't have a solution," Zura said trying in vain to calm her son.

"No, mom, it's not okay. I'm fifteen years old. If we let this situation continue, the probability of there being a world that is habitable when I'm as old as you, is pretty much zero. Actually to be more precise it is .12 to .15 but that is close enough to nothing." Stephen stood up with his coffee and left the lab.

Stephen reversed his steps to exit the science center. As he walked through the tunnels that led to their unit, trying to keep his coffee from spilling, he could feel himself becoming more frustrated. He didn't understand them. They'd rushed to put in the pump system to solve a problem that they'd created. At the time, it was the easier fix and much faster given they could reuse some of the existing infrastructure. Now no one wanted to be responsible for it or what it was doing to the planet.

He entered their unit and walked past the aging furniture Zura had personally picked out before they were born.

She'd changed the art and knick-knacks out once when they were about ten years old but no one had done much since.

Right now, he didn't see any of that as he walked past it and into his room, shutting the door hard behind him.

He felt silly for wanting his sister home, but he did. He needed someone to talk to. Someone who would understand.

Stephen banged his head on the wall a few times and then rubbed the red spot on his forehead. *That does hurt.* He then remembered Stella asked him not to do that since it gave her headaches. Spent of any other ideas of what to do, Stephen turned and flopped onto his bed.

Touching the small shiny black band around his wrist he projected it to the wall. Within a few seconds a half awake face with a hand over an eye trying to get the sleep out, appeared in front of him. The young man had serious bed head from falling asleep at his desk. Stephen was annoyed that Marco could pretty much look like that when he woke up. He could spend all day grooming himself and still just look completely average.

"Hey Marco, how are you? I need to ask you about something," Stephen said rushing in without even letting Marco answer. Marco rubbed his eyes.

"Hi Stephen. What's going on?"

Stephen paused and stared at the screen. He realized he needed to talk to someone but hadn't thought it through. Telling Marco what was going on wasn't something he could really do. Neither was it possible to ask him for advice, even hypothetically. He couldn't talk to anyone else about this at all, except Stella and he'd have to wait for her to get back.

"I'm sorry Marco. I made a mistake. I'll talk to you later."

Marco swore under his breath and rolled his eyes as Stephen hung up. He'd fallen asleep at his desk doing some research of his own, when Stephen had come through. Marco had his own work he needed to finish if he wanted an edge on his competition.

The walls stared back at Stephen. He had never decorated them like Stella. They'd been painted a bluish grey color when he was a little kid and he'd left it that way for more than eight years. The maintenance staff touched it up every year with the same color and for the past three years had asked if he wanted a new color. The blue still comforted him and there was no need to change it despite everyone else's suggestions.

The only picture displayed on the wall was of his family on a vacation back in his mom's native home, Hankura, on the western coast of Southern Liberty. They went back to visit her home with their grandparents nearly half his lifetime ago. It had been taken the same year his room was first painted. Since that time he'd only been back once, but he could still remember how beautiful it was.

The people were so full of life and the colors were vivid. Stella had taken nearly a thousand pictures trying to somehow capture and take with her the warmth of the people, the vibrant hues of the buildings and the trees, and anything else that would remind her of Hankura.

One day he planned on returning to attend The Southern Liberty University's West Coast campus. It was one of the best universities in the world for science and scientific research and it was where his parents had met, where they met Mave and eventually Rupert.

Otherwise, his room felt bare. Built-in dressers and a personal disposal unit for garbage gave more floor space and his bed took up nearly half of it. The handle for the PDU was near the door one and a half feet from the floor. The ARC's system collected all the waste in units such as that for recycling, composting, and conversion into fuel.

Aside from that the only other furnishings were his chair and desk with a projection area where he could have his system read and organize his written notes. He didn't understand why his mother wouldn't use hers. Instead she'd have all that paper, everywhere. He sat down at his desk and launched the projection. He scanned the report his father had run that morning and added it to the data before projecting it to the wall.

For hours he sat again with the information, re-running scenarios in his head and recalculating probabilities, hoping to decrease the probability of occurrence or increase the timeframe of it happening. He'd done something similar the night before, but tonight he optimistically hoped to find something different. He was searching for the answer to the burning question his mother had asked and every other person in the room had thought. What could be done?

No matter what scenario he ran, he kept coming to the same conclusion. It wouldn't matter what they did on their end if the International Association of Corporations, known as UniCorps, didn't act. They couldn't act if they didn't know.

He turned off the projection. There was nothing more he could do now, but he would show Mave what he ran tomorrow.

CHAPTER TEN
Right

Antarctic Research Center

AS STEPHEN TRAVERSED the pastel painted tunnels with sconces placed near the ceiling as well as tracks of lights running along the top, the path to the science center felt ridiculously cumbersome. A never-ending puzzle with twists and turns.

The genius of his father's honeycomb to honeycomb design meant that it could easily be closed off section by section if heating went out or if there was any other type of emergency. It also meant getting anywhere on the ARC took twice as long as it should.

When he finally arrived at the door to the science center, he startled them. They were huddled together talking quietly but it was quickly followed by a sudden hush the moment he entered the doorway. Mave went for the coffee pot as was her nervous habit.

"Good morning, Stephen," Zura smiled. "Come on in. It looks like you've been up late again."

Stephen looked down at himself and realized he had woken up, grabbed the notebook and his watch, and run out of his room. Navy blue cotton pajama pants and a long-sleeved sleep shirt hung loosely off his slender frame. They weren't his usual clothes to start the day but it didn't matter.

Stephen had marched out of his room, anxious to show his parents, Rupert, and Mave what he discovered in his number crunching the night before. He was convinced that once they saw this, they would have to tell someone. There was no way they could keep quiet at that point.

"Yes. I was up late. I think you'll want to see this. Yesterday, you said you needed to get a closer look at the data. I took a closer look to see if there was something that could be done that would make the outcomes better. I kept changing the assumption and rerunning the models but kept getting the same or very similar results. They were all bad., that is until I started changing some of the other variables. Variables that we've continued to hold constant." Stephen picked up Zura's tablet and copied his report to it before handing it to her.

"What are you saying Stephen?" Johan asked stepping over to take a closer look.

"I don't think we are going to be able solve this without looking at population, location of population, the number of pump holes, location of pump holes, and how much is being pumped.

"Those are things that we don't have any control over and honestly, they don't give it much support as far as research," Zura responded.

"I don't see how anyone can ignore it. There are twenty billion people and there is a lot of waste from production to support those twenty billion people. Because people are spread out companies either produce in more areas to minimize transportation or they have to ship to more areas and thus put more load on fewer pump holes. Either way, we can't keep pumping into the earth at the levels we are without these tremors and earthquakes getting even worse. Then there is even the issue of volcanoes. We are already seeing this happen. In the short term, the only solution I see is to close the pumps." Stephen stopped speaking.

He didn't want to go any further and looked at Zura, wanting his mother to take it from there. He then looked at Johan.

"Here," Stephen said, handing the paper and the data chip to his dad and walked out. "I need to get ready for the day."

"What the heck Stephen?!" An exasperated Zura yelled after Stephen as he walked out of the room and back towards his room. Sometimes he drove her crazy. She could never really figure him out. Stephen figured that this was their problem. Johan put up his hand to Zura. After letting Stephen get a few yards ahead of Johan followed.

Stephen didn't answer his mother. He didn't want to talk to her or anyone else in that room. He was still a kid and he wasn't supposed to have to think about things like that. He wanted off this forsaken sheet of ice. He wanted to tell someone what was going on and maybe have someone who hadn't already sold out look at the data with him.

Exhaustion hit Stephen hard as he crossed the threshold of the door to his bedroom. His bed called to him, reminding him that he'd ignored it the night before. A light knock on the door made Stephen roll over on his back to and strain to see who was three through dreary eyes.

"Hey dad."

"Hey Stephen. How are you?" Johan asked and then sat down on the edge of Stephen's bed.

"Tired and upset."

"I bet. You were working pretty late on this weren't you?"

"Yes. Very late."

"And you didn't get quite the response you were hoping for did you?"

"No. There should be only one response, dad. There is one simple answer. Stop pumping emissions into the ground, move the people in the hot zones, then fix the problem. You can even propose your solution again, right?"

"I wish it were that easy Stephen, believe me. For every one person you see that we answer to, there are two or three more that you don't see. Unfortunately, every single one has different interests. Maybe, just maybe, we are getting somewhere with all this. Maybe we have enough data finally to make a case that they can't ignore. Then, maybe they'll listen to what I've been suggesting for years," Johan smiled at his son.

He hoped to lighten Stephen's mood. It wasn't fair for Stephen to have to be involved like he was, but he was involved and he needed to be. Stephen was right. What was happening affected all of them, Stephen included. He had a stake in the outcome, perhaps more than even either he or Zura.

"Enough of that. Anything else exciting happening?" Johan asked, trying to shift the focus from work.

"No. It's supposed to be Spring break but it doesn't seem like it, especially with Stella gone. I'm tired dad and I need time to think," Stephen said, rolling onto his side.

Johan stood up and avoided stepping on the paper Stephen had let drop to the floor.

"Well, get some rest and then come back down and see us when you're ready. Okay son?"

"Okay. Can you close the door please?"

"Sure. Talk to you soon." Johan gently closed the door and Stephen collapsed onto the bed, landing on his stomach.

His eyelids were heavy and the dark circles underneath were now evident from the multiple nights of lost sleep. His cheek lay against the bed and his hands fell beside his head. The small light on his watch pulsed blue. He pushed himself up just enough to reach it with his other hand.

Stella had sent him a message. She'd gone exploring at camp and would tell him about it when she got home in a couple of days. Stephen looked at the ocean life calendar Mave had bought him. Only two days were left. Sleep beckoned him as he lay sprawled across the bed. He would have given into it but he felt compelled to continue working. His dad might be right - maybe they were close. He also felt guilty after he'd rushed out of the science center the way he had.

Stephen let himself tumble off the bed and stumble into the bathroom. He peeled off his pajamas and stepped into the hygiene closet. He took a deep breath and put the plugs into his ears and nose. No matter how many times he did it, he still hated the feeling of the rubber nodules pressed against the skin inside his nose and ears.

He dragged his legs over the short wall and stepped inside the small closet, letting the door close with a click before pressing the button to let the sanitation begin. With his head leaning against the wall in front of him he rested his hands on the sealed, smooth, concrete wall above him and spread his legs as if preparing to stretch for the marathon that would be the next month of his life. The hygienic wash and rinse would begin soon and with it, ninety seconds of peace.

As the pea gravel sized holes in the hygiene closet opened and began to squirt the anti-bacterial foam onto the top of his tense neck and back and then down the back of his legs, he forgot where he was for a moment. The foam would stay on him for thirty seconds releasing the tiny beads that tingled against his skin, revitalizing him. The infrared light shining from above his head, beside him from the walls, and up from the floor killed other germs.

The faint sound of a beep brought him back to where he was and he turned to face the other way for another thirty seconds. He loved the rinse the most. He had set the rinse power so it felt like standing out in the rain on a Spring day back in Northern Allegiance.

The final rinse removed all of the anti-bacterial solution and left him feeling clean and refreshed. He always opted to turn off the heated drying element in the hygiene closet. It was too warm and sucked the moisture from his skin, especially when the moisture in the air was already so low. Besides, he preferred the cooler air outside of the closet, and a thick towel.

He grabbed his oversized navy blue and white striped towel from the hook just outside the closet door and stepped out onto the cool white clay tile. Now that he was feeling a little more alive maybe he wouldn't be such a curmudgeon when he went back to the science center. He was already feeling restless, knowing there must be something else; something he was missing.

Mave looked towards the doorway as Stephen appeared again. This time he was fully dressed and looked as if he'd been in the hygiene closet.

"Hi, Stephen. Welcome back."

Stephen walked in and sat down by Mave.

"Hi Aunt M," he tried to say calmly. "Did you see what I brought earlier?"

"No, Zura took it. She and Johan have it in there." She pointed toward the door leading down to the ROC room. "I wouldn't go in there yet if I were you. I don't think they like what they are seeing and I don't think they agree on the next step."

"So what does that mean? What am I supposed to do?" asked Stephen confused.

"Right now? Nothing. Wait. Things will work out. In the meantime, you can help me do some of this prep work so we can get reports for when we are gone. Believe it or not it's almost time to leave this ice nest and it's almost birthday time for you and Stella. I'll be a bat's uncle, well aunt, if I'm in this place ever again in Winter." Stephen looked at her with a strange smile.

Sometimes Mave said the craziest non-sense things. Since she'd starting working on not swearing she said whatever other craziness popped in her head.

"You'll be sixteen this year and para-adults. It's a big step and I have something special for the two of you. However, my dear, it won't happen on Antarctica."

"What is it?" Stephen asked.

"It wouldn't be much of a surprise if I told you, now would it? You'll just have to wait and find out, but don't worry, it is out of this world!"

"Okay. Fine. I'll help you. You don't have to make all kinds of promises, Aunt M. You know I don't like surprises. What do you need me to do?" Stephen said.

Mave slid over with coffee in hand letting Stephen take command of the programming station.

"Why don't you run the program to get data on the sea creatures first," Mave instructed.

Stephen looked at her and protested, "But I want to work on the seismic activity program."

"I know. That's why you have to do the sea creatures first. I know if you start with that seismic activity program I'll have a hard time getting you to stop and do anything else. By the way, make sure when do the seismic program you are getting data from all of the regions. I don't want us to miss anything," Mave smiled at Stephen who gave her a look of frustration before turning a corner of his lip upward.

They could work together for hours. Sometimes it would be in silence, yet whenever he was around Mave, he always felt safe and connected to something bigger. He knew what he was doing wasn't for nothing.

CHAPTER ELEVEN
Answers

Antarctic Research Center

IN THE ROC room, Zura and Johan both looked out the wall of windows towards the never ending ocean. Zura felt lightheaded from everything that was happening much too quickly and all Johan could do at that moment was hold her. This was their life's work. This whole program was possible because of them.

They were supposed to be saving the world. All of their hard work and sacrifice was for what surrounded them and for the nearly twenty billion people sharing the planet with them. If they screwed up, they would be responsible for the fallout and that wasn't an option either wanted to consider.

The pressure seemed to push into Zura's shoulder blades and crept into her neck. She was the lead, this was her project, and at the end of the day she was responsible for what happened and for all the lives impacted by their work and the information they had. She felt the weight of the world pressing into her neck and back, even if she didn't have to bear it.

She took in a deep breath and as she let it out slowly she was reminded of the little ball of light that had appeared when she'd been working just two and a half months before the twins were born. She had never told Johan about it, but that message, along with Mave's insistence, had kept her pressing on with the mission she sometimes couldn't seem to grasp.

The message she got that day kept her committed to making sure the twins knew their worth. Their premature birth and that message were why she said yes to the serum during her labor. It was why she had risked everything. The ARC and all of the sacrifices she, Johan and everyone else had made along the way couldn't be for nothing.

Zura whipped her head away sharply from her embrace with Johan. She'd felt as if they were no longer alone, but as she looked around the room and behind her confused husband there was no one there. She stood back from Johan and looked around again, trying to shake off whatever was causing the hairs on her arms to stand up. She could feel a shift of energy in the room but only she and Johan were there.

"We have to do something, Johan," Zura finally spoke. "We have to send a report with our suggestions to both the UniCorps and the World Consensus Science Branches. They have to know what we've found so they can do something. I will not let this kind of blood be on my hands or our hands."

Upstairs in the general science room Mave suddenly sat up erect in the chair beside Stephen, a calm look coming over her face. She smiled and said, "I think you'll be happy with your parents."

Mave continued to work with a little more pep. A couple of minutes passed and Zura and Johan stepped out of the decontamination chamber and were coming up the steps to the science center workroom where Mave and Stephen waited expectantly.

"Hi, Stephen, Mave," Zura said as she slipped on her shoes. "Glad to see you seem more yourself this time, Stephen. Mave, can you and Rupert begin putting together easy to understand charts using the data we have? I don't want anyone saying that what we provided wasn't clear. I am going to start drafting my report. Johan, I need you to keep an eye on the subfloor activity. Get in touch with your global associates to get regional data for all global activity over the past eighteen months," she instructed.

"That may not be enough," Johan responded.

"You're right. Make it two years. In fact go back until you can see where the data begins to show a new trend and then go back further so they can see that something wasn't there and then it was. We need something that shows there was a change. It could be two or three years, but I know it's there." That was all she said before she sat down at her station and began to type. She was in her own space again.

"Stephen, you can keep working on what you were doing," Mave said before walking out of the lab in search of Rupert who was supposed to be taking the morning off.

He'd been up later than Stephen analyzing data. Mave knew Rupert well enough to know that without any rest, he wouldn't be much good but there wasn't time to sleep now. She had only slept three hours herself, but she got by fine on a pot of coffee a day and the occasional moments she took for rejuvenation. She knew the coffee addiction wasn't good for her, but it was one of her few guilty pleasures since coming here.

As Mave left the lab she figured that Zura wouldn't miss her for at least fifteen or twenty minutes. She'd be so wrapped up in her work she wouldn't even notice that she and Rupert hadn't returned.

Mave wandered through the tunnels looking behind her to make sure no one was following her. She desperately needed a moment to herself. She went into the hall leading to the living unit she shared with Rupert. She passed the main living areas to make it to her own bedroom. She opened the door and quickly closed and locked it behind her, making sure it didn't make a sound.

Before she let herself retire to the comfort of her bed for a few stolen moments of peace, she tested the door again to make sure it was secure. She could feel the tension that was in the science center all through her legs, back, shoulders, arms, neck, and head. She needed to recharge and clear all that tension out before going back in there for another round. She unbuttoned her uniform top leaving her undershirt and pulled off the cargo style pants, before she stretched out on the bed.

Mave took a deep breath in, closed her eyes and exhaled. She could feel the life of the breath fill her chest and throat before leaving again. She continued just breathing, circular breaths, round and round. In a few moments she felt her body warm up from within. Soon her body seemed to radiate, just a little at first and then enough to give off a faint glow. The light that circled her body got bigger and bigger until it filled the whole room.

Mave was one of the Connecteds. Connecteds were all over the world, placed on every continent to serve as a connection between the earth and its people with the Unseen and those like the Council.

After the World Consensus took over and the voting power of corporations exceeded that of people, the Connecteds were forbidden to publicly share any information they received that might affect the citizen's positive perception of the World Consensus or the corporations. They had even gone so far as to say that it was punishable by loss of Citizenship. They could become part of the homeless population.

Anyone who was suspected of being a Connected was to be reported if there was evidence of suspicious behavior, such as having knowledge or abilities that couldn't be scientifically or physically explained. This law had the desired effect of convincing most Connecteds to not speak or act openly about what they knew in certain areas of government, politics, and power.

Mave successfully avoided being targeted or reported as a Connected, despite being from a place called India in the Eastern Way, where many Connecteds came from. Her science background and quick wit helped her find answers and communicate what she knew in a way that wasn't too out of the ordinary or suspicious.

Of course, there were times when she simply had to remain silent because her mission here was too great to be compromised by ego or anything less than being a part of the movement.

Mave lay there peacefully, basking in the glow. It felt like a warm hug that washed away all the stress, until there was a knock on the door.

"Mave? Are you in there?" It was Rupert. Mave muttered something as she came out of her blissful state.

"What?" he asked through the door.

"Give me just a minute. I was just catching a little bit of shut eye," Mave said with a huff of slight irritation. She then forced herself to sit up. It was time to get back to work and at least it was Rupert at the door and not Zura.

Her moment of relaxation was over. She pulled her uniform back on, trying to focus through the feeling that she was still floating. She stepped into her boots, pulling the laces snug and then went to the door. She turned back towards the bed and smiled. She could still see the lingering light begin to fade and disappear.

Mave opened the door and greeted Rupert with a kiss on the lips. "Oh? I think you need to get cat naps more often," Rupert laughed. She didn't know what had come over her, but it was done.

This woman is amazing in every way, Rupert thought. He looked at her like he often found himself doing. He would have followed her to the ends of the earth. As he thought about it, he realized he had, and she still wouldn't let him be her official unity partner.

"So, we have some work to do Rupert. Zura has decided to do the right thing like we suspected she would. I am pretty sure we got some extra help on that one. Of course that means you and I have to help get everything she needs to really make the case. She's working on the formal report and we've got to pull together the charts and graphs that support what we've found," Mave said in one breath.

Rupert smiled. "Great. Are you ready? It's going to be another long night." Rupert was glad he was able to get in a few hours of sleep before starting the cycle over again.

They headed back to the science center where Zura was still hunched over her desk. Rupert glanced over at Mave who simply shook her head. It was best not to interrupt her when she was like that. They had enough of their own work to do and they all realized the urgency that surrounded getting this to the right people.

Rupert and Mave decided it was best to work in the ROC room so they could discuss what they were doing and not disturb the lioness that would be Zura if they made more than a whisper. As they were preparing to go through the door leading to the chamber and ROC room Rupert dropped a shoe on the floor, making a loud plop sound.

Zura spun her chair around and gave him a look. "Can we get some quiet in here, please? We've got a lot of work to do." She turned her chair back around and glanced one more time at Rupert and Mave as they walked through the door, shoes securely in hand.

Once in, Rupert rolled his eyes. "I'm glad we don't have to work in there right now."

"Yeah, well, we will have to be back with her soon and it better be with a plan of what we are able to show. You are my data man, so let's pull this together," Mave said.

She sat down beside Rupert as they pulled up the data using the same projector Zura had used earlier. Together they began paging through it month by month, noting the anomalies.

"This might take a while," Rupert said before stopping and looking at Mave from the side. "Mave, what do you think is going to happen once UniCorps sees this report?" Rupert asked, wanting her honest opinion.

"What I think doesn't really matter at this point. But, since you asked - I would love for them to read it thoroughly, get their scientists right on it to investigate the impact of pumping on the fault lines and tectonic plates, and then unanimously decide to enact the changes that are most likely to solve this issue without lives being lost. You know, stop the blasted pumping program. Then, for us to have averted a global catastrophe and to have fulfilled our mission. I would love for them to finally consider and start working on Johan's solution for pollution control as well," Mave smiled knowingly at Rupert.

"BUT…I doubt it'll work out quite like that. There is a lot riding on the ARC project, the emissions project, the corporate interests, and people's desire to feel everything is alright, even if it's a lie. So, does that tell you enough of what I think?" she finished with smug smile crossing her full lips.

Rupert just looked at her for a moment. "Smartass."

"Yes, I am. Thanks for noticing," Mave smiled at Rupert teasingly. If she hadn't fully committed to this life and mission she would've taken things further with Rupert. But she didn't have the luxury of that kind of life. She'd made the choice and not sticking with it could cost too much.

"Mave, we are going to have to go back about two and a half years to get to the start of this. Do you remember when the representatives and other Region officials voted to expand the drilling of emission pump holes?" Rupert asked turning to Mave.

"I think it was about ten years ago right? They were concerned that they were overusing the existing ones and convinced the Citizens Review group that more holes spread out would solve the problem and not cause issues of too many emissions being dumped in one place," Mave answered as she tried to remember the details from a decade before.

"That's right," Rupert added. "It went into effect almost immediately, they started drilling, and within a year the first holes in the second phase were operational. They've been bragging about how well it has worked and all the while it has just been like a festering boil just below the surface."

"Maybe they got excited too soon," Mave said.

"Clearly. We looked at the older holes and their spikes are higher, and the first signs of damage started nearly ten years ago, right after they approved the new set of holes. Those first holes are five to six years older. So it took about seven years after they started being used for us to see these spikes.

"So basically we know that if we are seeing this with the two dozen initial holes, we can expect to see the spikes show up in the same pattern for the newer ones," Mave nodded pensively.

"And, some of the older holes from the second round are what show up here," Rupert said as he let himself continue processing what he was seeing, what he knew, and what he could predict when he started putting the pieces together.

"They can't make any more holes, Mave and it is dangerous to continue using the oldest ones, just like you and Stephen said."

"I know. Can you show that in a picture, graph, or chart? Make it clear as the water out there?" Mave pointed at the ocean outside the window.

The view outside of the windows reminded Mave once more about why they had to choose this place to set up camp. Then she remembered and shuddered as she thought of the people funding the program and the ARC. It was safely away from any fault lines and its location in the coldest place on earth, meant that even with global warming it could remain habitable, for a time.

The Antarctic Research Center sprawled above ground and beneath the surface across nearly two and a half acres, and two submarines could be anchored to it from the main control areas where the science lab and science center were located. The main building itself was nearly 70,000 square feet with enough living units to house just over 800 people. Four additional outpost buildings totaled another 10,000 square feet and could house up to another 220 people.

Every month, when supplies were delivered, an extra portion was delivered to the long-term supply storage. This area was kept under tight security and was accessible for emergency purposes only by a limited group of cleared personnel. The ARC, along with the long-term storage, was subject to inspection by UniCorps and the World Consensus when they sent representatives from the respective Science Divisions at the end of each work season.

They'd be coming soon and before arrived they would have received all of the information being pulled together. It spelled out barely a sliver of hope in what was a mountain of doom.

Mave sighed as she thought about the children. She realized that most of them were no longer children but were crossing over or had already crossed into the status of para-adults. She and the other Keepers had been assigned to them to ensure they were guided towards their collective mission. They were the most important part of her own personal mission.

They were eight children with their own missions that they didn't even know about yet. She sometimes worried for them, but she and the other Keepers could only guide them. Their choices and actions were still their own, unless it became an issue of life or death, or became mission critical, then the Unseens would step in.

Mave faulted her generation and the generations before her for more than two hundred years, that had put them all in this situation. The mindset that led them to the pile of mess they were now trying to dig their way out of went even further back than that. They had failed to stop the madness of excess when they had the chance, and had just kept pushing it down the line. Now they were running out of time.

Rupert stopped and put down the tablet he held to stare at Mave. She was somewhere else. He'd been sitting there talking to her for nearly a minute before he realized she wasn't paying any attention to him.

"Are you coming back anytime soon?" Rupert asked, interrupting her thoughts.

"What?" Mave asked. She didn't realize how long she'd been in her own world.

"I think I found something else. Look at this map from our survey the year we started this project. Now look at the one before they started the last twenty holes. Now this is what we measured this week." He paused letting her take in the images. "Notice anything?" Rupert asked.

Mave looked at him confused. "Give me a hint what I should even be looking for."

Rupert brought up the definition of some of the lines, highlighting them in a bright yellowish orange. "Look at the fault lines. I just made them brighter for you." He stepped back letting her get closer.

"Am I mistaken or am I seeing what I think I'm seeing? Are those lines bigger? And there," Mave said pointing to a line that ran from the northern tip of Southern Allegiance down and across the top corner, "is that a new one?" she asked with a wide eyed look that blended recognition and confusion. *This couldn't really be possible.*

"You are not mistaken, my dear. This is the proverbial smoking gun," he added.

"Rupert, what does that even mean? Smoking gun? Where do you come up with this stuff?"

"It's an old saying. Never mind. What's important is that we have it."

CHAPTER TWELVE
Motion

Antarctic Research Center

"STELLA WILL BE at the hangar in an hour and sixteen minutes. Are you still going with me to meet her?" Stephen asked his dad before turning back around in his chair. Although it didn't show on his face, Stephen was relieved and happy that it was finally time for her to come home.

He played with his yellow cup filled with hot chocolate. At least it was hot an hour ago. It had since cooled to room temperature and was no longer appealing as he gently twirled the ribbons of chocolate around the top with his index finger. He'd finished his part of the report and was now at a loss of what to do next, aside from wait.

There was no one to talk to since everyone was running around as if it was the end of the world. Occasionally, someone would ask him to run some data or look at some probabilities or enter something or even make coffee, but otherwise he was nearly invisible.

Sleep was hard to relax into with all that was happening. Even after letting it claim him the night before, he'd woken much earlier than normal that morning. Waking so early had given him plenty of time to get work done on his class project, which he'd based on the work he was doing on the ARC.

He'd waited until after he knew others would be up and working before he meandered through the halls to the science center to keep an eye on the progress and for a little company while he waited for Stella to return. When he'd gotten to the science center he quickly realized that everyone had been up early that day.

He waited anxiously for confirmation that they were really going to do something – the right thing. After waiting more than an hour, Zura finally came out of the ROC room with a look of satisfaction.

"I've got it all together. We are ready and I think it'll make sense to our funders, thanks to all of you working so hard." For the first time in months, she looked content with the work they'd done but Stephen was waiting for whatever else she would say next – what he assumed would be orders.

"Can each of you take a section to review before I send it off?" she asked Johan, Rupert, and Mave.

"Do you all think we should wait until after the Gala to send this? Or do we send it before the Gala and ruin the party?" It was evident that Zura had already thought about it but was hoping that what she thought of as the best idea was shared by her team. The annual Gala was the one time every year she felt like they actually did something fun as a group.

The ARC had more than a hundred people working hard to keep it running. Most of the staff she saw hardly more than once or twice a month, if that. They were working behind the scenes and in the field. Their grueling schedule and demanding work made it so that she rarely got to tell them thank you and honor them face to face.

If she sent the report before the Gala, it would mean being on with UniCorps and the World Consensus science divisions instead of with her people celebrating their hard work. Even better, she actually might get to spend some time with her kids if she delayed sending the report for just one night.

"Zura?" Johan said louder. He'd started answering her question and realized she hadn't heard him.

"Yeah? So what do you all think?" she said, still not really listening. She was nervous and her hands shook ever so slightly as she tried to push off the other feeling just beginning to tickle at the back of her neck - fear.

"Why do you want to wait, Zura?" Mave asked.

"I didn't say I wanted to wait. I was just asking what you thought about the timing of delivery. Before or after the Gala," she said trying to be casual.

"Zura, we all know you better than that," Johan said, with a soft smile trying to let her know it was okay.

"What if they get this report tonight, before the Gala, and they start reading it immediately? I can't send it without marking it Urgent and so they *will* open it up. Once they open it up, they *will* read it. Once they read it, they *will* call me for a teleconference, and then I *will* have to pull all of you, well most of you, into a room and out of the party to answer questions and get drilled. So instead of enjoying the one fun thing we do the entire time we are on this block of ice, I have to pull everyone out of the party to be on a teleconference." Zura caught her breath and sat down, frustrated. She hated feeling owned, but they were all owned.

"Why don't we plan to send it ridiculously early the next morning? There's not much that we can do or they can do if they see the report tonight versus tomorrow morning. After all, it is the weekend and most of their staff will be gone. Just the jerks who run the place, I mean the officers, will be interested enough to open it," Mave said confidently.

"She's got a point, Zura. Waiting what amounts to ten or twelve hours won't matter. Not in the grand scheme of things. Trust me," Johan agreed.

Zura suddenly felt better. She didn't know what she would do without either of them, even if Johan did get under her skin sometimes.

"You're right, both of you. We get one night a year when we can celebrate as friends, party, toast, and have a good time. Let's not ruin it. There'll be plenty of bad days ahead so why add one more any sooner?" Zura forced a smile.

"Okay, you three," she said looking at Johan, Mave, and Rupert, "you've got your parts to read and get back to me by the end of today. Johan are you going to the hangar with Stephen? I still need your eyes on this too and we don't have much time. I mean you should go, but can you please come right back?" Zura didn't hesitate to take charge when it came to their work. Her eyes lingered on them as they went off in their separate directions. She missed them. All of them.

"Dad, wait. We need to head towards the hangar in twenty minutes to get Stella."

"Yes, Stephen. I know. I have the time too," Johan said before putting the report down on the desk. "I'm going to get my outside gear on and you should too. I'll meet you by the hangar's exit door in fifteen minutes okay?"

"Fifteen minutes," Stephen said checking his watch again. He started out of the science center and Zura followed behind him into the tunnel.

"Can I walk with you?" Zura asked as she caught up to him.

"You're my mom, mom. You also run the place," Stephen said with a confused look on his face.

"Stephen, I need you to do something for me while you are out there in the hangar. Is that okay?" Zura said searching his eyes rather than saying anything more.

"Yes. What is it?" he asked.

"I need you to take something with you. I need you to give it to the pilot, Jonathan Adams. He's the only one you can give it to. He's a longtime friend of mine. It's very important that you keep it safe and that you don't say anything about it. Stephen, look at me. I am trusting you with this." Zura's eyes penetrated his. She was more intense than usual, which worried Stephen.

"Why don't you ask Dad to do it?" Stephen asked worried. He looked at the palm of his hand which held a tiny microdot used to store data.

It was attached to the outside of a small silvery candy wrapper that camouflaged it.

"I can't. He can't do it. Only you can. It's better this way. I need you to trust me." Zura closed Stephen's hand around the candy wrapper. She searched his eyes for a sign of understanding. Stephen looked at the candy wrapper then back at Zura before nodding once and walking away.

He strode quickly to his bedroom, closed the door abruptly, and put the candy wrapper down on the desk. He only had ten minutes left before he was supposed to meet his dad. Before he did that he had to know what was on the microdot. *What was she giving to the pilot and why?*

Stephen put on a coat warm enough for the cold air that got into the hangar. He then checked the lock on the door before throwing himself into the chair. He opened up the reader sitting near his computing system and placed the silver piece of candy in the holder. He directed the laser scanner over the dot and quickly made a copy of it to his own microdot before opening the single folder stored. It simply read 'Noah'.

He clicked the folder name and more files than could fit on his viewer showed. It would take time he didn't have to think about where to even begin. The ARC was so big that he would need all two minutes he had left to jog to the hangar, where he would meet his dad and wait for Stella.

Stephen closed the folder and removed the original microdot from the reader. He placed it inside of a small plastic bag and into his coat pocket. His curiosity raced ahead of him as he stood up from his seat and prepared to leave. Stephen pulled the door open, pausing just long enough to move his copy of the data to a hidden storage compartment under his desk.

Stephen walked out of his bedroom door quickly. He now had to hustle down the network of tunnels, past the great hall where they were preparing for the ball, to the end where he would find the hangar's exit door. Stephen inhaled deeply taking in the smell of the cakes and pies already baking. He wasn't excited about the gala but they always had the best desserts.

Stephen pushed against the door and as it released under his pressure the cold air hit his face. He hadn't used the door since Stella left at the beginning of the week. There was no need to be cold if you didn't have to be, even if you could handle it better than most.

"You made it. Her craft should be coming any moment, based on my tracker," Johan showed Stephen his watch with a small light beeping on a tiny screen resembling a radar. "They are all ready for her." Johan stuffed his hands in his pocket. He could handle the cold just as well as Stephen, but Zura would balk if either went out without their coats.

There was no way Stephen would have missed it or even been late for Stella's return. He was more excited than anyone else that she was coming back home.

"So what are you going to do the rest of the day? You should finally have some free time. Your mom didn't give you a job today," Johan said with a smile that said he already knew.

"Stella is coming home. I'm going to spend the free time with her."

"Of course. What was I even thinking?" Johan joked to a dead- pan faced Stephen.

Johan and Stephen monitored the skies outside the hangar door for the six person aircraft that would be carrying Stella. Soon, a small shadow began creeping along the snow packed ground and then the craft came into view of the short runway. It slowed down and came to a hover as it entered the open hangar.

Stephen left the corner by the door where he stood with Johan, partially protected from the cold wind. Knowing Stella, she'd step off that craft with a regular jacket rather than a coat meant for late fall in Antarctica.

He was right. The door opened and steps lowered to reveal Stella in her lighter jacket. She came off the craft waving with one hand and carrying a small suitcase with the other. A man who looked like the pilot came off behind her, carrying what was clearly Stella's other suitcase.

Stephen walked over to Stella and gave her an awkward hug, lightly tapping her back. "Why aren't you wearing a real coat? You're gonna get pneumonia," he said worried.

"I missed you too, little brother. Besides, I do have a real coat on. It's all I need to walk forty yards to the door," Stella said as she gave Stephen a hug.

Johan walked up behind Stephen giving her a big welcome home hug before he took the bags from Stella and the pilot. Stephen read the name J. Adams on his uniform. *That's him*, thought Stephen. As Johan walked towards the doors to go back inside the main building, Stella lingered, watching Stephen.

"Hi Mr. Adams. I haven't seen you in a few years. Usually, you must be on the larger runs when I don't get to come out. Can I see your craft?" asked Stephen.

"That's right. Is it Stephen?" Adams asked.

"Yes. Stephen."

"Come on up. I've got a few minutes before turning her around," Adams said, inviting Stephen up the steps.

"You guys can go ahead inside where it's warm. I'm just going to check out this craft for one minute and then I'll be right back inside," Stephen said as he walked toward the aircraft.

Stella looked at him with her head tilted just slightly, before following Johan back to the door he and Stephen had walked through minutes before. Once inside Stephen was legitimately impressed. The craft was small but clean and neat. He knew the craft was still on and being powered, but the power source was quiet, only giving off a vibration that could easily be ignored.

The windows, tinted from the inside, displayed the outside and inside temperatures on the tempered glass panes. The seats were modern and streamlined but had cushioning covered by a soft smooth material. He ran his hand over the chair and then sat down turning it all the way around and then back again.

Adams watched him with interest. "So, do you like it?" he finally asked. "I've been flying this girl for just over a year when I have lighter loads, usually chartered. She's small, fast, and efficient."

Stephen stood up. "It's really nice, Mr. Adams. Wish I could fly in it, but when we leave we'll have to take the air bus since it'll be so many of us." Stephen felt inside of his pocket on the small piece of candy and pulled it out slowly. He looked behind him and out the windows of the craft.

"Mr. Adams? My mom wanted me to give this to you. It's only for you." He handed the candy wrapper with the attached microdot over to Adams, all of it still in the plastic baggie.

Adams took it and looked at it closely for a moment before he placed it in the inside pocket of his coat. "Do you know what it is?" Stephen asked Adams.

"Yes, I do. Thanks. It is important. You better get back to your sister and dad. I'm sure they are waiting for you," Adams said peeking out the window. "Enjoy your last couple weeks on the ice. I myself have gotta fly." He patted the pocket on his jacket.

Adams watched Stephen walk out and down the few steps to the ground below and then waved towards Johan and

Stella. He lowered the door and walked toward his pilot's seat. Once in his chair, he reached in his pocket and took out the baggie and candy wrapper. Adams removed the microdot and candy wrapper from the small baggie and he quickly scanned it with his portable reader.

The folder Noah popped up. It was there. He put away the reader and placed the candy back inside the baggie, putting it back safely inside his coat pocket. Things were in motion.

CHAPTER THIRTEEN
Connected

Antarctic Research Center

NEARLY SIXTEEN YEARS had passed and still Mave had never told Zura or Johan that she'd known all along that their twins would be born in Antarctica. Stephen and Stella were the only ones who could have been selected for that place and arrive in the needed time.

The Unseens had chosen to split the Chi into two bodies. They had decided it would have been too much energy for one to handle and it was too great a risk to the mission for the person they'd chosen to become overwhelmed and dysfunctional.

Twin souls could work together, help each other, and balance the Chi. The Unseens and the Earth Council had given generous leeway with how things happened, as long as certain key things happened along the way. One of those key things was that a child had to be born on each of the seven continents, which were now represented by the seven regions.

Each region held an energetic blueprint and each of the chosen children embodied the energy of the region. Together they would be strong enough, powerful enough that even the World Consensus and UniCorps would have a difficult time stopping them. It would require that they had their own Awakening and were guided by the Keepers until it was time to act.

Just like Mave and the other Keepers, each person had a role, a part to play. Some greater than others, but all critical to the success of the mission. It didn't matter what the part was, but when the time came, they would have to play it. Everyone would have their moment.

Mave considered herself fortunate. She was one of a handful of people, all Connecteds, who had some powers in common and some unique gifts that allowed them to serve their mission. All five also went through the 'Awakening' when they were ready to understand and act on what they'd been sent to do.

For her the Awakening happened soon after becoming a para-adult. She'd gone to camp one Summer for science and technology and met some other very interesting people. While at the camp, she learned that they'd been brought there on purpose, under the direction of the Council.

It was during that camp that Mave met Y Chang and Canson Pritchard for the first time. She'd also met Dr. Lima who now served as a Director for a University program that provided camps in science and technology to teens and university aged students.

Canson Pritchard was a teaching counselor at the camp the year she attended and was already working in the science field in education for one of the virtual schools. The camps were a way for him to earn extra income when school was out.

Y Chang was around the same age as Mave, but Y Chang had been much younger when the Awakening happened for her. She was just seven when she'd had hers and like Mave, she was from the Eastern Way. By the time Canson received his Awakening he was nearly thirty years old.

As far as Mave knew, the fourth Keeper still had not gone through the Awakening. The Council was concerned he had been lost to the temptations that claimed so many other Connecteds. Mave and the other Keepers weren't told exactly who he was but had been told he had chosen a difficult role and been born into power, wealth, and privilege.

The Earth Council had agreed to allow this power along with certain personal attributes. To them it was worth the risk in order to have access to and affect those in power and to serve as Keeper for one of the eight who was to play an integral role in the mission. The eighth was also closely associated with the world of power, wealth, and privilege.

The Earth Council had chosen not to reveal either of their identities to the other Keepers so as not to interfere with free will. While Kean was uncertain, the others still held out hope that his free will would lead him to the path they needed him to be on.

Dr. Lima had brought them together in a special book club that summer, where they discussed literature, world history, social science, and science. She'd shown them how it was all woven together. Dr. Lima was Mave's guide and mentor and had been critical to her own Awakening. She recalled Dr. Lima's talks and discussions about the use of the Connection.

Dr. Lima once said "there are some who use the Connection for good. There are others who use the Connection for purely selfish gain. Yet, most are still unaware that they are Connecteds and so aren't using their power for anything at all."

When she started camp that summer she had no idea that it would change her life. Mave had been in that intimate club with Y Chang and Canson. Yet, even then, Dr. Lima always seemed to be waiting on someone else to show, but he or she never did.

Mave remembered how Dr. Lima looked around at the three of them as if she were thinking deeply, considering them on some other level. She then told them a story about the Festival of Lights. It was a story that had been passed down to Dr. Lima from her own Keeper.

Many nights when she lay in bed at night, unable to sleep because of the weight of everything she had to do, she'd recall that story.

Dr. Lima began by telling them of a wondrous Festival of Lights that happened every year at the Winter Solstice.

"Let me tell you all a story," she began. "One that I was told around this same point in my life. Pay close attention to this magical tale," she'd told them as she began changing their lives that evening.

"The Festival of Lights was a celebration of the coming light and of choosing to help brighten the dark. Where we are here in the Southern Allegiance Region there was a traveling caravan. People would hang colorful, handmade lanterns on their vehicles as they drove, to let others know which way to go. It was quite a sight. Especially, as the people got closer and closer to the festival. The line of lanterns coming in gave a clear path for anyone who may have gotten lost along the way."

Mave remembered that Dr. Lima paused then for a moment to let just that part sink in to her book club members.

"You know, it didn't matter who you were. People gathered from every corner of the world at the point where the sun is closest to the Earth. Some would arrive before the festival was to begin and craft lanterns. As the legend goes, at midnight the clouds would part and the sky would clear. Within moments, there would appear millions of stars. The people would light their own lanterns and release them into the night sky to join with the stars."

Dr. Lima waved her hands towards the sky, where the first sign of stars had started to show. She put her hands in her lap and studied them before continuing.

"As the story goes, there would be so many lanterns, shining so brightly, it would appear as if dawn had come early. The glow could be seen from miles away. After the lanterns had all been released, then the fun would begin. There'd be a celebration filled with music, dancing, singing, drinking, talking, and all kinds of celebration in anticipation of the new day coming. It was when the morning star would cast off the remaining darkness and be with them longer and longer each day." At this point, Dr. Lima smiled.

Her face lit up as if she were watching it all in front of her at that very moment, her very own show. Her eyes went somewhere else as she experienced the magic of the story.

It was early in the evening two days before they were set to leave, and after they'd heard the story. The four met on the far side of campus and rolled logs over to sit on before gathering sticks to start a small fire. The fire was more for light than for warmth and Dr. Lima had insisted. She loved a good fire.

Dr. Lima had continued the story by telling them that at the festival, there were always some who just watched and enjoyed the beauty of the lights, but chose not to participate in lighting their own lantern and releasing it.

That evening as they sat listening to the end of the tale about the Festival of Lights, Dr. Lima stopped and looked each of them in the eye. Then she forced the three to lean in to hear her as she whispered what Mave remembered felt like a secret.

"You are all lanterns," she said leaning into them as well. "You can choose to light the lantern or not, but that doesn't change the nature of what you are."

Dr. Lima then sat back on her stump and picked up a super-sized marshmallow and shoved it onto a stick. As she stuck the stick in the fire. Mave could see her smiling.

On that warm July evening Dr. Lima said a great deal more but when Mave was in her darkest moments and doubted her choice, she remembered that she'd chosen to light her lantern. The choice had cost her some of the simplest pleasures of life, but she'd made it and was committed to it.

After those two weeks of camp they all went their separate ways. Dr. Lima remained in Southern Allegiance, Mave returned to her home in the southern part of the Eastern Way. Canson left for his home in Australia and Y Chang returned to the main continent of the Eastern Way.

They all went back but none of them were the same. The time spent with Dr. Lima. Canson, and Y Chang had ignited something dormant in Mave and that fire continued to burn. It wasn't much later that Mave would have the talk with her mother in the garden that brought it home fully and deepened her conviction.

Mave exhaled deeply. Long ago, when her hair didn't shimmer with strands of silver and her eyes weren't artfully embraced with lines that gave a memorable mark of the joys and trials of life, she settled on the realization it was better not to know, especially if they weren't prepared to use it, than to know and abuse it. She adamantly believed that with power comes responsibility, and too many Connecteds had abused their power or had allowed themselves to become corrupted by it.

Since that camp all those years before, Dr. Lima had been assigned as a Lead Guide, helping the Keepers who were selected to guide the Chosen eight. The time was coming soon when they would need to meet again and they would discuss the newest developments and move forward with their plans.

***

MAVE WOULD HAVE to report on what the data showed and she knew they weren't yet fully prepared to address the speed at which things might progress from that point. There were certain measures the Earth Council tried to refrain from using because it began to border on their laws of order and that would be out of line with the Unseen.

She would just have to try and remain focused for the time. There was nothing she could do except be prepared and that wouldn't happen by worrying.

Part of that preparation was the special event Mave was planning for the twins. She wanted it to happen when they were back in New South City. With all that was going on, she wasn't sure she would have enough time to make it work or that it would make sense to her no nonsense Stephen.

Between the findings, the reports, the visit from the science divisions of both the World Consensus and UniCorps, and that evening's annual ARC Gala, there was very little time for thinking about or planning anything else.

Mave hoped she'd have enough time once they were back in Northern Allegiance and in their other routine to pull it all together. Once back there, they were always more scattered. Their schedules were harder to keep track of and she couldn't just walk over to their living quarters.

She couldn't do it on her own and, as she considered it further, realized she shouldn't have to. She would get help from their parents, plain and simple. They couldn't afford to lose time since she had to coordinate more than just the twins for this surprise.

With a few taps to her watch, Mave sent a quick note to her longtime friend Canson Pritchard. She needed to make sure he was on target for his next part, which if things were going according to plan, would be happening fairly soon. He needed to help her send out the signal for what would be a not so coincidental coincident.

CHAPTER FOURTEEN
Ren

New South City in Northern Allegiance

LONG SINEWY MUSCLES strained against the metal restraints. Rennold growled, bearing his clenched teeth as he struggled to get free. He looked at the needle the technician held with the tube at the end to collect this month's sample. It looked even bigger this month than it had last month.

The technician eased closer to him slowly and he continued to struggle against the heavy duty restraints, his muscles tensed. The band squeezing around his arm felt sinister and inhumane as it made his veins bulge despite his protest.

The gag in his mouth prevented him from yelling to let them know how angry and resentful he was for being treated like a lab rat. The gag was relatively new, having been added to the regimen after he'd torn flesh from a technicians arm, three months ago. Since then it had been added to the protocol for the monthly blood sucking and bloodletting procedures he was forced to endure.

The two way mirror hid her from view, but Ren knew his mother Kim was watching. In the room away from his judgmental eyes, tears slowly ran down her face. When she saw him afterwards she knew the evidence of her crying, the puffy eyes, the red cheeks and nose would still be evident. Even after all these years, coming here with him and having the tests run and his blood taken still upset her.

All these years and still there was nothing. They were no closer to an answer. He was different, forever changed, and she knew why. Knowing this did nothing to control the anger or the outbursts caused by the raging levels of testosterone and serum that coursed through his veins. She'd been convinced to receive one of the earlier doses of the same controversial serum given Stella and Stephen while she was pregnant with him.

She'd met Zura and Johan years ago as part of a select group of would be parents who'd volunteered to help understand a life changing serum and to allow their children to receive the first benefits. It was a second round of studies that had been abandoned a generation earlier. They'd all been found and recruited by Dr. Claudia Lima.

Mave came into the picture soon after, talking about how important Rennold was and why it was important that he be protected. The years had gone from a bad dream to a nightmare once he hit puberty and even more hormones flooded his body, but Mave seemed to have some magical power over Ren.

Whenever she was around him, he changed and seemed to stop fighting everything and everyone as much. She wasn't sure leaving him in Mave's care would be the best thing for Ren, but nothing else had helped so far.

As Kim peered through the glass she saw her son's eyes get that wild animalistic look again. They were done taking the blood for this month, but no one wanted to let him out of the restraints. She would have to go in and soothe him first.

She prepared herself mentally for the unpredictable reactions she witnessed each month. Some months it was easy as soothing and going home and in other months they both left screaming and in tears. It could take twenty minutes sometimes, but if she didn't go in, he might really hurt someone. He'd gotten so strong and his anger could become so extreme, if he really knew his strength he would be out of the restraints already.

Ren's eyes softened when he saw Kim walk through the doors to the lab. He slowly stopped struggling against the restraints and she could see his tensed muscles relax. He hated being tied down like an animal, having his blood taken and having them give him shots to see if it would help calm him.

For more than five years he'd been coming here every month and nothing had come of it. Nothing. He was ready to be done and try something different. He hoped Mave could help. He was nervous about the ceremony and even more nervous about leaving home without his mother for a month.

Since his change, he hadn't gone anywhere without Kim. She was his safety net when he got overwhelmed and his natural survival instinct of fighting kicked in. He might not be able to get back to calm without her and could wind up killing someone this time.

Kim ran her hands over his blond hair, saying nothing. She wished she'd never agreed to the trial, but it was too late. There was no going back. Whatever was in him was there. It had already fully integrated into his system years ago, the doctors had told her. All they could try to do now was manage it.

She nodded her head to the man behind the two-way mirror to release the restraints. They unlocked and Ren shot out of the seat. He looked at the mirror and threw up his middle finger before grabbing the tech's chair and hurling it at the glass divider.

"You bastards! Come in here when I'm not restrained! You think you're so tough when you have me tied down!?" he yelled through the shatterproof glass. He grabbed his uniform shirt, pulling it over his head as he stormed out of the door.

"Ren, they are just doing their jobs. They're trying to help," Kim said.

"Don't defend them mom. If they were trying to help, they would have helped by now. Instead they still just treat me like a freak after five years. Five years of getting my blood drawn every month by rude imbeciles who treat me like an animal," he yelled the last part, turning his head back towards the mirror so he was sure they'd hear him. "Five years of having them give me drugs like a lab rat and nothing to show for it! Nothing!" he yelled. Kim stopped and stepped back from her son who was raging again.

He huffed, then looked at the fear in her eyes. She'd done this to him. She thought she was helping but she'd ruined his life. "I wanna go home," he said more quietly. "I need to get out of here. This place makes me crazy."

* * *

PERHAPS THE AWAKENING Ceremony would help. Mave had been trying to convince Kim to let Rennold go through it since he'd had his first incident at thirteen - the incident that had forced him to undergo testing. The same testing that hadn't found any solutions in more than five years. At almost nineteen he was just a couple years from being an adult and possibly being condemned as unfit for society. Ren was afraid of what that meant.

He'd lost so much from his earlier life and already had to change so much of his life to accommodate the effects of the serum that lived in him. They'd moved across the country to where they could get better access to the treatments, even if they weren't working. In a fitful rage over what seemed a minor argument now, he'd hit his father. The blow to his chest sent him to the hospital in cardiac arrest. After that, Kim knew he couldn't continue living like he was.

He'd left his father and that damaged relationship and all of his friends to live in New South City. Ren had stopped attending regular school at fifteen when medication couldn't control him and he'd had to finish his studies with private tutors and online courses.

Now his mother thought he would suddenly be able to function without her, around other teens. Though he hoped she was right, he was still scared he might lose it. Scared she might be wrong.

CHAPTER FIFTEEN
Heat

Antarctic Research Center

BY MIDDAY THE service craft arrived with the special menu items and serving staff for the Gala to be held that evening. The pastry and dessert staff had already prepared a mouthwatering display of delicious treats, leaving the kitchen open for the other courses. They'd spent one night on the ARC and could now return on the same craft that had brought the others to finish with the rest of the party preparations.

Soon the great hall was buzzing with energy as people flew around the room setting up for the evening's gala. There was a team in the large kitchen prepping the food, stacking dishes, organizing silverware and napkins. Another team was working in the great hall setting up tables for the party and putting together the dance floor that was stored onsite for the annual event. After the first two years of having it brought in, they'd purchased their own that stayed on the ARC for future parties.

A group from the decoration team was busily hand-making centerpieces from fresh cut flowers and ribbons in spring colors for all of the tables. Outside the wall of windows that lined the external walls of the great hall there was the reminder that they were still in Antarctica - ice sculptures being finished. Stella looked around the room at all of the activity. She couldn't wait for the party to be over.

There weren't any other kids on the ARC besides her and Stephen so these parties were always filled with boring talk of the weather, literally, and what people were planning to do when they got back home. Of course, everyone was just going home to do more work. It might be slightly different work, but it was still work related to this work and Stella found it nauseatingly boring.

Stella was searching the room now for Ms. Ida. Ms. Ida had been coordinating the Gala as long as Stella could remember. With all of her colorful eccentricities, she was a breath of fresh air to Stella. She was from Northern Liberty and was full of spunk considering how old she must have been. Stella guessed she was pretty old, at least fifty. She also spoke with a beautiful accent that Stella had gotten pretty good at emulating whenever she spoke to her long enough.

Ms. Ida never just wore the uniform. She always added handmade, knitted, and even crocheted accessories like scarves, leg wraps, arm bands, neck grabbers, and even ear piercers. Sometimes she'd show up wearing all of them at once. She said when she came here she needed everything, just to stay warm.

Ms. Ida always made her something special and she was the one person Stella actually looked forward to seeing and talking to during the Gala. The one year Ms. Ida hadn't come, was the year Stella turned thirteen, and also the year Ms. Ida's mother had passed. Since then, Stella always liked to check and see if she was there when everyone was setting up. She had something for her this year too, picked up from the science camp campus gift shop. She knew Ms. Ida would love it since it was as colorful as she was.

After looking around from the door for a minute she still didn't see her. Ms. Ida might be in the kitchen, but Stella wouldn't be able to find out. The staff, Ms. Ida, and her parents had banned both she and Stephen from the great hall and kitchen until party time a few years ago.

It was after the incident when Stella and Stephen were twelve and tried to sneak cupcakes out of the kitchen. Instead of making a clean escape, one of them, Stella always denied it was her, knocked the perfect cupcake pyramid off the counter along with a tray full of cookies shaped and colored like animals in the Antarctic. Stella still thought everyone had overreacted. Besides, now they were nearly sixteen.

Even outside of the great hall the ARC was buzzing with activity. Zura was heading down towards the great hall looking for Stella. She'd barely seen her since she got back and she knew Stella would be looking for Ms. Ida. Unlike many days when she might only pass her family, today Zura was passing people from her other teams on the ARC. Some of whom she hadn't seen in weeks.

There were two maintenance teams, an engineering team, collection team, a classification and preservation team, a health unit, a special operations team, and a team who worked with each Region to monitor ground and submantle activity. There was also a team that Johan managed that did some other research and collection work related to embryonic research and sustainability as far as she knew, but they rarely participated in anything.

During the Summer months the ARC had close to a hundred people working on it. Most of them were off that day to rest and prepare for the celebration. Usually a representative from UniCorps came but this year they declined the invitation. They'd elected to instead come to the larger semi-annual year end meeting happening the following week. It would be the last important meeting of Zura's team before everyone left the ARC for the Winter.

Zura was relieved with their decision to not participate at the gala. It would have ruined the party if they came, considering the pending news. She tried to push all of that out of her head for the time and reminded herself that she couldn't do anything about it now.

As Zura rounded a corner with a split she nearly collided with Stella. "Oh, there you are," Zura beamed. "How's my star child?" she asked putting her arm around Stella.

"Hi, mom. I'm fine. I was just seeing if Ms. Ida was around. Have you seen her? Oh, how are you? Ready for the party?"

Zura shrugged. They hadn't had a chance to talk to Stella about what was happening and she needed to tell her before she heard it from Stephen. "I haven't seen Ida. You heading back to your room now?" Zura asked.

"Yeah, I'm tired. I was up too late last night. We were having so much fun mom, we didn't want to go home so we stayed up as long as we could together. I met some of the most nine people ever and we are definitely all going to keep in touch. Well at least some of us, I guess," Stella said before being interrupted.

"What's a nine person?" Zura asked confused.

"Mom, cool, light, fun, peps. Anyway, there were people from all over the world - the Liberties, the Allegiances, the Eastern Way, and even Australia. That's where my number one new friend is from. Her name is Alexis and she is absolutely, well, she follows her heart. They even had an old pump on the campus, like the ones we learned about in school."

"Take a breath honey," Zura laughed.

"Okay," Stella smiled, "I breathed. So the old pump was right in the middle of the courtyard and it was so cool. I threw a rock in just to see how far down it would go, but I couldn't really tell. Oh, and I even made a few guy friends too. I mean we're just friends. They were great to hang out with. Wait, I got you something Mom. I think you'll like it. It's totally antique type vintage. You know, old. You won't believe it. It was in the educational materials' section of the campus shop. They had some really old things in there. They even had a whole special section of just old stuff to look at. We couldn't buy it since it was just a display. I can't believe people had to live like that in the 2000s. I think I would have just died."

Zura walked along with her daughter, just smiling and listening. She loved to listen to Stella talk, even if it meant she didn't get more than a few words in. At least today she was talking to her. Stella had shut both Zura and Johan out when she left at the start of the week. She was upset about having to go to camp, but it seemed she had gotten past that.

Stella opened the door to her room just enough to look in. She shrugged as she opened it the rest of the way. "Sorry, I kinda just dumped everything in once I got back. Stephen wanted to show me something but I told him I didn't want to do anymore science stuff, not today. Besides, I was going to look for Ms. Ida. I should probably see him and at least see what he wanted. Ugh. Did I mention I am not in love with science, mom? Why doesn't Stephen have to go to art camp or music camp? So not fair." Stella flopped on the bed dramatically.

"Stella, I am so glad you are home. I missed you," Zura said, closing the door and sitting down next to her. "I do need to talk to you too."

"What's going on?" Stella said, forcing herself to be quiet.

"We've been working almost around the clock here this past week," she started.

"And that's different from normal, how?" Stella asked, smiling at her mom.

"Okay, maybe that's true. We discovered something in our data that we are going to have to report. It's a big issue and next week all the reps from both UniCorps' and the World Consensus' science divisions are going to be here. They would be here anyway, but it is going to be much more intense. What we are about to report to them, is really big and they aren't going to like it." Zura stopped to let that much soak in.

"Well, what is it?" Stella prodded.

"Let's see, how do I explain this? The ground is getting weaker. Our pumping of gas and emissions into the earth over the past almost fifteen to sixteen years has caused a sort of fracturing of the earth beneath the ground where the holes are. It's kind of like veins splitting off and they seem to be drawn towards existing fault lines, where earthquakes are already likely to happen."

"So does that mean we are making more earthquakes?"

"Not exactly. Or, at least, not completely. It does mean that the more we pump the more veins are made and the more pressure there is on the ground where the earth is being pushed to the side. There is only so much room to wiggle before something has to give. We're already starting to see the effects with increased tremors and the migration of sea life away from the most effected zones."

"What do you mean?" Stella asked sitting up suddenly more interested.

"What's happening below the surface is impacting where sea creatures are giving birth, which impacts where other sea creatures go for later feedings. It's just a nasty web and we are pretty certain that the earthquake in Southern Allegiance happened as a result of this. In fact, I'm pretty certain the increase of all these smaller earthquakes are because of this." Zura looked at Stella while rubbing her temples. She knew Stella would see it in the simplest way.

"We stop the pumping and then we'll stop the splitting, right?" Stella said, just as Zura had anticipated. It should have been that cut and dry.

"Yeah, basically, that's what would need to happen. However, it isn't a guarantee but it would be the best start," Zura said looking down. In reality, it wasn't quite that easy.

"What's the problem then? Start with shutting down the pumps," Stella said as she studied her mom's tired eyes and the bags hanging over her cheeks.

"I wish it were that simple Stella. That we'd just turn off the pumps tomorrow. Unfortunately, I don't think our funders are going to simply say, 'turn it off' without having a way to solve the problem in their favor."

"In THEIR favor? What about everyone else? Everything else? Excuse me, but what the hell? They can use dad's idea!"

Zura could see herself in Stella at that moment. She could see the heat rising around Stella's neck before Stella spoke, her temper beginning to flare.

"Stella, watch it," Zura warned.

"I am watching it mom. I'm watching as someone tries to destroy the world, again, and everyone is too scared to say something. Again! Ugh. What? The water crisis and ten percent of people dying wasn't enough? Let's shoot for twenty this time!"

Zura chose to let her rant. She had every right to be mad.

"I know you're upset Stella, but there is one more thing. This is classified information. You can't share it with anyone outside of the core science research team – that's me, your dad, Mave, Rupert, and of course Stephen. That means no one else on the ARC, no other family, friends, no one else can know what we've found."

"It's a secret?" Stella asked incredulously. "Of course, it's a secret. Okay. Well what can we do? I see what the problem is, but who's working on the answer?" The fire had risen to Stella's face.

"We are looking at some options, but for today, let's not worry about it since it'll be up to UniCorps and the World Consensus to decide which direction to take. I just wanted you to know and to find out from me. There's nothing we can do right now." Her mom stood up and took a deep breath.

"So, what did you bring back for me?" Zura asked plastering a smile on her face, but she couldn't hide from Stella the worry and concern that were imprinted on her brow and inside her head.

CHAPTER SIXTEEN
Ready

Antarctic Research Center

RUPERT FIDGETED SLIGHTLY as he smoothed his clothing and ran his hands over his neatly styled locs. He stood outside of Mave's door dressed in a handsome formal outfit. It was finally time to head down to the ARC Gala.

He wasn't sure he really felt like going or that they really had time for it this year. It was their eighteenth year and in that time the ARC had grown up, in a way. Much like a regular eighteen year old, there were still some challenges as it tried to figure out what it wanted to do.

The door to Mave's room opened and what he saw nearly took his breath away. He stood there staring at her like he'd seen an angel.

She was stunning in her long red dress with gold beads lining the edges. A long matching red silky wrap draped over one shoulder. She had on the earrings he'd bought for her two years ago on her birthday. She'd only worn them once before, at the Gala last year. In his eyes, she was the first and last. She had no idea what she did to him.

"You look absolutely beautiful." He gave her a kiss on the cheek despite wanting more than anything to touch his lips to hers, even if it smudged her lipstick, but he wouldn't.

Her streak of silver made her look even more refined and elegant and he loved that she didn't feel the need to change who she was naturally.

"Are you ready for this?" Rupert asked after taking all of her in.

"If by 'this' you mean the Gala…no I'm not but let's go and try to have fun. We only get this once a year. We've worked hard these past few months and it's going to get even harder. How about we take one night to relax, handsome? We deserve it," she smiled at him and smoothed his tuxedo.

If only she weren't already committed. She sighed and took his arm as they walked toward the great hall.

***

STEPHEN BANGED ON Stella's door impatiently.

"Can I come in?"

After talking with him earlier, Stella had gone into her room to sleep. She'd only gotten up an hour earlier to get ready, and he doubted she was, but thought he'd check.

"Hold on," Stella answered through the door. She needed to zip her dress. She only bothered wearing one because her mom ran the ARC and she was asked in past years not to embarrass either of her parents too much. She got it up and zipped. Despite it being a dress, she had to admit that she liked it and she liked how she looked in it.

Of course almost anything was less boring than the regular assigned uniforms with their stain friendly three color options. *Would you prefer grey, black, or navy blue? None, thank you.* So tonight Stella was wearing a pastel blue dress that dropped just below her knees and her favorite boots, similar to what the SEP Agents wore but in a darker hue of blue. Her curls were free with the exception of a butterfly hairclip pinned on the right. She even decided to put some lip gloss on. Anything more was too much trouble.

"I'm still holding…" Stephen knocked again. Stella had forgotten he was out there as she looked in her mirror admiring herself.

She opened the door. "Sorry. So should I wear the matching jacket or should I wear this scarf Ms. Ida made me?" Stella held both of them up.

Stephen looked at them and then looked at her. "Do you really want me to choose?" he said with a confused look on his face.

"No. I guess not. Are you wearing that?" her nose wrinkled as she pointed to his outfit.

Stephen looked down at himself in the black slacks and plain white dress shirt before answering with a shrug. "Yeah, it's my more formal wear and it meets the requirements for the Gala. It is mostly comfortable so I think it is suitable." Stella just shook her head.

"Close the door Stephen," Stella ordered, sounding like Zura. "I want to ask you something about the report and all the stuff you all have been doing. I don't know for sure but I'm not feeling so good about this whole situation. Mom is worried and I don't know how I know but I don't believe any of these people are really doing something that's going to fix it. I'm afraid that when we are actually grown up there'll hardly be any safe place to live. What if they decide to just bury it, so to speak?"

"Well, they could try but I don't think it can stay buried. The evidence will speak for itself. It is nearly impossible to hide an earthquake. Besides there have already been a couple of earthquakes, and the one in Southern Allegiance was above a five on the Richter scale. It's not a major earthquake, but it's more than can be ignored, especially considering the fact it wasn't even on a known fault line."

"But you can bury the truth and not give people options to avoid those earthquakes or bury it and not have a way to prevent them from happening in the first place," Stella snapped back, unsatisfied with Stephen's response.

"What did I do?" Stephen backed away. "I'm in the same situation as you Stella. I don't know exactly what's going to happen. I know what we are reporting for the most part, but no one has all of the answers. What I do know is that it isn't practical to think that you or I can just march into UniCorps or the World Consensus and say to them 'stop pumping, or else'. The probability of that giving us a positive outcome is essentially zero."

Stella rolled her eyes and pressed her lips together. She decided to check the time instead of attempting a response to Stephen. "I guess we better get down to the great hall. Mom will be giving her speech in just a few minutes. It'd be rude for us not to be there. Besides I'm up right after that." She grabbed the jacket and a small bag and followed Stephen out the door.

"I hope Ms. Ida is here. I think she's going to love this." Stella opened the bag and let Stephen look inside.

Stephen furrowed his brow. "What is it?"

"It's a piece of body decoration from the early twenty-first century, before they began using stones and gems almost exclusively for conducting energy. A private owner donated her collection to the school and they put them in the shop as collector items. I think you put it on your finger. I've seen pictures of people wearing things like this in museums.

"Is that what you needed the extra lubles for?" Stephen asked, taking a guess.

"Yes. Don't tell mom, but I didn't really use any of those forty lubles on snacks. I spent all of it plus some I'd saved on this and it was worth it. I know Ms. Ida is going to be excited when I give it to her. She's going to love it."

CHAPTER SEVENTEEN
Gala

Antarctic Research Center

THE TWINS COULD hear the sounds of talking and the live band coming out of the great hall as they tread quickly through the corridors. Once they arrived at the doors they looked at each other and walked into the great hall together.

Johan marched over to meet them as soon as their faces crossed the doorway and hurried them over to their table, near the front of the hall beside the small stage where the band was set up.

Stephen tried to take it in but it felt overdone and was too much for him. There were so many people working the event compared to the number of people actually there from the ARC for the party. Stella took her seat between Stephen and Johan.

Zura was sitting beside their father looking at her notes on her tablet. It was a beautiful sleek clear tablet that she could write on, read on, take notes on, and more. Despite having had it for months no one had ever seen her pull it out until now.

Johan touched Zura's hand and she looked up with a slight jump. Even with all the noise in the room, he'd managed to startle her. She loved her work and was great at it. That didn't change the fact that she hated having to stand in front of all of them and talk about how great they were and how important the work they were doing was, and remind them of why their sacrifices mattered and why what they did mattered, and so on.

This year felt even worse, knowing what was at stake and keeping it from them.

If she thought it would be okay, she'd simply say, "You're all amazing and we are all doing our part to save the world. Thanks everyone for another hard working year. Let's dance!" After the thought about it, she laughed. *That would be easy enough. Yeah it would be.*

Zura looked at the time and stood up. As she began to walk toward the stage she could feel everyone's eyes following her. She carefully climbed the few steps to the stage and the band quieted, along with the guests and service staff. Now, they were waiting on her. She regretted not taking a drink of water before getting up.

Her mouth felt like she'd taken a teaspoon of cinnamon. She tried to clear her throat. Her eyes focused on the short speech she'd written on her tablet and with one more glance at her waiting audience, she began.

"Good evening everyone. Thank you for being on the ARC for another year. I can hardly believe it's been eighteen years since we first came here with a vision for changing our world for the better. Because of you." She paused realizing she couldn't say what she'd originally written and decided to take the much simpler direction.

"It's because of you that we celebrate tonight, your commitment and your sacrifice. I want to thank every one of you for another year of hard work. Tonight, we're going to party!" Zura was surprised by the applause and appreciation for the short remarks even if she wasn't done.

"Before the band begins again we're going to start the party off tonight with an upbeat and very special piece from one of our younger people on the ARC, my daughter Stella. She's performing a classic piece from the mid twenty-first century on the piano."

Stella pushed her chair back and inhaled, letting the breath slowly move out of her as she walked over to the beautiful baby grand piano that she'd fallen in love with years before. Every eye was on her. She sat down and slid her fingers across the keyboard, feeling it, becoming one with it.

For this song, she didn't need to look at the sheet music. She'd learned to play it by memory two years before and had continued to practice until she felt she could play it smoothly, her fingers having memorized every movement. She'd even snuck away to the auditorium at camp to practice, when she could get away.

She lined her fingers up at the starting point and began to play. The first notes filled the room and the music filled her, creating a magical experience. As her fingers slid across the keys effortlessly she seemed to radiate. She could see the rainbow created from the notes as sound became light waves in motion. With every key stroke she created her own light show.

It didn't bother her that no one else in the room could see it moving through the air and all around them as she played. It was beautiful, like the Aurora Borealis, just more vivid and filled with every color of the rainbow. They all correlated to the notes Stella played using the vibrations of the baby grand piano. They couldn't see it, but they felt the chills as the music vibrated around them.

Mave would often look up and around into what seemed like empty space. She could see something but it wasn't an experience she could share. Stella's fingers continued to dance along the keys, graceful, strong, and sure. She'd begun playing before she could write and even if many other things didn't make much sense to her, this did.

Stella finished her piece and sat there another moment taking in the applause and watching the colors fade. She then stood with a bright smile across her face, curtsied politely and then threw up both her hands as if to say 'yes, look at me'. *That's*

Stella, Johan and Zura thought simultaneously. She bounced back to her seat the smile staying with her.

The band filled the room with music to eat and dance to, and for the next three hours everyone on the ARC had the chance to forget all of their worries and just enjoy the night. The food was delicious, the drinks flowed freely, and the dessert table was all but raided by the twins.

Stella found Ms. Ida shortly after her performance. She was standing near the back of the room watching the party unfold and making sure her staff were all on task. Once Stella spotted her she made a beeline to her with the bag in one hand and pulling Stephen along with the other.

"Ms. Ida!" Stella gushed giving her a huge hug. "How are you?"

"I am just fabulous. As are you! You are getting better and better every year Stella. That was absolutely beautiful. ABSOLUTELY Beautiful! I just loved it. I remember grinding my teeth through your pecking out Chopsticks for the first time and now that!" Ms. Ida said gleefully. Then she turned to Stephen. "Oh Stephen, and how are you doing? Anything exciting happening?"

"I'm fine. Nothing exciting's happening," Stephen answered almost incoherently before putting his head down.

"I went to camp last week. I just got back this morning actually, but when I was there I found something I thought would be just perfect for you so I had to get it because I just knew you'd love it." Stella handed Ida the bag. "Go ahead. Open it," Stella said anxiously.

Ida chuckled at Stella's impatience. "Okay. Okay," Ida said as she reached in and pulled out the ring.

"It's body decoration!" Stella said almost squealing.

"It is, isn't it? It's gorgeous. It's a ring." Ida tried a few fingers before finding one it would fit. She held her hand out for the twins to see. "This is absolutely stunning. Almost too special. I have to know, where did you find it?" Ida asked.

"It was in the campus store at my science camp in Southern Allegiance. A private owner donated it to the school and they had it in their campus store. When I saw it, I thought of you. Do you love it?" Stella could barely contain her excitement.

"I love it. Thank you," Ida said and gave Stella another hug. "I've gotta get back to work for a while. I'll see you again tonight, though. Promise?" Ida said before hugging Stella once more. "Thank you again, Stella."

Ida walked away with her long flowing fuchsia dress, bangles, arm bands and wrap going with her. She had a big fuchsia headband with feathers in her silver blonde hair. Stella could see the individual feathers moving as Ida breezed away.

"Stephen, we have maybe one and a half hours before everyone starts breaking away from the party. I want to see that folder or file or whatever you were talking about, before people start wondering where we are. Let's go look at it now."

"You go ahead of me and I'll follow you in a couple of minutes. I'm going to grab another cupcake. Do you want one?" he asked.

"Grab me a cookie. Two cookies. Be there in five minutes Stephen. Don't get caught in a conversation. No statistics tonight," she said escaping through the side door. Stella walked quickly back through the corridors, to their family unit.

Stella hurried down their hallway and stopped at Stephen's door. She tried the handle. He hadn't locked it, as usual. She decided to go in and wait there instead of her own room. Everyone was at the party, and she wanted answers. No, she needed them. She had to see it and process it for herself so it would really make sense. Stella plopped down on Stephen's bed, shoving a pillow behind her then immediately stood back up and started pacing around his bed.

Stella looked out the window but quickly remembered that out here, there really wasn't anything to see. She sat back down and waited. The days were beginning to change. It was no longer daytime all day and instead the sun was only up almost all day. The sun was beginning to fade and shadows were forming outside where the building cut off the lowering sun.

Stephen pushed the door open with his hands full. He had two cupcakes and a plate full of cookies. They'd be almost sick in the morning but neither of them cared. It was worth it. Stella often joked that she had a separate stomach just for dessert.

Stephen carefully set the plates down on the edge of his desk before sitting down in his chair.

"Look away, Stella," Stephen ordered.

Once he was sure she wasn't watching him, he slid his hand under his desk and took the memory microdot out of its hiding place. He used the reader again to open the storage and project it to his smart wall.

The folder 'Noah' showed up and he clicked on it to reveal the many files under the folder.

"Wow," said Stella. "Those are a lot of files. Have you looked at any yet?"

"Not that many," he said. "I haven't had much of a chance but there are a few I wanted to start with. You see this one? It is called ARC Reborn." Stephen clicked on it and it opened schematics of the ARC layout including residential units on the main site and then the smaller satellite sites.

"Look at this," Stephen said. "Have you ever seen or heard of anything besides this level and the one below? Did you know there was another level down?"

"The ROC room and lab are down a level so I guess it's not unreasonable that there is another level, right?" she reasoned.

"Yes, but from these images it looks like an entire floor running the length of the entire ARC that is all below the level of the ROC room. The ROC room is on the same level as the storage and supplies and that safe room dad showed us. I didn't even know that the level we did know about was the same size as the main level," Stephen said while pointing to the diagram on the wall.

"I wonder what that next level is for. Maybe in case there is a change in weather above ground, it's a little more protected under there," Stella suggested, searching for an answer.

"Okay, we now know there's a second level and it's much bigger than I thought. There's a whole third level that's the same size. I wonder what else there is," Stephen said curiously before going back to the Noah folder.

"What about this? HPT folder?" Stella asked a she pointed over Stephen's shoulder.

Stephen clicked on it and there were files of human population trends and projections for the past two hundred years with projections for the next two hundred years. There was a map showing density of where people lived around the globe, and another one showing the fault lines.

"This isn't good Stella. I want to see something."

Stephen pulled out his other memory microdot and opened up his analysis on where earthquakes were projected to happen and the impact on population.

"Look at this Stella. If we just continue doing exactly what we are doing, we could make this whole area of Southern Liberty unlivable. That would mean everyone living here would have to relocate. That's one of the most urgent area. It's showing a lot of activity."

Stephen moved the images and panned out to the southern hemisphere and then the globe. "But it's not the only area with some scary activity happening. There are hot zones everywhere and the northern tip of Southern Allegiance may also be at risk, but there haven't been as many reports."

"What's that?" Stella said pointing to a region near the Northern edge of Southern Allegiance.

"It's another hot zone possibly," Stephen said before pointing to other areas dotted around the map projected of the world.

"And do those colors show the population density?"

"Yeah, the darker the color, the more people. When you put it all together you'd have to relocate nearly half of the worlds' population to keep them from being swallowed by an earthquake or swept away by rising water levels. Or even burned alive from volcanoes."

"Do you even think these other areas could handle twice as many people? We are already living on top of each other," Stella questioned.

"No, especially since some of those areas are where we grow a lot of our food," Stephen said as he panned out on the map.

"What are we going to do about that? And there are still the holes in the ground? What about where all that waste is going?" Stella asked looking over Stephen's shoulder at information she only partially understood.

"I don't have the answers for those questions, Stella. What I found when doing my models was that people would need to move closer to the center of continents, away from where existing fault lines are and where volcanoes are. Those are the highest risk areas. That type of population movement is not easy. It would mean a lot of work for The Relocation and Population Management Division, the World Consensus, and Regions to relocate what amounts to billions of people over a matter of a year or two," Stephen said as he continued to click on population files.

"How do you even build residences that fast for that many people?" Stella asked.

"It would be very difficult. The cost alone would probably bankrupt the government and that would be bad for UniCorps and its members. They won't like that solution. Anything else and... well," Stephen looked down at his hands, choosing not to continue.

"What happens if the people aren't relocated Stephen?" asked Stella with hesitation.

"Do I really need to say it Stella?" Stephen stood up and started pacing.

He needed to talk to someone who would be able to help him figure this out. He thought of Marco again. Then he thought of his rude call and realized he needed to talk to him anyway and maybe even apologize.

"I think we should talk to Marco from Southern Allegiance. You know the one in my Science in Life class? If anyone knows how to open some of these restricted files, he will know how. I'm going to make another copy of the data on this microdot and put it somewhere safe. Someplace no one else will even think to look.

"Where's that?" asked Stella before realizing she already knew. Stephen looked at her and knew she knew.

Stella looked at her watch and realized most of the time their time had already passed. "We probably need to get back and let someone see our faces. Someone is going to start looking for us and then start asking questions."

"Why don't you head back and I'll be there as soon as I'm done. Then you come back and I'll sneak out again so we can finish." Stephen gave Stella her jacket and opened the door to let her out.

When Stella slipped back in the side door to the great hall she did it with grace, sliding along the wall with the hopes that no one had spotted her. She was allowed to leave and come back if she wanted; after all, she was almost sixteen. She also knew it was better and easier with no questions.

She saw her mother talking in one group and her father across the room talking to another. They seemed to be having fun.

"Good," she thought. "The world may be ending, but let's eat, drink, and be merry. For tomorrow we just may die."

CHAPTER EIGHTEEN
Racing

Santoria, Southern Allegiance

"GET BACK HERE! Now! Marco! I said get back here. It is….Errr!" the woman, Teresa Garcia, paused, waving a helmet. "You are going to get yourself killed and when you do, don't blame me!" she slammed the door in frustration.

Marco looked back with a grin and zoomed around the side of their unit. He darted around the corner and then around another before coming on a long stretch of road.

Out here he could breathe. Even with the residential towers lining the street, he felt free when the wind was in his face and his hair. He could feel the ground beneath him and knew he was kicking up tiny pebbles and dirt as he rode through the streets. The helmet was just one more thing to get in the way of him being a free man.

Almost a free man, at least. That didn't matter though. What mattered was that Alexis had invited him over and he wasn't missing his one chance to see her before she went back home and back to school. Alexis had finished school early and gotten a jump on college. She'd even decided to take a special camp course in science and technology in Santoria that Spring break. Otherwise, he wouldn't get to see her for several more months.

He would have been at University with her already if he had taken his final year, last year, seriously. Instead, he still had three classes to finish and only two had been available that year.

He was hoping for a summer school miracle on the last credits he needed.

As he was turning into Alexis's residential building lot, his watch beeped. He stopped his bike and checked to see who it was, hoping it wasn't Alexis canceling, again. It was the goof from Antarctica. He had not forgotten that Stephen had called him just a couple days ago, waking him out of a dead sleep to say absolutely nothing.

He wasn't letting him ruin his night. Not that night. He let the call go. Once off his bike he stopped by the front doors of the sky rise building built in a smooth silvery grey finish to check his reflection in the glass. It was another repurposed hotel like so many others. He fixed his uniform jacket and hair and flashed a smile to check his perfect teeth. Satisfied that he looked good, he pulled the door open.

"Name?" the security guard asked as soon as Marco walked into the building. "And which unit are you going to?"

"Marco Garcia. Alexis Murray-Cruz in unit 14-4. Please."

"Identification." The security guard held out his scanner to read Marco's fingerprint for registration. "Have you been cleared already as a secure visitor Mr. Garcia?"

"I'm guessing I have. I was here a few months ago and even before that. I'm pretty sure you were the one who checked me in both times," Marco said trying to mask the irritation in his voice. He wanted to go up before Alexis had a chance to start the fun without him.

The security guard seemed to be taking forever to add info in his tablet before hitting the button to call Alexis for approval to let Marco come up. Marco peered over the desk and grinned when his screen flashed from red to green.

"You can go on up now. Elevators are out of order, but you can take the stairs," the guard said sitting back down behind a desk and pointing through the lobby to a rear door.

Marco turned and began walking quickly towards the stairs, just past the elevators. He was pushing the doorway to the stairs when he heard the ding of the elevator doors opening and saw a woman step off. He looked at the security guard who had a smile on his face.

The guard chuckled at Marco. "Sorry. I thought they weren't working. Didn't want you to get stuck."

Marco ran back over to the elevators to try and catch the doors before they closed. He just missed them and shot the guard another look. Waiting would still be faster than climbing the fourteen flights up. He pushed the up button and stood, uncomfortably as the security guard kept looking up with an annoying smile on his face, mocking him.

His watch started beeping. He looked at it and saw that it was Stephen, again. *Not tonight.* He wondered what was suddenly so important.

The elevator dinged again as it arrived in the lobby. Marco sent the call away and jumped on the elevator once an older couple exited. He took advantage of the mirrors that served as the elevator walls. Now he could see himself well enough to really fix his windblown hair and check between his teeth before stepping off.

Once at the fourteenth floor, Marco stood taller and walked down the hall a few doors to unit four. He placed his index finger on the scanner beside the door and it turned green and sounded the doorbell.

"Hold on, I'm coming!" Alexis called out a few seconds later. Inside the unit Alexis was hurriedly stuffing clothes into the closet and throwing away paper plates and cups. Several minutes passed before Marco finally heard her click the lock and pull the door open slowly.

Marco stepped inside and gave her a huge hug. He'd missed her over the past three months since their last break. She grabbed his hand and pulled him back to the bedroom. He could tell she was excited. Her parents were gone for at least a few more hours so she had the unit to herself. They could really have fun and hopefully not get into any trouble.

Marco took off his button down shirt and threw it on her bed, leaving just his uniform t-shirt underneath. They both walked over to the desk where they pulled up two chairs and sat down in front of what Marco considered his dream computer setup. Alexis had a system that was so fast she could get the advantage over him every time when they did the code and upload race.

Tonight they were planning to hack into the science division of the Southern Allegiance Region's conservation and preservation unit, where reports from the seismologists were sent each month. Alexis wanted to go for the World Consensus science division but Marco didn't want to get into trouble internationally. Besides, it was supposed to be just for fun. That was what they kept telling each other. There was no need in completely risking their freedom for what boiled down to a game.

As para-adults they could get into a lot of trouble and get her parents in trouble. If they were caught it could mean being prosecuted by Southern Allegiance and sent for behavioral modification. Their parents could be punished by being fined and imprisoned.

Marco stretched his back and shoulders and shook his fingers as he readied them for the race. His attempts to impress Alexis were met by her laughter. She knew him well enough to know his stretching was only so she'd notice his muscles. Alexis wasn't sold on Marco as more than a good friend. He was smart but unfocused and too arrogant, at least for her taste.

"Are you ready?" she smiled.

Marco looked at Alexis and said, "Let's do this."

Alexis began entering code on her computing system and Marco did the same. They would try to get in two different ways, and hopefully confuse the Southern Allegiance system. Since the funding from private organizations and the support staff available through UniCorps, the World Consensus, and the regions had first class talent in their programming departments.

It was all part of the challenge and the fun. Alexis mumbled as she worked. She couldn't stand losing or giving up. It just wasn't in her nature. Marco couldn't stand the idea of losing to Alexis. That was no way to impress her and losing wasn't part of his vocabulary.

"Hey, I just thought of something. I think I met a girl at camp this week who you might know. Her name is Stella. She's got a twin brother. Do you know her?

"I might. Do you know her brother's name?" Marco asked not slowing down a bit.

"Soren, Sle, Stephen. Stephen! They live in Antarctica right now. Who the heck lives in Antarctica? Ever?"

"Ha! Yes, I know him. We take an online science class together. He actually called me today when I was on my way up here. Small world. What's his sister like?" Marco asked trying to sound nonchalant.

"She's nice. She's got pretty, big hair. What I'd do for hair like that! Why?" Alexis looked at him out the side of her eye with a raised eyebrow. Her fingers never stopped moving.

"No reason. Just wondering. Normal question." Marco paused and looked at what appeared on his screen. "I think I'm getting close. I think we are almost in. We're gonna need you to work your magic next. I hope you are ready over there."

"Don't worry, big shot. I'll be ready," Alexis teased back.

Marco's watch started beeping again. "Why do you have that thing with sound on? So annoying…and distracting," Alexis moaned.

"Speaking of the devil. Well, I guess in Antarctica it's too cold to be the devil, but it is Stephen. I'll call him back when we are done. It's the third time today. I wonder what's going on?"

Marco had barely glanced at his wrist, not wanting to slow down and miss the pace Alexis was setting. After the repeated calls he was becoming curious about why Stephen was trying so hard to reach him.

"Hmmm. Maybe he forgot what his work was for the break and figures you'll have it. Don't know why anyone would think you'd have it, but …" Alexis let her voice trail off and let the thought dangle. She never left him alone for slacking off in school.

"Are you almost ready? Do you have everything up over there? I'm about to go for the migration so our systems talk to each other for the breaking of their password key. Remember, it changes every seventy-five seconds. Get ready with the passwords and the key. One. Two. Three. Boom!"

Alexis hit a button and the screens began mirroring each other with code and data flying between the two as if they were talking. Marco and Alexis were silent, waiting for the confirmation that they had gotten through the password so that the system could match the correct key. Then they'd be in. This time, they would get what they were coming for.

"Come on. Come on. Hurry up. I thought you said you had one of the fastest systems, Alexis!" Marco charged irritably.

"I do. Faster than yours for sure. Their system's faster and probably five times as expensive, so don't get pissy with me."

"Wait. Wait. Ha! We're in baby. We're in!" Marco exclaimed and turned, giving Alexis a kiss on the lips. He surprised both of them as they both leaned back and got back to their own seats.

"Okay…well… you've got nice lips but I've got work to do. Let's get in and get out. Fast. You sync the files under 10-86 and I'll do the UP1K file."

Alexis and Marco started synchronizing the folders when Marco's watched beeped again. Alexis rolled her eyes at him.

"It's him. Again," Marco said with a shrug before accepting. "Hey, what's up? What's the emergency?"

Stephen looked blank for minute trying to think of where to begin. "Do you have a minute Marco? Oh, I'm sorry about the other day. I wanted to talk something over with you but had to get my thoughts together better first. Is now a good time?" Stephen felt desperate and he was sure he sounded that way too.

"I've got a couple of minutes but I am in the middle of something. What's up? Oh, before you start, you'll never believe this. My friend Alexis met your sister Stella at camp this week. Crazy, right?"

"Yes that is a coincidence. Did you hear that Stella?"

"Wait," Alexis chimed in, "Stella's there? Put her on."

"Hold on," Stephen said, walking away from the view. A moment later he returned. "I'm back. Stella's here."

"Stella! Hey it's me. Alexis. Such a small world!" Alexis grabbed Marco's wrist, pulling it closer so she could talk.

The moment Stella heard Alexis say her name, she bumped Stephen out of the way so she could get in view.

"Oh my god! Alexis! How are you here? I thought you were going back to Australia," asked a confused Stella.

"Long story. You know my dad and stepmom are here and since I avoided really being here much all week, I'm here for now. I leave tomorrow morning. They are much too in love for me."

Stella was about to say something when Stephen nudged her and interrupted. "I know the two of you want to talk, but we have something more important to talk about. Stella and I need to talk to Marco, privately."

"Alexis can stay on Stephen. She was my roommate this week at camp. I trust her and she might be able to help us."

Stella felt certain that the four of them being there was no accident. "Besides, we don't have much time. The party is going to be over soon and you know mom and dad will be coming by before heading to bed."

Stephen nodded accepting Stella's logic.

"Okay. You both have to swear yourselves to secrecy. Do you swear that you will not speak of or share this information with another living soul outside of the four of us? Sharing it with anyone could result in death," Stephen threatened.

"Stephen! Stop being dramatic. Just promise you won't tell," Stella said shoving her brother.

"I would rather not know anything that may actually cause me death," Alexis complained.

"You can leave now then if you want to Alexis. There will be no hard feelings," Stephen said firmly.

Stella rolled her eyes. "Just start talking Stephen," she said nervously.

"I need them to promise they won't share this information first. Do you both promise?" Stephen said, remaining firm.

"Yes. I promise," Marco said anxiously.

"Fine. I promise too," Alexis gave in. She was curious about what could be so important.

"You probably both know our parents work down here on a project funded by the science divisions of World Consensus and UniCorps. They do a lot of different things in monitoring, collection, analysis, climate monitoring, ecological systems, and engineering. The ARC is its own little world, in a way. We've recently started more detailed tracking of things like tremors, earthquakes, volcanoes, fault lines, and ocean life and following those trends to understand them better. They have access to data that goes back longer than we've been alive and have other historical data from even further back. It's a lot of data," Stephen said before pausing.

"And, it's a lot of talking. Stephen, you are putting me to sleep. Get to the good part," Stella said over his shoulder.

Stephen ignored Stella. "Over the past six months or so they've been looking at data from over the past couple years much closer. It was tremors and earthquakes, especially around the pump holes; you know where they dump the emissions and gases."

"The fault lines closest to the holes are more active than the ones far away. There's a trend and Stephen and my mom's team have finally started making sense of it over the past few months," Stella said smiling smugly at Stephen.

"Wait, why were they even tracking the earthquakes? Isn't that what the Science Institute is for?" Alexis quickly jumped in.

"They didn't use to track the tremors and earthquakes that closely. It was only when it directly impacted our main work we had to look at it too. There were too many changes in ocean life to not look into it more. It's getting worse," Stephen said before Stella could try to explain.

"I'm not the expert but from what I've seen, it's to the point that something big could happen, like a serious earthquake or even a volcano sometime soon. When it happens, because, yes, it probably will, it could kill a lot of people," Stella chided.

"And there is more than one place at risk so we are talking a lot of people," Stephen jumped in again.

"Serious as in worse than what happened here?" asked Marco who was now looking at his screen as the files were populating. Stephen managed to peak his interest, but he and Alexis were in the middle of something else – their little fun game with potentially serious consequences.

"In reality that wasn't a major event Marco. It was bad enough, with the structural damage, but very few lives were lost. To answer your question - yes, possibly," Stephen said bluntly.

"So what's it all mean?" Alexis asked.

Stephen scratched his head. "It means the need for mass relocation of billions of people in a short period of time." Marco and Alexis looked at Stephen, waiting for more.

"And that is hard to do. It costs a lot of money and there is no place for them to live." Stella stepped in realizing her brother wasn't picking up on the cues.

"Oh. That's rough," Marco said rubbing his chin distractedly.

All of the data they were after was in and it was time to finish up and get out. "Hold on," Marco added.

He stopped the video feed and sound. Alexis and Marco had to quickly make sure they had everything saved. The files being synced must have been over one hundred and they were forced to jump through the interspace of the subsystem in order to protect the two hackers.

Marco looked at the remaining time left to completion. He could tell someone was trying to track them right now and they risked their location being compromised the longer they remained tied in.

He smiled to himself as he thought of the person on the other end who was probably swearing right now as the files floated across space and time. Eight. Seven. Six. Five. Four. Three. Two. One. Complete. He immediately disconnected everything from the Region's system. They were done.

Alexis turned to give him a high five. "We did it. We actually did it. Crap! I can't believe we did it. What if they are still trying to track us? What if we get caught? I could lose my funding for school, or even get kicked out, or worse. Marco. What if we made a big mistake?" Alexis continued, feeling both exhilarated and scared at the same time.

"Al, calm down. This isn't even like you. We did everything right. Just like we planned for months. If what Stephen is saying is true, this could be even more valuable. Don't worry, we aren't going to get caught and you are going to be fine. Besides, I," Marco stopped talking as his phone beeped.

"I forgot I put Stephen on hold," he accepted the call again.

"Hey. Sorry about that. We had to finish something up over here. Now what was this again about relocating people and time and money?"

Stephen was irritated, noticeably and Marco wasn't helping. "Look Marco, we have a situation where it is very likely that the earth is going to crack and swallow up millions or billions of people or it's going to explode and make lava structures out of millions or billions of people. It's not likely anyone can get that many people relocated before our projections show the first series of serious earthquakes. You know earthquakes are triggers for volcanoes." Stephen was almost breathless having said all of that without a single inhale.

Stella stood in the background waiting with Stephen for Marco's response. Of course, he could have said anything and it wouldn't have mattered. She just liked looking at him.

He had these soul stirring brown eyes and thick wavy hair that dusted his forehead. His skin looked like he'd lived near the equator his whole life and she could imagine he had his pick of girls. After all, he was there with Alexis. Perky, persistent, pretty, persuasive Alexis. Whatever they had going on, Stella reasoned she didn't stand a chance but it didn't hurt to appreciate the view.

"And you are telling all this to me because?" Marco didn't get what he had to do with any of what Stephen was saying. Stephen was unsure of exactly how to put the next part and afraid of saying anything else over his regular communication.

"Can you log into our science class chat site. It uses a secure system? I think it's better if we talk there."

Marco got on Alexis' system and pulled up the portal to the chatroom for the classroom. At the same time, Stephen was connecting in through his system. He had state of the art equipment like everyone on the ARC.

Stella didn't even try to hide her boredom as she sat behind Stephen. "So, Alexis, how do you think you did on your final project? I passed mine, which was enough."

"I got a really high mark. While you went down and played on that piano I was studying. So yeah, I did well," Alexis teased her. "Are you still going back to civilization with all this new stuff happening?"

Stella looked at Stephen. That question wasn't even something she'd considered yet. "I don't see why not. They can take all this info home with us, right Stephen?"

Stephen looked over at Stella. He hadn't been listening. "What?"

"We can take all this home and you guys can keep working on it from there, right?" Stella asked again.

"Yes. It will go home with us," Stephen answered quickly.

Stella suddenly felt like there was something else going on or someone watching but didn't see anything on Stephen's screen to show someone else besides the two of them. It was like a ghost in the system. She could feel the energy but didn't know where it was coming from.

Stella spoke into the class chat portal where she could see Marco and Alexis. "Guys, could someone else be watching what you write here but not show up in the chat? You know, hide themselves?"

"There's not a setting like that I've ever seen. Then again, I don't usually go in here for fun, you know?" Marco replied sarcastically. "If someone wanted to, there's always an invisible in. You just have to know the vulnerabilities, the weak points, and then you start there. Why?"

"I feel like someone may be lurking in there. Watching. I know it's silly - strange and I can't really explain it, but when I get this kind of feeling, my hands tingle and get warm. Is there any way you can check?" she wondered.

"If you think something's there Stella, we should probably pay attention to it," Alexis said turning to Marco.

"It would be hard to do unless you have the teacher code and I've never had a reason to get those because it's just never been that important to me," replied Marco.

He knew there was a way to do it, but didn't see why anyone would be in there this time on a Saturday night, for no reason, in an invisible state. Like him, most people had better things to do with their time.

"I doubt we have anything to worry about Stella," Stephen said hurriedly, wanting to get going. "Look, we are both in and I see you. Make sure you put voice on. Turn the video off, just to be safe and I'm going to disconnect this other video."

Stephen abruptly shut off the video that Stella and Alexis had just used to talk and turned his attention back to the chat room he and Marco were logged into.

"Seriously, Stephen? We are in a class chat with our classroom IDs used to log in and with our voices on here and you don't think they can figure out who we are because we don't have the video on?" Marco asked and Alexis laughed in the background.

"Fine, you put your video on if you want. Mine is staying off," Stephen huffed.

"I think you are forgetting that you need to show him some things on this side and you will actually need the video," Stella reminded him.

She was getting a little tired and annoyed. It was already late and with all that was happening, nobody was going to be sleeping in tomorrow, even after the party. It was going to be all work, even if she didn't do anything there'd be too much going on for her to sleep.

Seeing Marco and Alexis's faces reappear brought a smile back to Stella's face. They could see her and Stephen too. "You ready over there?" Stephen asked before going on this time.

"Ready. Now what is the big deal?" Marco asked.

"Ok. We have to report all of this to the funders at the science divisions of UniCorps and the World Consensus. My mom is sending the report tomorrow morning. I'm afraid they won't do anything about it. They'll try to deny it, say the science isn't right, or just bury it."

"Why do you think our government would do that?" Alexis asked sarcastically. "They have a policy of honesty and service. It's in the creed." They all laughed.

The creed had been established when the World Consensus had been created nearly eighty years before. Before the World Consensus, the government had become so corrupt and dishonest that no one outside of the government knew what was going on.

When the World Consensus was formed it was with the promise to be different. The founding leaders promised transparency so people knew what was happening and trust could be rebuilt. Shortly after the new government came to order, there was a great amount of money and investment put into science, research, education, social programs, health issues, and the environment.

They began investing in schools for everyone. Their grandparents retold stories from their parents who'd lived through the earlier years of the World Consensus. They'd lived through the transition from individual nations to one world but Marco, Alexis, Stephen, and Stella had only read about it in reports of history.

"I need to make sure we don't lose this fight. We have to make sure they don't bury it. We have to make sure people know the truth if they do try to bury it. They have a right to know," Stephen pleaded.

There was silence for a moment and then a sound that almost seemed like static. It was a faint electrical pulsing and then it was gone.

Stella turned to look at Stephen. "What was that? Did you all hear that?"

"I heard it too," Alexis added. It was like something else was happening in the background.

"Hold on. Let me try something. I'm gonna disconnect and reconnect. Maybe what we were working on earlier is causing some kind of interference. Be back in just a minute," Marco said.

Marco disconnected from the class's platform and rebooted his entire system.

"Alexis, make a copy of what we got from Southern Allegiance on a microdot. I have a feeling it may be important down the road," he said, turning to Alexis and continuing to disconnect out of the school's entire system.

"I think it just might too. I'll keep one and give you one."

Alexis started putting the data on two separate microchips. Marco finished the disconnection only to start reconnecting again so they could get back on with Stephen and Stella. *She does have big pretty hair just like Alexis said,* Marco thought.

Stephen disconnected and reconnected too, just in case the issue was on his end. He paced back and forth in front of the display and Stella lay on the bed. She was tired after her early morning and the end of camp party they'd had the night before. She needed to rest but from what she could tell, that wasn't going to happen. Her mind had too many thoughts running around and she was picking up on some strange things.

"Stephen, I don't think that was Marco causing the interference. Someone was there. Like a ghost in the machine. Someone or something was there with you and Marco in that chat room. If we hear it again, we should just ask who it is," she muttered in a voice that sounded tired.

The screen came back up and then it showed one other user in the room. Marco's face popped back up and then immediately began to break up into pixels.

"Marco you are coming through broken up. What do you think's going on?" Stella asked.

"Not sure. You're doing the same thing. There is definitely interference. Let's hurry up. Can you somehow get the data to me, Stephen, in a safe way?" Marco asked quickly.

"Do you have a system with a secure virtual pass connection that goes through the interspace?" Stephen asked.

"Of course I do. Do you?" Marco asked back sounding insulted by Stephen's question.

"Yes. I am going to copy it into a virtual pass through file. It takes a while, but once it reconnects on your end, you'll have to use a password to pull all the files back together. I'll start the copying and I'll send you the password encrypted. We can't use this room but," Stephen was cut off by a sharp static sound and his image once again was broken up.

"I'll be back in touch in five, the other way. Get outta this room." Stephen shut off the connection abruptly.

"Let's go say good night to mom and dad now, so they don't try to say good night later, Stephen. Come on. Maybe it'll give your system time to work any bugs out." Stella grabbed Stephen's arm and drug him out of the room. Their parents would be coming for them soon and she didn't want to be surprised.

***

MORE THAN FOUR thousand miles away in Australia, Canson Pritchard had lost the connection, again. He hadn't been able to get in without interrupting the class chat session. He was certain Marco had done something to the chat room that blocked other users from coming in.

Marco was too good and now Canson had missed his chance, a unique chance that could have helped the mission leap forward. He wasn't sure he'd end up with a chance like that again. He took comfort in knowing the groundwork was being laid and the pieces were falling into place just like the Earth Council had planned. He knew another way would open up.

CHAPTER NINETEEN
Static

Antarctic Research Center

STELLA SAT IN anticipation on the bed behind Stephen as he sent a message to Marco that he was ready to talk again. They didn't have any other way to talk besides the classroom chat site and he hoped what they'd done would make it secure this time.

The four had all agreed that the second they heard or felt anything strange, they'd disconnect. Stephen was already nervous, checking and double-checking the connection, the site, and what he was hearing in the background.

He didn't want to break the law by sharing this information or have his parents get in trouble, but he had to know what was going on and what the secure files in the Noah folder were. The only person he knew who could do it was Marco.

Marco sat down in front of his system and camera. He could see Stephen in front and Stella behind him.

"Hey Stephen, Stella. So I got the file and the encrypted one. I take it you want me to try and open them?" Marco asked as he made copies of both on his side.

Stephen looked around as if someone might be there unexpectedly. "Yes. I can't get into them. I thought maybe you could. I need to get access to everything on there. I am pretty sure something is being hidden from us that is important," Stephen answered in a loud whisper.

"I can try," Marco said looking at the small microdot in his hand.

"I think if we can find out what's on there, we can figure out how everything connects and why these people are acting like they are," Stephen said before stopping at the first sound that hinted there might be interference.

"Talk later," he said abruptly and disconnected. "Who do you think it is?" Stephen asked Stella.

"Or it could be a what," Stella suggested. She thought it was strange that the interference happened again.

"Turn off your camera completely and disconnect from everything. I don't want someone tracking or hacking us," she added.

"Good idea. I still need to understand who it is. Can you send Marco a message for me from your system?" Stephen asked Stella optimistically.

"Yeah, but someone may be tracking that too," Stella answered.

"I'll set it up for you so that it's a one sided message with a mid-way source scrambler. Nothing can come in that way, the source will be hidden, and only you can send out. Once the message is out, I'll switch it back," Stephen assured her.

Stephen and Stella scooted out his door, checking the hallway for their parents and anyone else before scurrying into Stella's room, closing the door and locking it immediately behind them. Stella resumed her position, on the bed, while Stephen took the chair and got back to work.

"You can just send the message yourself. You know what you need to say, I don't," Stella said while looking at the back of Stephen's head.

"No. I'll tell you what we need to say to him. I need you to write it out in your words. You'll say it different than I would," Stephen said.

A few minutes later Stephen stood up and backed away from Stella's desk.

"It's ready for you," he said. "Okay. So we need to give this message but make it sound normal. Are you ready?" Stephen asked.

"I guess so," Stella said confused. "What is it you want to say?"

"I'm trying to say that we want to talk soon. That we want to hear what he might have found out. That you are sending this message with a scrambled source. That he can send one back that way. That the thing we can't talk about is earthquakes and volcanoes about to happen," Stephen said, hopeful Stella could make it sound like it needed to.

Stella sat in front of his system for and tried to make sense of what he'd just said. They were twins, but wired completely different.

"Okay. Here's what I'm sending. 'Hey, all scramble brained over here. Sorry, I had to cut out but would love to talk again soon even if I can't talk about what's got me all cracked up and ready to explode. Ever felt scrambled? I'm sure you have.' How's that?" Stella turned and asked Stephen.

"I suppose it will be sufficient. It gets the message across that we need him to receive."

"Can I go ahead and send him the message now?" Stella asked back. She was proud she'd made sense of his message which sounded a little creepy.

"Yeah, go for it," Stephen said to Stella nervously. Stella sent the message, stood up, and sat back down next to Stephen on her unmade bed.

"Are you ready to go back home?" Stephen asked Stella as they waited.

"Definitely. I am ready for a normal Summer - one that doesn't require a parka. I'm ready to be off this continent and see some kids our age. I'm ready for our birthday party and getting our new status as para-adults, too," Stella said almost daydreaming. She'd been ready to go home since before she'd left for camp.

"You know we don't get anything as para-adults. The only thing new is that we can get in more trouble for doing things. Things like what we are doing now," Stephen said correcting Stella.

"That's not true Stephen. You're being pessimistic. We get new freedoms, a later curfew, aggregated voting rights in local elections, we can get our first license, and more. Plus, we get an upgrade on our watches which raises the programs we can access to the para-adult programs. Even if we do something wrong or get in trouble we don't get in as much trouble," Stella corrected him.

"I think you are being overly optimistic," Stephen argued back.

"Oh, I forgot to tell you about what happened at camp. Alexis, some other kids, and I saw something really strange. We went into the teacher's cafeteria, I think, behind Dr. Lima and these three people. They were strange and scary but in a cool mysterious way," Stella beamed.

Stephen looked at her appalled, "You snuck into a building on the university campus? What if you'd been caught?"

Stella cocked her head to the side and ignored his question. "We snuck in because we needed to. Once we got inside, we heard the strangest conversation between Ms. Joykill, also known as Dr. Lima, and these people. We had to run out of there because Ms. Joykill must have heard us. Oh my god, it was so exciting. Makes me want to go exploring," Stella said with a broad smile.

"You shouldn't have been snooping around and going into rooms you weren't supposed to be in Stella," Stephen admonished her.

"Like I said, I had to. Have you ever thought about what else was here in the ARC? This place is so much bigger than either of us ever knew and then with all of the off limit areas and locked doors, aren't you curious?" Stella asked Stephen.

"Of course I'm curious, but I'm not going to go in locked rooms or areas that say off limits. That would be bad citizenry," Stephen said with a look of surprise that Stella would suggest it.

"Don't act all high and mighty Stephen. Just because it's not a physical door you are walking through, what do you think you are doing with all this trying to break into files and get access to data that has restricted access? Same thing," Stella retorted.

"I disagree - it's not the same thing. I think we have a message back. Hold on." Stephen was happy for a change of subject.

It bothered him that what Stella said was possibly true. He was behaving like a criminal and putting himself in the position of risking the loss of his full citizenship status because of being overly curious. It didn't make him feel much better that he was doing it because he had to, not just for fun.

Stephen paused. "What if we get in trouble? What if someone finds out?" he asked Stella.

"Well then, do it soon, before you are sixteen," Stella smiled. "We can't stop now. We may be breaking the law, but it doesn't mean we are doing something wrong." Stella always had a way of making him feel...confused.

"Marco just sent us something. He says, 'We'll talk soon. Feeling scrambled too and a little overwhelmed. So much to think about and I just need a little time to sort things out. You'll be the first to hear from me when I'm ready. Stay warm.'

Stephen looked confused. "Oh, I get it. Okay," Stephen nodded.

"Yeah, I got it too," Stella smiled. "So how do we actually get the files once he gets them open?" Stella asked Stephen. "How do we receive anything safely?"

"We have to use the same process as before. If Marco can open them maybe it'll be safer to wait until we are home for him to send them. We have access to more systems and networks there so it wouldn't be as traceable."

"Don't you think if Marco can manage to open up these blocked files, he can manage to send something without it being traced? My worry is us opening it up or having it show up on our side," Stella said.

"Yes, you are right but there is still much more risk here," Stephen nodded.

"So you think we should wait until we are home to have him send it?" Stella asked confused.

"Right. Tell him that Stella," Stephen said to his sister who just stared at him.

"Stephen, if we don't get it until we are home how can we use it to figure out the ARC?" Stella asked Stephen.

"We will just have to wait until we're back or study the files from home," Stephen answered.

"Between you, Marco, and Alexis we can figure this out. We're gonna have to risk it. Everyone is going to be so busy the next few days they won't notice anything. You know how to clean up the network. So as soon as you get it on something safe, just get rid of any trace of it. You can do that right?" Stella smiled a sneaky smile and then her eyes got wide as something dawned on her.

"Stephen, what if someone or something is trying to tell you something in that chat room but can't get in?" Stella asked, as the idea dawned on her.

Stephen looked at her. She was making no sense.

"I mean, Marco put that block on the class chat room so no one else could get in besides the two of you, right?" she asked.

"Yes," Stephen said with a pause.

"What if the staticky sound is someone or something trying to get in, but being blocked? Aren't you curious about what it is?" She smiled mischievously at Stephen.

Stephen lied, "Not that curious, but I get what you mean. We don't have much time but I could go back in and see if anyone is there."

CHAPTER TWENTY
Coincidence

Antarctic Research Center

THERE WAS THE sound again telling him someone else was there. He sat up quickly and tried to speak.

"Hello? Hello?" Canson Pritchard said.

Canson had been disconnected from the room the last time he'd tried to get in. He needed Marco and Stephen to know he was there.

"This is Mr. Pritchard, from the advanced science and technology class. Your science in life class. Who is this?" Canson waited for a response. He was hopeful one of them would answer.

On the other end Stephen and Stella sat staring at the screen, their eyes wide in panic. They hadn't turned on their side of the video and quickly muted the sound.

"What should we do?" Stephen asked Stella.

"I don't know. It's your teacher. Will you get in trouble for using the class chat room?" Stella answered him back in whisper. She got up and stood in the corner by the door where she would be out of the picture.

"Hello?" Canson's voice came through again. "It's okay. You're not in trouble. Are you still there?" Canson tried to calm the person on the other end.

Stephen looked at Stella once again and then turned his voice back on.

"Hello?" Canson's voice cracked with nervousness.

"Hello. I'm here," Stephen finally said, clearing his throat and sounding a bit calmer.

"Who is this?" Canson asked.

"Ummm. I'm in your class. I'm sorry for using this room to talk. I, we, I-I just didn't, we didn't know," Stephen stopped. He was stammering all over his words. "I needed a secure place to talk to someone, Mr. Pritchard. Please accept my apology."

"I see. Do you mind telling me who you are? I can't quite catch your voice," Canson prodded. He was curious what Stephen would say.

"I'm sorry Mr. Pritchard for using this interface. It won't happen again."

"Wait! Don't go. I know who you are. I know who the other kid is too." Canson paused and Stephen considered disconnecting again, but his sister in the corner urged him to talk.

"I'm here," Stephen replied.

"I need to talk to you Stephen. It's important."

"Hold on, Mr. Pritchard," Stephen said and put his voice back on mute. "Get Marco back in the chat room Stella. Hurry. I think it's going to be okay," Stephen said before turning his voice back on.

"I'm back. What's going on Mr. Pritchard?" Stephen asked.

There was a moment of silence as Canson's eyes seemed to look straight at Stephen even though his video was still off.

"Stephen, I need you to listen very carefully. What I have to tell you is very important and may not, well, probably not, make any sense. It has to do with you, your sister, Marco and a girl you haven't met, but your sister has, named Alexis, Ren, and two others."

"I met Alexis, sort of," said Stephen. Stella walked out of the corner and sat back down on Stephen's bed. "Stella is here too," Stephen told Canson who was glad she was there to hear what he had to say as well.

"What do you need to tell us?" Stephen asked, leaning in. The staticky sound came to an end and then Marco appeared on the other side of the projection showing on Stephen's wall.

"Hold on," Stephen said wanting Marco to hear this. "Marco, I have our teacher Mr. Pritchard on the line. He has something to tell us. It has to do with that friend of yours too, Alexis."

Marco wasn't sure whether to speak but Stephen had already called out his name. He figured he'd take a chance. He was pretty sure there was no way this would end well, but nothing he was involved in at the time was likely going to end well.

"Yeah, what's going on?" Marco asked reluctantly.

"Marco, thanks for coming back. I was trying to get in on your connection, but I'm guessing you two did something to block me," Canson said. Both boys were silent. They actually liked their teacher but they could still get in trouble for what they did.

"Anyways, the three of you here, you two, and Stella, are a part of something bigger. The fact that you all are connected isn't a mistake, an accident, or coincidence. We've been working very hard to get Alexis and Marco connected and then connect them with you and Stella," Canson paused, letting what he said ruminate for a moment.

"Can I get Alexis on my system? Seems she may want to hear this too," Marco asked.

"Sorry she can't get into this room. It's for registered students only," Mr. Pritchard said but Marco had already sent her a message to have her open up a transmission with him. She'd be able to hear everything going on in the room and at least see him.

While Marco went to get Alexis connected, he, Stephen, and Stella were all wondering what this was all about. When Marco saw Alexis come up he quickly caught her up on the conversation, leaving out the fluff. She'd have questions but he would let Mr. Pritchard answer them.

"We're back," Marco said. "Alexis can hear us but she can't see you," he added.

"No problem," said Canson as he readied himself to continue. He understood why he was the one who had to get them prepped. With everything going on with Mave he had to fill in the gap. It didn't make him feel any more comfortable. He took a deep breath.

"Again, this may not make any sense but you are all together, so to speak, for a reason. You are part of a small group of kids designed to perform a certain mission." Canson stopped again trying to find words that would make sense.

"Designed? How are we designed?" Stella asked, sitting up behind Stephen.

"That's a good question. I can try to explain but it's much bigger than me. You were made with certain, hmmm, qualities that you can use when the time is right. Then you were given a serum before birth to enhance these natural qualities. They aren't fully developed yet because before they can be fully there and usable, you have to know they even exist," Canson sighed, pleased he'd managed to find words that might help them begin to understand.

"So each of you have some general talent or gift or ability that sets you apart from others. For example, Stella, you can get a sense of what is happening before it happens and a sense of what people are thinking. Not exact but their motivations, fears, you know? It's just a part of who you are."

"Are you saying we're like part cyborg or something? Or we aren't all human?" Stella asked worried.

"Yeah, what do you mean? How do you mean we were made?" Marco asked.

"It's something you have to feel more than me just telling you. Each of you has it and the rest do too. Next month when Stella and Stephen are approaching their sixteenth birthday we want to hold a special ceremony for all of you.

"How many of us are there?" Alexis's voice broke into the conversation from somewhere in the distance.

"There are supposed to be eight of you. We have managed to reach seven of you. The status of the eighth remains uncertain," Canson said back to Alexis and the others. "But we want to get you all together, in a way, so we can help you better understand your mission."

"This is bull. Is this some kind of new project you are doing for school Mr. Pritchard? Technology and society or science and society?" Marco asked.

Stephen just sat and listened silently. He was following the sequence of incidents and coincidences that led to this point. He tried to reason that it was just coincidence but the likelihood of all of the random events truly being just random kept falling outside of his range of likely probabilities.

As he settled on accepting that perhaps Mr. Pritchard wasn't lying his thoughts turned to something else. That there wasn't anything really special about him. Sure he was smart, but a lot of people were smart.

"Mr. Pritchard, you said we all have special qualities. I don't have anything special," Stephen spoke up awkwardly.

"What are you worried about that part for Stephen? He's saying we are here for a mission. That we were designed! Doesn't that seem a bit stranger than whether or not you have a special quality? And besides that, of course you do but that's not the point," Marco said, bewildered at Stephen.

"All of you were given something shortly before birth, a booster shot so to speak. The full effects of it haven't really been seen yet. You'll see a difference when the time is right and after the ceremony. I need you all to trust me, trust those who have always been there for you. We will all participate in this. It is my plan to go through this with Marco and Alexis. Stephen and Stella you'll be with Mave.

"Mave! How is she involved with this?" Stella asked while moving in closer. She now wondered just how much she didn't understand.

"Mave is like me. We have been assigned to you," Canson said, offering no further explanation.

Instead, Canson continued with his original thought. "Some details are still being worked out and I'm glad to say that isn't my area, but until then, keep searching for the truth of what is going on."

"Wait, Mr. Pritchard. Maybe you can help us with something," Stephen said.

"What?" Canson asked curiously.

"We have some files we can't open. It's really important because it has to do with some work we are doing here and stuff happening in other places and we…"

Mr. Pritchard cut Stephen off. "I can't help you with that. I believe between you, Marco, and Alexis you have all the skills you need to get what you need. Besides, as a full adult the consequences are much worse. You've got a few years before you turn twenty-one."

"Can I ask you something?" Stella asked Mr. Pritchard.

"Sure."

"How did you get involved? What part do you play?" she asked him.

Canson looked at Stella and Stephen. They were so innocent and on the ARC they had lived much more sheltered lives than the others. He wondered if they would understand.

"I was chosen as well to serve as a guide and help things line up. I'm called a Keeper. There are things happening beyond what we can see with our eyes or hear with our ears or feel on our skin. I am a part of that, walking sometimes on a fine line between there and here."

"Are you a Connected?" Marco asked.

Canson hesitated for a moment before answering. "Yes, Marco. I am."

"This is unreal. I've heard about Connecteds but I've never met one," Alexis said with a sound of wonder in her voice.

"Wait...how do we know you aren't just saying crap and messing with us or that this isn't some kind of class experiment to see how a group of kids react in a strange social situation?" Marco's eyes narrowed. He wasn't very trusting after what happened to his father.

"It's not a social experiment and it's not for class. This is real. What you do will impact society but at the same time you will learn from it," Canson answered trying not to feel offended by Marco's accusation.

"Wait. Back up. You said 'we'. Who is 'we'? Are there more Keepers?" Alexis's voice broke in again.

"I did say 'we'. 'We' is hard to explain but there are more Keepers. You know Mave already, Stephen and Stella. You will meet the others, in time. I'm sorry if I'm leaving you confused. I sense there are many more questions and they will be answered but there is a process for understanding," Canson said. He offered nothing else as they waited.

"Darn right we have more questions, Mr. Pritchard," Alexis said hoping he heard her clearly. "And if we are so involved, we deserve answers," she argued.

"In time. You'll get answers in time."

Canson had ripped the lid off the box and there was no putting it back on. He hoped it wasn't too soon for them to be getting this hurried intro. He hoped they'd trust him and what they were already feeling enough to follow along.

"And keep working on that file. I believe it's important too," Canson encouraged them before returning his attention to Alexis. "About what you said before Alexis - I am sure you have met other Connecteds. We are all Connecteds. Stella and Stephen, Mave is assigned to you two as well as Ren. I'm assigned to Alexis and Marco with a connection to Stephen to connect those dots. The two who are in Southern Liberty have another Keeper."

"How are we all Connecteds? I've never heard of anything like that?" Alexis questioned further.

"Just because you haven't heard of it doesn't mean it isn't true. I need to go but I will be in touch. Stephen and Marco, I'll see you both in class next week. The room is yours. Oh, you cannot speak of this to anyone who does not first speak of it to you. Good night." Canson was gone.

The group was silent for a moment. "I call B.S.!" Marco said forcefully. "What do you think his game is?" he added.

The others were quietly trying to process the unusual and surreal exchange.

"Do you think he's trying to get the information we have on the files without getting in trouble?" asked Alexis.

"It's possible. Can you find out who else he works for or who his connections are, Alexis?" Stephen asked.

"Are you all really asking that question? You do realize he said Mave was our Keeper, assigned to us? Isn't that weird? And he is assigned to Marco and Alexis?! Doesn't it bother you that we have...stalkers?" Stella said with concern. "And we aren't supposed to speak to anyone about it? Doesn't that sound strange too?" she added, waving her hands in the air for effect.

"Yeah, it does sound strange, but I trust Mave. She's always been there for us Stella. Even when mom couldn't be," Stephen said defensively.

"I think it's all fine and good we've got some really important mission to do, but right now we have to open up these files, Marco and I have a small project to do, and Summer break won't be here for another month and a half. So, we have other things we need to worry about, right now," Alexis told them. "We really don't have time to waste."

"You're correct, Alexis. Marco, I need that information as soon as possible. My mom and her staff are having an important meeting here in the next week or so with the people who pay for this research center to be here. I need to know if there is something in those files that can help us make our case. If we don't..." Stephen stopped in the middle of his sentence. He didn't want to even think about what would happen if they couldn't make the case.

"Can you do it?" Stephen finished.

Marco's project with Alexis needed his attention too, but after hearing the problem from Stephen he thought they might be related.

"Alexis, I think you can help with this and it might help with what we are working on too. Stephen needs to get into some files that are protected. When you see the data there is a folder called Noah. He can access some of the files but there are a lot that are protected and he can't get into them. I know if anyone can get into them, it's you." Marco was betting on Alexis not being able to resist a challenge like that.

Alexis thought about it for a moment. "If you think it'll help us figure out what we have going on from the other project, I'll help. Send me what you have Stephen," she said, almost happily.

"It'll be easier for you to get it from Marco. He has it. Once you get in, send it back using a scrambled source," Stephen instructed.

Alexis rolled her eyes at Stephen's request. "I know. Do you think I'm stupid?" she asked rhetorically.

"No. Not at all. You wouldn't already be in university if you were stupid," he answered seriously.

"Guys, we gotta go. Thanks for helping, Alexis and Marco. It was good seeing you, Alexis. We'll talk soon." Stella broke the connection and looked at Stephen. "Not every question deserves an answer."

"I know you are special Stella, but there isn't anything particularly special about me?" Stephen said still considering why he was a part of the chosen group.

"What do you mean. Of course there is. That brain of yours and I need you to go ahead and turn it on for me. Help me make some connections and figure out what this is all about," Stella said, smiling at Stephen as she tried to cheer him up.

Stephen turned everything off, double-checking that he wasn't connected to anything. He then rolled his chair away from his desk so he could face Stella. She sat perched on the edge of her bed, hands on her chin, leaning forward expectantly. He'd already been making connections in his head. He didn't think the same way most people did and it sometimes made it hard to tell others what he was thinking, including Stella.

"Stephen, what if there are no accidents, no random coincidences? Like Mr. Pritchard said about us all being connected somehow. What if it's planned and we are just players in a game?"

Stephen was curious about where Stella was going with this. "Yes. I'm listening," he said, willing to listen to her.

"So if there are no accidents or random coincidences, then it must be on purpose and ordered coincidences," she added. "Stephen, what if it's no accident we are brother and sister? That mom is our mom, dad is our dad? That we were born on this big block of ice or that our parents head up the ARC? Or that Mave has always been around? Even before we were born. What if none of that is an accident or random coincidence?" Stella said curiously, her brain busy.

"That's a lot of ifs and that would take a great deal of planning that probably goes back a few lifetimes or generations.

On the other hand, it could be an accident and a series of random coincidences and we just happened to wind up together at the right place at the right time with the right parents," Stephen said not completely convinced himself it was coincidental.

Stella considered that possibility too. "What about Mave? Mr. Pritchard said she was our Keeper," she asked.

"She could have been made our Keeper after we were born or once they knew she was going to work on the ARC," Stephen tried to reason.

"But who is 'they'?" Stella then retorted.

Stephen pondered the question for a moment.

"Come on Stephen. You are the one who can see all these probabilities. What's the probability of all these ifs?" she asked Stephen.

"I don't know. Those are past not future probabilities. Those things were in process before you and I were born."

"True. Maybe we should talk to Mave. I'm sure if she is our Keeper she won't mind," Stella suggested.

"Good idea. Should we go now?" Stephen asked.

"It's too late tonight and in the morning they'll be dealing with that report. We should probably wait until things settle down and she has time to talk," Stella suggested.

The sound of a light tap on the door made Stephen quickly disconnect from everything. He rolled back from Stella's desk towards her bed where she sat with the plate of cookies, one in her hand.

"Come in," Stella said, taking a bite casually.

CHAPTER TWENTY-ONE
Sent

Antarctic Research Center

ZURA ROLLED OVER reluctantly and looked at the time on her nightstand through blurry eyes. The time, 5:00 a.m., looked back at her in a glowing blue light. She had barely slept since she finally crawled into bed beside Johan at one o'clock in the morning. She'd been tossing and turning throughout the few hours she'd forced herself to lay in bed. The same dream kept waking her up and she couldn't shake it.

She managed to find the floor with her feet and shimmy her tired and worn body off the bed. She slipped on her plush white robe and her slipper boots and opened the bedroom door. She shuffled through the bedroom door trying not to disturb Johan who she'd left sleeping on his back, one arm on his stomach the other on the night stand. Everything happening now would eventually fall on them. Zura hated the idea that they might have failed these two innocents, and everyone else.

After the night he'd had, Zura knew Johan wouldn't want to wake a moment earlier than he absolutely had to. He would want to get the extra hour and a half until his alarm went off at 6:30 a.m. She'd asked her core team to meet her at 7 a.m. in the science center to finish prepping for what she was certain would be coming later in the morning.

Zura walked across the living area to the hall where Stella and Stephen slept to check on them before they woke for the day. As she passed through their living quarters on the ARC she was reminded of when it was being built and how her husband had taken time to help design their unit to her specifications.

Her children's bedrooms were next door to each other and just on the other side of the family room and kitchen. The design of the overall ARC, similar to a honeycomb meant going around to the other side of their bedroom to Stephen and Stella's hall.

As she approached the first door, she naturally began to tiptoe. She didn't want to wake her children. As she got nearer to the door she slowly turned the handle to peak in on her sleeping son. She couldn't believe they'd be sixteen in what amounted now to just days. She hadn't even finished plans for the birthday celebration they were expecting, and this was a big one.

She turned the handle on Stephen's door and quietly pushed it open. Stephen nearly fell out of his chair, hitting the bottom of the desk with his knees as he stumbled backwards.

"Mom!?" Stephen gasped.

"Stephen, what the heck are you doing up at five o'clock in the morning?" Zura demanded.

Stephen scrambled to close his screen while stuttering something incoherent.

"I said, what are you doing up at 5:30 in the morning Stephen?" she asked again.

"Umm, I couldn't sleep and wanted to get some work done. Why, why are you up?" he asked back.

"I'm asking the questions. What are you working on and why are you in such a hurry to hide it? You know I don't like secrets or sneaking," Zura warned.

"I was just working mom. I wanted to get a jump start on a project that is due when I get back. It's an important class, the online science class. I couldn't sleep and figured I'd just do some stuff on it, that's all," Stephen tried to reassure his skeptical mom.

Zura looked at her son. He was a terrible liar and she knew he was lying. His eye twitched against his will, under her probing gaze but she wouldn't press him this morning. It was too early and he rarely lied. If something was keeping him up at this time of morning she didn't want to press him and make him lie about it more.

She mostly trusted him, but she'd have Rupert check both the incoming and outgoing communications and systems that were accessed that morning, as soon as she had time. Trust but verify was her motto. It was one of the reasons she was where she was.

"Turn it off and get some rest for the next hour, okay? You aren't going to be any good to us if you are falling over asleep." She waited for him to lie back in his bed. "I'll see you soon," Zura whispered and closed the door.

She hoped Stella was sleeping. She turned Stella's handle to find her asleep on her bed. Her head was hanging almost over the side and her arms were dangling. She figured she'd be lucky to see Stella before noon. She gently closed the door and walked back down their hall and to the small family kitchen.

Zura needed to feel normal this morning before everything went to hell. She made herself toast and coffee and ate in silence taking in the view from the windows above her. The sky was still light. She had to admit she loved that it was never really dark during the months they were there. It made her feel like she had all day to get things done. When she finally got back home to Northern Allegiance she would crash and sleep for a couple of days, but while here, she couldn't spare any time.

She finished her toast and carried her coffee back to her room. She needed to send the report out before her funders were awake. It would be there mixed in with the slew of other late night and early morning messages when they checked. It might help it be a bit more buried and buy them some more time.

She'd already crafted the message and attached the file. Zura tried to ignore the feeling in the pit of her stomach as she sent it all off to her contacts at the science divisions of UniCorps and the World Consensus. Once done, she walked in circles rethinking through everything. There was nothing left for her to do before her team's morning meeting at seven.

Zura went into the bathroom and looked in the mirror. She looked tired. She felt old even if the years didn't show it. She was in her late forties and suddenly wondered if she'd somehow made a mistake with the past twenty plus years of her life. It had been eighteen years with the ARC project and even more preparing for this role she considered to be a once in a lifetime opportunity.

Zura stepped into the hygiene closet and hung her robe on the hook just outside the closet door. She stood in the middle of the small sanctuary, exposed, as she stared at the little holes in the walls. She pressed the small red button to start the sanitizer, letting it do its work as she rested her forehead against the wall in front of her. After years of having to be strong this was the only place she ever let herself cry anymore. She slid down to the cool floor with her hands on her knees and her head down as the foam covered what it could reach.

Alone in that room that somehow made everything clean again, she wept. The sanitizer session ended. Instead of coming out she reached up to the red button, pressing it again to let it start another round. She had to be on and ready when she stepped out. She stood up and let the lasers do their job.

Zura lifted her arms up and placed them against the wall and just let go for a moment. All she could do now was breathe deeply. When it beeped telling her it was over this time, she unlocked the door and pushed it open. She reached for her soft robe and put it back around her, hoping for a little more comfort.

Zura could hear the alarm going off and was sure Johan would be coming in soon. She'd be able to go in the room to dress without worrying about waking him. Zura could hear him hit the snooze button and she rolled her eyes.

She walked into the bedroom and got her uniform from the closet, not bothering with any attempt to be quiet. Coming out of the clothes closet she noticed her dress from the night before draped over a chair in the bedroom. It had been a tolerable evening that lasted too long.

"Johan, time to get up. You've got less than twenty minutes now to be in the science center," she nudged him once she had her uniform on. Looking at the time that now read 6:42, she bristled at the thought that he'd already hit the snooze once and that she'd spent more time in the restroom than she'd thought.

"And after your night you are gonna need some coffee before you show your face in there."

He rolled over and moaned. "Ughhhh. I'm getting up. Why the hell did you call a 7 a.m. meeting today, of all days?" he complained.

"Because, we are gonna have UniCorps and the World Consensus crawling all up our backsides in a few hours and I refuse to not be ready. See you there. There's still some coffee in the kitchen." He could see Zura set something down beside him before she grabbed a folder and walked out of the room, leaving him just barely sitting up in bed now.

His head throbbed and he lay back down on the pillow for just a moment to help ease the pounding and keep the light from the bathroom from making it worse. He shot up as he heard the sound of the alarm beginning to go off again. *Crap! 6:50.* He noticed Zura had left him a tiny tablet to take for the headache. He hit the clock repeatedly trying to turn off the annoying sound before finally dragging himself out of bed and to the bathroom. *"What a crappy way to start a day that is already going to be crappy,"* Johan thought.

The headache was already starting to go away but the throbbing hadn't subsided. He knew Zura wasn't happy he'd had a few too many drinks, especially with what was happening and who would be coming that morning.

The wife in her let him sleep until his alarm went off and gave him something for the headache. The boss in her expected him to be there on time and ready to work. If he wasn't, he'd pay for it with both the wife and the boss.

Johan was grateful the sink had running water. He splashed his face with cold water and walked into the small room to be sanitized. A couple of minutes later he was out and dressed. He'd done pretty well getting ready all things considered. He pulled the door open and walked out, letting it close gently behind him.

He'd grab a coffee before heading down and make sure Stephen was out of his room too. He hoped Zura wouldn't get on him too much for being a minute late. He knew the kids had been up late talking and catching up.

Stephen came past the kitchen, walking quickly, as Johan poured himself a large black coffee. "Good morning, Dad. We're late," Stephen said to his dad's back.

"Morning, Stephen. Wait up. I'm headed that way," Johan said. "So, did you have fun last night?" Johan asked.

"It was okay for a grown up party," Stephen answered. "I'm tired though," Stephen added as he checked the time on his watch and hurried his pace.

Johan just sipped his coffee carefully, trying not to spill it as he walked too quickly for the headache he was nursing and the coffee. Johan wanted to ask what he was doing up so late, but just the sound of their voices seemed to bring the headache pangs back. Instead, he just walked with only the sounds of boots against the floor, hoping the medicine would take full effect before they hit the center and that Stephen would be okay just walking together.

When Stephen and Johan reached the door to the workroom Zura, Rupert, and Mave stopped talking and looked at them. Zura then looked at the time. "You're late," she snapped.

"You're right. I'm Sorry," Johan responded. She was his boss right now and the full team was there.

"I sent the report soon after I got up this morning. I expect that some of the executives at UniCorps will be checking their messages when they first get up and so we might hear from them at any moment, but definitely before they go into certain profusion of Monday morning meetings. I'm hoping the World Consensus will be a little slower so we aren't ambushed all at once. I wouldn't bet on it though," Zura said already pacing lightly.

"I think we are pretty much ready, Zura," Mave said trying to bring down the tension that was already built up.

"Yeah, but we need a game plan and we need to stick to what we discussed so that we have measured response that makes sense for them and for everyone else. This needs to be a win for all. Got it?" Zura reminded everyone as she prepared herself. Everyone nodded, except Johan, who simply said 'mmm hmm".

"Now, Rupert, I need you to get the absolute latest reports on earthquake and seismic activity and where it is happening overlaid with population density. It will be just about the same as what we gave them but I just want the latest. I need it in a half hour, okay?" Zura requested.

"I'm on it, Z," Rupert said as he hurried to his workstation.

"Mave, I need you to call one of your contacts at the Science Institute. I know they are the main ones tracking the seismic activity and I just want to see if they can run another report. The last one we got from them showed the same thing. I just want that confirmation again, in case our funders push back. See what you can get them to send by 8:30 a.m.," Zura said, giving her second order.

"Stephen. You were probably up late working on some models. If I know you, you brought them and I want to see them. I also need to talk to you," Zura said.

"Okay." Stephen stood holding a memory chip, not sure what to do as his mother then turned to his father.

"I need to see you, alone, in the lab. I'll be in there in about ten minutes." Johan knew what that meant. He looked only slightly better than he felt.

"No problem. Do you want me to look at anything or do anything while I wait for you?" he asked Zura.

"No. Thank you," she said curtly. He was in the dog house. He took off his boots and refilled his coffee before meekly heading through the door and down the steps.

Once he was gone, Zura pulled Stephen over to a large table and they sat down.

"Stephen, I need to know if you found something, figured something out, or whatever you are looking for, I need to know," she said looking at him intensely.

He lowered his head from what seemed like her secret seeking eyes. She'd never really pursued developing it, but he knew that she sometimes just 'knew' and this was one of those times.

"I made a copy," Stephen said quietly.

"Uh huh. Ok. What did you do with it?" she then asked.

Stephen squirmed. He'd get in trouble if she knew he'd shared it outside the ARC and their circle. "Nothing. I showed Stella," he answered trying to keep his face from revealing anything more.

Zura looked at him, knowing he wasn't telling her everything, but she couldn't afford for him to shut down. "Okay.

Well, what is it that you were working on with what you saw?" she asked.

"Mom, there are files on there that even we can't open. We don't have the passwords or a way to decrypt them. What are they? Why are they protected even from you?" he whispered to her inquisitively.

"There are some things that are even above my clearance level and I have access to the things I need for my job," Zura said, glancing at Stephen. "I was able to get a hold of those other files. I am hoping someone else can access them," Zura said, looking worried.

"Is that why I gave it to the pilot?" Stephen asked in the same curious whisper.

"Yes. I think he knows someone who can help," Zura answered.

Mave was in the background confirming that the most recent report on earthquakes, seismic activity, and the underground fissures that they were noticing would be transmitted by 8:30 a.m. She hung up the phone and gave a thumbs up to Zura. Rupert was still pulling his report together when Zura stood up and got ready to go into the lab.

"Give us ten minutes, please," she said. It couldn't be more obvious that Johan was in trouble.

CHAPTER TWENTY-TWO
Hidden

Antarctic Research Center

MAVE WAS POURING her second cup of coffee and asking Rupert if he'd like another cup when an urgent transmission came through. Zura and Johan were still in the lab even though more than ten minutes had passed.

Mave read the message aloud. "Talk at 8:30 a.m. UniCorps and World Consensus. Confidential." Mave finished before adding, "Talk about abrupt. This isn't going to be a friendly gathering."

Mave prepared to enter the ROC room to tell Zura and Johan the update. At least their funders would get it over with soon and then get on with fixing the problem.

She slipped her shoes off and started towards where she knew Zura was lighting into Johan. Rupert stood to the side watching. He had no intention of walking through those doors with Zura, not if he didn't need to. Not that morning.

A few moments later, the door leading up from the ROC room opened again. Zura marched out taking her white booties off as she waited for Mave who was behind her. Johan trailed both of them. He'd sobered up a bit.

Zura looked at the time and then stalked over to Rupert. "How are things looking Rupert?" she asked, without stopping as she continued her short trek to her work station. "Mave, what do you have for me?" she asked without waiting for Rupert's answer.

Rupert handed Zura a small chip, which she loaded in the reader to pull up in front of them all. Not much had changed, but more importantly, she needed to document the full record before anyone had a chance to change it. She'd be holding on to that chip.

"Thanks Rupert. This is just what I needed. I need you to make one more copy and put it in a safe place." She gave Rupert a look to make sure he knew what she meant.

"I will. Don't worry," he said as he went to work on making a second copy of the data.

"Okay, Mave, give it to me," Zura said, turning her attention to Mave.

"They are working on the report as fast as they can. They should have it by 8:30 a.m. like I asked. We'll just need to be ready to receive it even if we are already transmitting with UniCorps and the World Consensus.

"As soon as it comes through, make a copy to give to Rupert. I want both of those to be kept safe. I'll keep the original transmission. We can't risk losing any of the data we have today. Do you all understand?" Zura looked at the time and then checked her reflection in the glass window.

"Okay, get the equipment ready. Johan, pick up your desk please, it's visible on the screen. Stephen, you have to stay out of the shot and stay quiet. Technically, you aren't even supposed to be in here," Zura ordered.

Stephen sat down reluctantly by the door and then got back up again and moved to the opposite side of where the transmission would take place. He took out a small device and propped it on the table beside him. He would line it up once everyone was on.

Soon there was a beeping sound. "Okay guys. This is it," Zura said.

The team was seated closely together around a small oval table. Zura pressed a button and in front of them appeared a large holographic image of a round conference table with Representative Gregor Magiro, Dr. Tomas Sporgsman, Dr. Sandy Ashby, and another man who seemed to obliterate the room with his presence. The latter was distracting with his twirling of his large mustache. They were all familiar with Mirkal 'The Stache' Dempstead.

Somehow they'd managed to pull both UniCorps and the World Consensus together in such a short time. As they looked at each other the sour looks on all of their faces made Zura even more nervous.

"Good morning, everyone," Zura said trying to sound cordial and friendly. She wasn't sure she could set the tone for the meeting given the seriousness of the report.

"Good morning Dr. Bello. Good morning everyone," Gregor responded, speaking for the room.

Gregor didn't want to waste time. He knew something was coming but wasn't expecting it to be this bad. "What the hell is going on, Dr. Bello? I wake up this morning to find this waiting for me," Gregor said pointing to a projection of a page of the report Zura had sent a couple of hours earlier.

"Yes, Gregor. I do understand the concern," Zura said. She pulled up her projection as well so that her team could see it.

"As all of you are well aware, the ARC project began more than twenty years ago. We've been collecting data before we ever built this place or put the first emission pump hole into the ground. Things have changed. When we started we weren't tracking the pump holes because those weren't even in existence then. Before this issue, we were looking at ocean health and using that as a way to measure environmental and ecological health in general." Zura looked at the team on the other side of the transmission to make sure they were following her.

"Okay. So what does that have to do with this? Sounds like you are saying that looking at all this isn't even really your job then?" The Stache jumped in.

"You may not know this, but once the pumps went in we were asked to watch for anything else unusual in the high risk areas around the tectonic plates and fault lines in addition to changes in the ocean's health. We aren't the only ones looking at that, but everyone else who is looking at it is not looking at the other things we consider."

"Doesn't anyone else see a problem with the lack of checks and balances here? Why are we paying all these organizations to look at the same damn thing? You want to talk about waste? There it is!" The Stache attacked again. Zura tried to ignore him so she could maintain her composure through the meeting.

"It doesn't matter who noticed this. It just so happens that we did," Johan spoke up in defense of his wife and the work they did.

"Right., and with what we began to see we had to step back and look at the bigger picture. We looked at as much as we could and kept track of it. We didn't see much outside of what we expected to see at first, but after some bigger disturbances and anomalies we decided to go back and look at our data. These disturbances and anomalies can't be explained away by the normal shifting," Zura said and waited for them to respond.

"That shouldn't have anything to do with our project. We dug those emission holes far away from the fault lines," Dr. Tomas Sporgsman from UniCorps responded.

"And you can't really say that without a doubt, this isn't normal or hasn't happened in the past," The Stache defended the pumping again, causing the muscles in Zura's neck to tense as she shot him a steeled look.

"We built them far away from the fault lines we knew about," Zura said back. "What we didn't know was that the fault lines we have known about aren't the only ones. There are new fault lines that can show up and small ones that can become larger ones." She paused before continuing, "And they are growing and what we are seeing is that some of them are developing fissures.These small cracks spread a little like tree branches, spreading out and connecting."

"That's not this program's doing. That's just nature," The Stache responded.

"Zura, can you definitively tie any of this to our emission pump program?" Gregor asked. He didn't want to agree with Mirkal's argument but he had a reasonable point. It needed to be as certain as possible.

Zura looked at Gregor. His concern was genuine, but she couldn't tell if it was because he was concerned the program might be causing the problem or because he was concerned his program and reputation might be at risk. Or both.

"Not absolutely definitively, but there is a very strong correlation."

"Correlation does not necessarily imply causation," Dr. Sandy Ashby said, speaking up in defense. "This has been a highly successful program in eliminating air pollution. Dr. Bello, do you really want to suggest that it is the problem?" she asked Zura.

Mave saw the report from the Science Institute come in but she couldn't do anything about it without disrupting the conversation. She shot Stephen a look and then tapped her wrist once. He would get the hint.

He left the small device on the table and spun around to pull up what had come through to Mave. He loaded it onto his system's projector so that the ARC team could see it but it remained out of view for the team in the Capital city.

Zura looked at the woman from the World Consensus. This was what she'd expected. "We don't want to blame the program. We want to make sure that we are operating safely and that we protect citizens who may become at risk."

"Are you suggesting we tell people about this Zura?" Gregor asked.

"If it gets worse, yes. They need to know if their lives are at risk."

"That would cause mass panic and consumer confidence would immediately tank along with our economy," The Stache said, giving the grimmest image he could imagine.

"Or we stay quiet and those people die, along with your sales to those consumers. Now that could also tank the economy," Mave shot back.

"Okay. Okay. This is the thing. You are suggesting that we have some time before this becomes really dangerous, right?" Gregor asked.

"It's hard to tell exactly. We've already had earthquakes in Southern Allegiance, ones that have rattled people and caused damage in Northern Allegiance, and other smaller incidents in Southern Liberty. No one is even talking about the earthquakes happening in areas where most people have already left. Some of these earthquakes have been pretty bad but not devastating," Zura said attempting to conceal the frustration that she could feel just under her skin.

"Take the most recent one in Southern Allegiance. There was very little warning, but what little they had was used to get people to safety. Thankfully, it was only a 5.5 on the Richter scale. Had it been worse and they weren't warned, it would've meant major casualties that could've been avoided," Johan added.

"The seismic activity we are tracking, the tremors, have really been one of our few real warnings, but we don't know when the next major incident will happen. It could be days, weeks, months, or maybe a couple of years. What we do know is that there are more of the underlying signs. We are seeing more connections," Mave said, nodding towards Rupert.

"We are seeing an underground map of what looks like these tree roots and they seem to be happening closer to the emissions pump sites than they happen the further away we get.

So to your point Dr. Ashby, no, we cannot prove causation, but there is too much correlation for it to be coincidence," Rupert said, as he pulled up an image that overlaid the pumps and their lines with the seismic activity.

"We think that the emissions being pumped into the ground are the cause of excess pressure and gas. This is building up and has to go somewhere. It appears to be pushing through the earth and causing these fissures. We can't prove it, but we can't see any other explanation," Rupert said, highlighting one of the graphs he'd put together.

"Dr. Bello?" Dr. Tomas Sporgsman called out before anyone else could continue. Zura turned her attention back to him. "I just want to remind you that you and your team, which means every person on this project and on the ARC, have signed a confidentiality agreement and a nondisclosure agreement.

There it was. What they'd all expected to be thrown out at them at the start of the conversation. UniCorps and the World Consensus held true to form.

"Sharing of any findings from research conducted on the ARC without approval from the funding committee is not allowed and is legally punishable. The sharing of this information may cause panic and social unrest amongst civilians and could possibly incite illegal behavior amongst civilians. Being a part of or contributing to any of those illegal behaviors is also illegal and punishable under the law. Do you understand this, Dr. Bello?" Dr. Sporgsman finished and awaited her response.

Zura could feel her nails digging into her hand the entire time he spoke his threat in the form of a warning. "Yes, I understand what the law is. Do you understand what our moral duty is to the citizens of the world?"

"Don't push this, Dr. Bello. We have obligations. UniCorps is obligated to protect the interest of our partner organizations and I'm sure you can understand that the World Consensus has obligations to protect the citizens. That means we can't allow anyone to incite civil unrest or anything that might endanger the immediate safety of those who entrust their leaders to protect them," Dr. Sandy Ashby added.

"Zura, you know that what you all proposed as a solution is nearly impossible, right?"

"No. It may be difficult, it may take time and resources, but it isn't impossible," she shot back.

"You all proposed the mass evacuation of major cities around the major fault lines because those areas are more likely to become active with everything else becoming weaker. I'm sure you know that most of those lines are centralized around the Ring of Fire. Of course you know, you're the scientist," The Stache said mockingly before continuing to denigrate her team and the work they'd done.

"There are only so many places people can go that aren't in danger. Besides that, we are talking about relocating nearly half the world's population in a matter of months or just a couple of years. I don't even think it is logistically possible. These people won't want to leave their homes at the threat of a possible earthquake or volcano happening at some unknown time in the future…maybe. You see? What you are saying and suggesting, doesn't make a whole lot of sense," The Stache argued as if everything Zura had said was laughable.

"That's enough Mirkal. For now, this remains completely confidential," Dr. Sporgsman said. "We'll talk more at the annual debrief next week. We need to talk on our side before anyone does anything," Dr. Sporgsman warned.

Zura looked back and forth between Tomas and The Stache. Their only concerns were about what this meant for UniCorps. The evacuation from just the one city in Southern Allegiance cost the government millions. Just one or two more cities that size and the government would be almost broke and UniCorps would have to support it even more, costing their stakeholders and corporations millions that they may never get back.

"We'll be waiting for your visit and to hear how we will move forward responsibly with this issue," Zura said. "If there is anything else I can answer for you, please let me know. Thank you."

Zura cut the transmission. She relaxed the pressure her fingernails were placing as they dug into the palms of her hands. She made sure they were gone before turning her attention to Stephen who'd been sitting silently.

"Did you get all of that, son?" Zura asked him.

"I sure did. Every word," Stephen answered with a smirk of a smile.

CHAPTER TWENTY-THREE
Revisiting

Antarctic Research Center

JOHAN TOSSED TINY rounded paper pellets at the small window in the room where he sat.

This had been his life's work. The work that defined all of their lives. The place that was built to help save them, now felt constricting, a prison of its own.

Johan had always been proud of the work that he and his team of architects, engineers, scientists, and technicians had done. It was a beautiful work of engineered art. Zura made sure it was also comfortable by hiring interior designers to make the space not just functional, but livable. They knew they would be spending a lot of time there over the years.

The idea for the ARC was begun more than thirty five years before as part of a global initiative to ensure the continuity of the human race. The scientists, technicians, analysts, engineers, and every person who worked on the ARC as regular employees had been carefully hand selected by the leaders of the collaborative that preceded UniCorps.

Someone else needed to know. The only person he could tell would be there any minute. Johan hoped it wasn't a mistake sharing this with anyone else not already approved, but keeping it to himself now felt too risky.

He looked out the oval window at the land that stretched out from the ARC. Though he and Zura owned their little unit, others who'd bought shares of ownership could lease a unit for Antarctic Expedition vacations. Most people never utilized this benefit and on the rare occasion that someone did they were usually placed in the outbuilding units. From the surface they looked like separate units but underneath, every part of the ARC was connected.

A light knock on the door brought Johan's attention back to the present.

"Come in," Johan said from his position by the window.

Rupert walked in and took a seat in the empty chair that rested near the out of place birch wood desk.

"You seem to have a lot on your mind these days, old friend," Rupert said without waiting.

"I do. We all do. I need to talk to you Rupert, about the ARC."

Johan sat down in the chair opposite Rupert and leaned forward. His graying hair showed his years - the ones he'd used getting to where he was.

"Things are going to happen quickly I think and I don't know if you know enough about the ARC, though by now, you should. I've been trying to protect you –protect all of you."

"What's going on Johan? Did something happen we don't know about?" Rupert asked concerned. He rarely saw his friend like this.

"It's more about what's been going on before now that I need you to know about. It might not make a difference right now, but I feel like it may matter, one day."

"I'm listening."

"Let me start with some things you may be familiar. Before becoming UniCorps a group of powerful organizations came together as a collaborative of sorts, to promote some of their joint interests in a more efficient way.

"That's well known. No surprise there."

"Well, that collaborative convinced the World Consensus to join in the efforts after making a convincing argument about continuity of life and the protection of natural resources, the environment, and the health of citizens."

"I read about those programs, even helped implement some of the earlier ones," Rupert said curiously.

"Once they got the World Consensus on board, they began finding the people who would lead the work and build the ARC, this place. They found people from all over the world, Rupert, who could and would be able to work together. They chose Zura to lead up the main work. They chose me to assist that work and to lead another project."

"Another project? The one you disappear to work on?"

"Yes, but that's for later. They gave Zura leeway over choosing other two members of her core team. She lucked up with Mave and Mave helped her get you."

Rupert smiled, knowing he had always been a sucker for Mave.

"They did a good job recruiting. Everyone I work with is highly rated, from top universities or from some of the most powerful private companies, including those under UniCorps. You should be happy that the ARC can attract and keep that kind of talent."

"I am, but what I want you to know is why it was all so important. Why they are willing to recruit and pay for the best. You see, UniCorps invested an unnamed amount of their own pooled money as well as an unnamed amount from the World Consensus budget for Security."

"Security? Is that why Mylar is so involved?"

"Yes. Exactly, though it's hard to see the connection."

"Yeah, it is," Rupert agreed.

"They are able to argue that Security includes the security of our environment – how safe it is so that life can go on. The push for the ARC came in earnest after reports on the changing climate, the water crisis, and concerns over the emissions and pollutants that had never been fully resolved. I'm sure you remember the initial solution for the emissions issue was pushed through by an overeager lobbying group. They did not want to disrupt production and sold the prior individual nations on creation of jobs. If I remember correctly, you yourself wrote a report on what we learned from that experience as part of your graduate school program."

"I did. Almost everyone had to address it in some way."

"So you know that the first solution lasted nearly one hundred years before people began realizing the problem and calling for an end to it. Unfortunately, by that time, it had already impacted the water and started poisoning people with lead. Nations built miles and miles of pipe that pushed emissions several feet under ground and then into cleaning factories that were designed to clean the air," Johan continued.

Rupert nodded his head. He knew the story. "Yes, the pollution above ground had been relatively well contained in the nearly airtight buildings, by using the deatomization process to break down the poisons. No one wanted to pay for the around the clock monitoring required or deal with the risk associated with deatomization. It made the air too unstable. After a couple small explosions, they started shutting them down."

"Exactly. They never tried to determine how to improve them. Even with the small explosions, the risks, we had the data that the benefits were outweighing the costs. No one ever got to the see that data," Johan said, feeling upset about the failure.

"We wound up with two issues. There was the instability of the deatomization process and then the poisoning of the water supply. That wasn't even something they'd thought about and didn't worry about much. They figured someone else would eventually come up with a better solution, before the pipes corroded. When they'd been put in originally, the pipes had an estimated life of about 100 years. So by the time the life of those pipes had worn out, the people who'd worked on them or been around when the pipes went in were also gone," Johan said as he thought about the lack of foresight that was being repeated.

"That's when people started noticing the water tasted funny and sometimes came out of the taps a strange color. We lost a lot of people in Southern Allegiance because of that," Rupert said, shaking his head and thinking of his grandmother's stories.

"Even the ones who'd maintained the pipes had been pushing for someone to fix the real issue decades before it ever broke down, but it wasn't broken then, so there was no outcry to fix it," Johan said as he considered the reports he'd read during his studies.

"Yeah, and no politician wanted to be the one to cause panic or a budget shortfall over something that might not even really be a problem. My grandmother was a local representative in her area and couldn't get anyone to listen at the time," Rupert said, shaking his head.

"Well, when the pipes began failing and contaminating the water supply it happened on a global scale. The solution of the pipes had been global and so was the problem. The world needed a way to manage and control it all and to work together for what was a global water crisis that soon became a global food crisis." Johan said standing up and looking out of the window at the clear water.

Johan and Rupert both considered what they'd learned about and read about as children growing up and as scientists. The era of the storms spanned nearly ten years with weather conditions so turbulent and unpredictable that people would be caught in tsunamis, hurricanes, tornadoes, and snow storms with barely enough notice to leave before it hit.

The casualties in those years had been astronomical, especially for the time. There were only twelve billion people living and nearly a billion had been killed in the era of the storm.

By the end of the water crisis, another billion had died. Rupert shook his head as he listened. Some of this was new to him as it hadn't been reported the way Johan told it in any of his years of school or as a professional scientist.

"It was the weather crisis that gave birth to the idea initially for the World Consensus. The water crisis became the policy window for the idea to catch on and go through. Those leaders, with the support of those who would become UniCorps, were finally able to act on the ideas and quickly proposed the solution of pumping the emissions miles down into the earth, below the water supply using a safe non-corrosive material. Rupert, I can tell you I have my own opinion about those crises, but let's just say that it seems very convenient."

"But out of that came a solution. Finally. It wasn't meant to be a permanent one and everyone agreed on that much, at the time. Now if we could just convince them or remind them that it was a temporary solution and we are now working on borrowed time because we still have to deal with the emissions problem and the current system can't handle it," Rupert said not convinced of where Johan was going with the conversation.

"The other solution isn't ready. It was the second part of deatomizing the particles that became a problem with the poisons being pushed so far down. Unlike the cleaning factories, there would be no way to access them directly or control how they spread."

"And this is where we are today. I know they argued it was better financially to start a new process rather than to replace the existing pipes with the new non-corrosive materials. I remember how vague everyone was around a long-term plan and long-term solution, but because people wanted the quickest and cheapest solution they agreed to it all. It wasn't long after that they asked if I wanted to be a part of the solution," Rupert smiled as he remembered how he'd come into this life.

"You and the rest of us got pulled into this mess Rupert. It was a problem scientists had been trying to solve for as long as it had been a problem. The ARC was supposed to be a part of that solution and we haven't solved a damn thing yet Rupert."

"Seems like there is a lot of talking about what needs fixing, but there's not a lot happening to fix it," Rupert said crossing his arms and leaning back.

"We have some ideas. In fact, what we have is better than just ideas on how to fix it long-term, but no one is listening. Rupert, I've started working on ways to improve the deatomization process. It's been a lot of years since then and the science has advanced so tell me why no one wants to look at it again."

"And if that technology to do it was created here, it belongs to them, doesn't it?" Rupert asked as more of a statement than question. He sat back, understanding Johan's dilemma.

"There is a solution. I know it, but it may not happen in either of our lifetimes. It's that tidbit of information that is only given on a need to know basis, and very few people know." Johan was now speaking in a low voice.

"Things like that take a lot of time to get right and it's not something that can be done and not be right. We can't take that risk and wind up in the same position twenty years from now."

"Of course not. With the right support, it could be done in a few years, but me, working alone in secret, it could take twenty more years Rupert. That's not fair to any of us."

"It will take resources committed to the research and to the maintenance of the infrastructure. No one wants to stop or slow production to make it happen. It'll never get through any vote to do that, but if the resources were in place, do you really believe it could be a matter of a few years before we started seeing success.?" Rupert asked Johan curiously.

"Yes. I do. We need a place to test and god knows we need more dedicated brains. I'm frustrated Rupert. I feel like a pawn in their game and it's not something I ever wanted to be. I only wanted to fulfill my duty, and help save us."

"I understand Johan. I don't believe it's over. There is still time for you to do that, but you can't bear it alone. You shouldn't have to. No one person got us into this mess and no one person is going to get us out."

Over the years, Johan had led discussions with UniCorps and the World Consensus about revisiting the inactive cleaning factories. He'd proposed that the cost of producing the noncorrosive tubes had gone down enough that it should be reconsidered as an option. He'd even offered to help lead the project of retrofitting the old pipes. He'd raised the offer again last year during their annual meeting and again he was shut down.

The reasons were always obscure and arguments poorly formed, ranging from long-term plans that would pursue alternative solutions to there not being enough research on the new materials to overall costs and anything else they could think of. It was clear they had no interest in the one possible solution that anyone had offered that had a chance of working. He understood why, as he was caught in the middle, having the answer while being a party to the problem.

"I just wanted you to know what was bothering me Rupert and where I am right now. Frustrated and I want to see something happen. I put too much of my life into this for it to all be in vain."

"Johan, we've all sacrificed for this. None of us want it to be in vain. If we want something to happen though, the demand for it can't come from here on the ARC. It has to come from out there, the citizens. They have to want it," Rupert said with a sigh.

"They'd have to know that they should want it first," Johan said as his eyes wandered to the small window.

"Johan, there is no choice but for them to know. Is there something else Johan? I've known you a long time and when you asked to talk to me, you seemed to have more to say. What you told me, most of it I knew already. So I'm wondering what it is you decided to hold back now.

Rupert was right. There was more. He looked into his best friend's face and smiled. "It's not important right now."

"Alright, if you say so," Rupert paused to give Johan a chance to say whatever was really on his mind. After a few moments of awkward silence Rupert nodded, "Well, you know your wife is on us constantly to get all this prep work done before we leave so I'm going to get back to it. If you want to talk again, Johan, you know how to find me."

"Thanks Rupert. I'll be back down there soon."

Rupert stood up slowly from his chair and limped ever so slightly to the door. He cast a questioning look back and then left the room.

Johan turned back to the report he was supposed to read, but now he was distracted. That wasn't how his conversation with Rupert was supposed to go. He couldn't put Rupert in the middle of something like what he carried on his shoulders.

Rupert hadn't asked for it and had already given more than he ever needed to. He'd barely told him more than what they'd all studied in school with the exception of the possibility surrounding a possible solution to the emission issue, which was important and Rupert did need to know in case anything happened to Johan.

He stood up, arms crossed, and looked out his window again shaking his head. *It couldn't all be in vain.* Years before, he'd trained and studied to become both a master engineer and scientist. He'd done his internships with the International Space and Time Exploration Program, (I STEP) and was familiar with the interest in and exploration of space and time. It was a topic that always held his fascination and intellectual curiosity.

Johan could still easily recall the excitement he had more than twenty years ago when he'd been chosen to lead the ARC design. He'd come up with the honeycomb styled chambers with central grounds for community interaction, dining, and more. Family units were integrated into the design allowing some semblance of normalcy in the event the ARC was needed to do what it was designed to be able to do.

Most people living on Earth had no idea of the progress made by all the research and investigations done in space and time studies. They'd had more success than they could publicly take credit for. He was forbidden to speak of some of what he knew, even with Zura and his children. He'd sworn an oath of confidentiality before taking the position and breaking it would be handled as treason.

As he sat back down in his captain-style chair in his private office away from the science center, he continued to look out onto the ocean. There were more fish and other sea creatures swimming in the Southern Ocean than before. He knew they'd come in escape, seeking refuge from what they could instinctively sense as danger.

The waters in Antarctica were warmer than even just twenty years before when they'd begun collecting the data. He watched them move through the waters and hoped that eventually people would understand it just as well.

Johan stood and thought about how this place, this project, had changed his life. He'd seen and heard things that he could never explain or share with anyone outside those privileged to know. There were things others would not understand and now he was faced with all of it actually mattering and becoming real.

Years of theory, planning, and preparation might finally have to be implemented. He was thankful for the residences they'd been granted as part of their agreements to work on the project, but leery of what might now be expected.

Johan tried to return his focus to the report, scrolling through the details of tremor reports leading up to the earthquake in Northern Allegiance that few outside of the region knew about. What he read from a personal source described the forced silencing of the news because they didn't want to panic the citizens.

There were no evacuation efforts at all, and while it didn't result in any direct casualties, it made Johan wonder whether others were asking what the long-term plan actually was. Was anyone asking the questions that would yield answers that could make a difference?

He shook his head in disgust. There had been signs and warnings well before the earthquake and the injuries that did occur could have been avoided, but he felt as if that was just a test. How would people react? If UniCorps and the World Consensus were willing to let that occur, what else were they willing to do?

Johan needed to make additional preparations to ensure the safety of his family and ensure that the others would be ready.

CHAPTER TWENTY-FOUR
Steady

University of Southern Allegiance in Santoria, Southern Allegiance

DR. LIMA STRODE across the beautiful historic campus. It was a warm Spring day with trees that burst with color. The endless blue skies were interrupted with little puffs of cumulus clouds. The reddish brown brick buildings held countless stories from more than three hundred years ago and had been one of the locations the Council had used since Yin joined it.

The dorms filled once again with the regular university students ready to finish the final weeks before July, when the one month Summer break began. Claudia Lima needed a break too. With managing the camps she barely had time to catch her breath even when the regular students weren't on campus.

There were so many balls in the air and simply trying to do her regular job at the University, help coordinate the ceremony and track down the eighth were keeping her hands full. She'd decided to postpone the follow-up meeting with the Council. There was no use meeting them when she had nothing useful to report.

That postponement ended today. She had to go back to check in after learning from Mave that Zura was reporting what they'd found to the funders. Dr. Lima already knew that both the World Consensus and UniCorps would balk at what they received.

She needed to ensure safe passage of information out of the ARC and into the right hands so that people would know the truth. For that she required the Council's help. They would also have to help her coordinate everything that needed to happen as they approached the Awakening Ceremony.

Dr. Lima continued her brisk walk across the campus as students headed back to dorms before the evening's special social activity. She'd arranged for a guest musician, a violinist, to come and perform that evening. His accompaniment was setting up now and soon she'd be able to move about more freely.

The entertainment was in the student social budget and it would keep most people out of the building she needed to use and out of the immediate area for the evening. She couldn't risk another incident like the one with Alexis, Stella, and the other campers.

She lingered in the courtyard watching the students disperse. Once only a few stragglers remained she began to walk again. There was a short window between the students returning to their dorms and then coming back out for the performance.

As she neared the glass doors to the building, she stopped to look around her. She wasn't very subtle but she needed to make sure she had no followers. She quickly pulled the door open and went through shutting it just as abruptly. She pulled a small grey bar down to latch the door from the inside, something she had neglected to do over camp but would not forget again.

Dr. Lima walked across the dimly lit empty staff dining hall, her arm hairs rising as she moved towards the double doors. She could already feel them waiting. Their Chi was so strong she could feel it pulling on her own, bringing her towards them. She walked through the doors on the other side of the hall and drew them tightly shut.

Dr. Lima fixed her uniform and checked her hair in the reflection of the glass in the door's window panes. She knew she was being silly as they wouldn't notice or care. They didn't see her that way.

She walked past three doors on the left before stopping in front of one where the faint glow of lights which activated when the building was closed, escaped under each of the closed doors. That was how those kids had found them, she guessed. They'd kept going by the lights until they'd heard them. As she approached the regular room they used, she could see the figures in the room through the frosted glass.

She checked the time before walking in. She would need to make it out and back to the campus concert hall during the performance but knew she would have plenty of time.

Dr. Lima scanned her finger to the panel on the side of the door and heard it click, releasing the lock. She walked into the room, softly closing this door too, behind her.

She walked into the room and sat with Yin, San, and Cho for her briefing. Three hours later, she pulled the door handle open to leave. She nearly stumbled out of the office. She stopped, remembering to return the lighting to the setting it was on when she'd arrived. She felt lightheaded as she fumbled her way through the doors leading to the faculty dining area. As dizziness set in, she sat down at one of the round tables, the meeting playing back in her head.

Things were in motion and if it all went well she could step back from all of this soon. She just had to get them to the next phase and then those responsible for that part of the mission cold take over.

CHAPTER TWENTY-FIVE
Evacuation

Rift Valley, Northeast Part of Southern Liberty

THE RIFT VALLEY had been showing significant signs of activity and tremors for the past few weeks. Delia had gone out several times over the past month measuring the cracks in the hole, sometimes with Lyn, sometimes without. She considered it her duty. She didn't know why she had to know and track this tiny change in one single hole in one city in one Region, but she did.

The reports from the news only motivated her further. She just had to know for herself if there was some connection, even if didn't mean anything to anyone else. There still had not been any official position taken. Those in charge continued to say that tremors were normal, blamed it on seasonality, and weather systems. Things that made no sense even to Delia, who wasn't very scientific, at least not in the traditional sense.

She and her parents thought it odd that no one seemed to be talking about what happened in Southern Allegiance. Her dad often speculated how there was no data or information anywhere about the patterns in Southern Allegiance leading up to the major earthquake. There had to be information but whoever had it was keeping it close.

"Dad, I've got six months of data from that old pump hole now. Is that enough for you to look at and tell me what you think?" Delia asked her dad Orbil as he packed a bag.

"I will take a look at it as soon as I can. Delia, with all that's going on, I can't make any promises and I don't want you out there asking too many questions."

In light of the changes that had happened over the past few weeks, she had to know if it meant something. She sent him a copy of what she'd recorded so far.

"I understand. Anything you see that might look strange, just let me know. I'm curious," Delia said trying not to pressure her father too much. They were still preparing as if they were going to go out on their regular mission trip to donate items to people in need.

"Are you all going to be back in time for the evacuation?" Delia asked looking at the bag Orbil was packing and the one already sitting near the front door belonging to Marie.

"I expect so. You just follow the orders. Everything will be alright," Orbil answered. It wasn't the answer Delia had hoped for. Sometimes their trips ran long and there wasn't much time until the round four evacuees would be called.

The RePM Division had told all evacuees that the evacuation was temporary. According to the RePM Division, it was a precaution only and the scientists and geologists were studying the issue. At the time, there was no cause for real concern.

There were more than thirteen million people living within fifty miles of the Rift Valley and all had to be relocated to safer areas. Each person was allowed to take one suitcase and a handbag only. Anything that couldn't fit into this small allowance was forced to be left behind.

The lines for passage were long, stretching the full length of the streets, spilling onto the sidewalks and the side streets that led to the main processing area. SEP Agents were charged with checking the paperwork of every man, woman, and child to be ported out of the area. This was all planned to occur in the span of just one week.

They were already a few days in and more than five million people were out of the area between the official evacuation and those who had taken the evacuation into their own hands. They'd left town in personal or chartered vehicles at the first notice.

Many in powerful positions had been evacuated if they had been able to leave work behind and get their families. Delia knew they would be the ones to get first dibs in the transports once in the main evacuation.

In the evacuation zone, just as soon as a hovehicle or bus was full they sent it off so it could make the return trip. The RePM Division had planned to be able to evacuate between 300,000 and 350,000 people per day with some taking private hovehicles and most in the extended capacity hovehicles and airtrains.

Delia only knew this detail because of Lyn, whose father held a respected position at one of the global corporations belonging to UniCorps. The math didn't work out and Delia and Lyn had both concluded that the evacuation would never really happen in the time they were giving. Hopefully, any danger was weeks away and not days.

When the agents had first come by to announce the evacuation and to begin preparing people, she remembered hearing neighbors ask the obvious questions. *Were there enough places to stay? Were there enough hovehicles and airtrains to get them out?*

And the SEP Agents had been ordered to give a specific response to the question that was on everyone's mind - *What happens if we don't all get out in a week?* The required response was "We are doing everything possible to ensure all citizens are relocated in the target timeframe." If pressed, they simply repeated the response, just firmer.

The SEP Agents lined the streets, spaced every ten to fifteen yards to ensure a smooth and thorough evacuation. The orders they'd been given was to ensure every person left the city within the one week allotted and this included dissenters and those who resisted leaving.

The hovehicles floated along the center of the streets filled with people and with luggage secured to the top. Behind the hovehicles were older buses that rode along the road.

Both the buses and the hovehicles were being sent to different destinations. People who had family in other places would be temporarily resettled there and were assured by leaders that they'd be able to return once the danger passed. Those who didn't have family would be sent to further less populated areas where they wouldn't be a burden on the already strained resources.

Every household received an assigned number during the initial phase with a code based on the day they were to evacuate. Delia's family, like most of her neighbors, had the code four. Lyn's family received the code two. Delia had been surprised when Ms. C said she'd wait to leave with the other neighbors. It was especially surprising since every day was another day closer to a possible earthquake.

The number arriving for evacuation each day seemed to border near 400,000 and once they'd already secured their homes they could not return. It was more than could be processed in a day, which meant each day there was an excess of as many as 100,000 people who were stranded at or en route to the evacuation hub. They slept in makeshift camp grounds, nearby churches, schools, and wherever else they could find shelter.

In addition to having the prioritized evacuation, the SEP Agents went back each day for that day's evacuees, despite the hundreds of thousands still waiting from previous days. The numbers of people awaiting evacuation wasn't on the news. That part of the evacuation wasn't being reported anywhere that Delia could find, but she saw it. They were being evacuated systematically, street by street and block by block, ensuring no person remained and that each only brought what was legally allowed.

Delia waited at home for her turn to leave. She hoped that what the SEP Agents and news said was true. That other regions and cities were sending down all available hovehicles and even their old buses to help get people out.

Delia was constantly reminded of the math. At the start of the official evacuation there were eight million people in the area. There was no way everyone could get out, unless they got more help. She hoped that the rest of the world would care enough.

The area that was now Southern Allegiance had always played support to everyone else. She'd learned in history how the land had been racked by others coming in to mine natural resources and how the people had at one time been used as laborers without pay. She didn't want her part of the world to be considered expendable. Not right now. Not when millions of lives needed the support of the world they had always supported.

CHAPTER TWENTY-SIX
Homeland

Rift Valley in Southern Liberty

THE SHRILL CRY of an inconsolable little girl pierced the air of the evacuation site, causing everyone to look around. On one of the hovehicles headed to Antes in the Northern part of Northern Liberty, a young girl with bright green ribbons strewn through her hair was having a screaming fit. They were forced to leave their family dog behind and her already frantic mom tried uselessly to calm her. Her crying set off a chain reaction of crying and whining kids who were scared.

"Get control of her!" an agent barked at the mother.

"I can't do anything. She's scared! What do you expect!" the upset mother yelled back.

"Get them outta here now. I don't want to cause a scene," The callous agent yelled at the driver sneering at the burdened mother and her daughter. The hovehicle took off in the midst of the cries and the angry mother's attempt to protest back was drowned out by the cries of the other children.

Most SEP Agents tried to be cordial and polite but always seemed intimidating in the shiny grey uniforms with exterior armor and helmets. Their faces were partially masked by a chin guard while the large agent issued reflective shaded glasses they wore hid much of the rest of their face. The glasses were specially equipped with the ability to read the tags of registered and unregistered citizens. All of the special gear made them appear a shade less than human, floating between a flimsy grey space of real and mechanic.

The agents' uniforms were also equipped with a bioshield that once triggered would encase their entire body and suit plus ten inches. The shield was designed to activate when any biochemical or smoke above a safe level were detected by the suit's sensors. Ten inches allowed them to form a protective wall when lined up shoulder to shoulder.

This defense system was touted as a safety mechanism for agents and other law enforcement officers, as well as citizens. The designers promoted the notion that citizens could stand behind them and escape to safety if there was an attack. The idea of the citizens benefiting had always been met with a little suspicion but the technology had been approved and the uniforms were already put in the budget without public input.

The shield technology was designed and invented by the UniCorps International Security Division after nearly a hundred thousand citizens and agents had died during the attacks by the homeless more than twenty years before.

The technology was heralded as one of the best inventions of the decade and every peace keeping agency regionally and on the international level bought the upgrade. It sent Unicorps's stocks and profits through the roof and with the enemy still out there, the demand for new technology and defense skyrocketed. The public was now at the center of the argument for keeping security developments funded.

Before the homeless attacks the world had become complacent and vigilance against evil had waned. There was little threat seen from those who would inflict harm on good people. The one world government had come with a stronger sense of peace and unity.

The accused attackers were originally sold on the idea of a united world and had thrown all of their support and effort into making it a reality. It was supposed to be a world that worked for everyone. They helped to push the idea through politically and were essential to garnering public support for one government in the prior decades. It was the men and women who were now outcasts that had been critical in the election of the first Supreme Leader by all those able to vote.

Soon after forming the World Consensus, people wanted more power, more identity. They wanted to be from somewhere and have associations with others that were tied to a place. The corporations and media played on this desire and soon, there was a campaign for the Homelands.

At first it was fun and entertaining. The Homelands campaign was a way to have friendly competition in production of goods, services, academia, the arts, and athletics in order to support the World Consensus.

Several years passed with the loose identification with Homelands. Once people became used to identifying with a Homeland, more structure was added to it and they became official areas governed by Region Leaders. The institution of the Regions strengthened the power of the World Consensus and made them a more formidable threat on a global scale.

The homeless were called that because of their refusal to choose a homeland in a world that supposedly had no borders. It wasn't what they'd fought so hard to accomplish. They were now much older but they still believed in one world and were against forced association with a Region and homeland.

The final straw for the homeless was the requirement to register with a Homeland and have a second identification based on their registered homeland. The Regional Leaders had proposed to the United Congress that every citizen be legally required to identify with a Region in order to more accurately meet the needs of the citizens, both regionally and globally. Registration would allow them to collect accurate information on official citizen counts which was argued to aid in making sure each region was given their share of resources.

The World Consensus no longer held the promise it once did and had again allowed for and even facilitated divisions based on regions and place of birth.

The punishment for refusing to comply with registration was banishment from the region. No other region would accept the homeless as official citizens so they would truly be homeless and forced to live without any legal identity or resources.

Prior to the attack, the government had already managed to greatly reduce the overhead for prisons and chose not to jail them due to costs. The homeless could not receive any benefits and were only permitted to work in jobs that no one else wanted. They were forced to pay a penalty tax for the burden they caused on society for refusing to comply and be accurately counted. They were also charged for a second type of uniform which identified them as being without a regional registration.

And for greater insult and embarrassment the homeless were required to turn in their regular World Consensus government issued uniform. This clothing was phased out in favor of regionally specific uniforms. With the exception of those on government assignment, or attending approved private clothing functions and events, the regional uniform was required for all daily wear.

Immediately following the attack, the United Congress hastily drafted a bill which was just as swiftly voted into law. It said that every person was required to register and every child was to be registered upon birth. After the fear instilled through the treatment of the first wave of homeless, very few people had chosen to resist the registry.

The homeless were forced into hiding or to prove, many unsuccessfully, that they were not a part of the attack. Most wound up in the repurposed jails and prisons, now working the menial jobs for no pay. The government justified this forced labor by stating the attackers should be grateful that the death penalty had been abolished and that they were receiving room and board.

They were stripped of all but basic human rights and had their World Consensus citizenship status reduced from basic to fringe. Not only did they take the adults who had pushed the homeless movement, they took any child sixteen or over as a para-adult and the rest were sent to the Agency for Orphaned Children.

Children over ten were sent to a special program meant to remind them of their responsibilities and commitment to being a World and Regional citizen of the World Consensus. The younger children were eligible for immediate adoption to parents who were vetted to be strong and responsible citizens.

It didn't take long for those who chose to be homeless but had not been charged of any crimes to realize they were still being counted and still working in the system, without benefits. They could join a region if they chose but would have to pay an additional penalty tax for being reestablished as a full citizen and yet they could not receive benefits for the subsequent year. It was blackmail.

In a matter of a few years all they'd worked for had been destroyed and returned it to what it had been, but only worse with all power aggregated. The corporations had bought the governments in all but name before anyone who was alive had even been born. They'd bought the healthcare system and controlled the jobs, food sources and food chain, media, and every essential good needed to live.

The formation of the World Consensus simply gave them a more efficient way to leverage that power. Each Region Leader was also a high ranking official at one of the macro corporations that belonged to UniCorps.

The homeless who escaped capture were now outlaws and harboring one would mean loss of full citizenship at a minimum and possibly land a citizen in prison with fringe status.

The homeless who escaped or who chose to remain outside of the system, removed their internal registrations and now roamed the areas where no one wanted to live - the deserts, hills, and the old oil fields that were now dried up and abandoned.

They set up camp where they could but most groups could never settle due to the ongoing searches by SEP Agents and the World Consensus. They were generally left alone as long as they stayed out of sight and out of the way, unless tensions flared or someone was needed to blame for a crisis, an attack, or even economic issues. Then the agents would begin hunting the homeless again.

Those who had found the least desirable areas had the best chance of being left alone, but there were never any guarantees.

CHAPTER TWENTY-SEVEN
Edge

Antarctic Research Center

THE ENERGY ON the ARC created a recognizable buzz in the air. Everyone was on edge and tempers flared with little to no cause.

"Rupert, I need you to clean up the data and store everything new securely. No mistakes," Zura barked orders.

"Of course. I've got it under control," he answered in as easy a voice as he could muster.

"Johan, will we have everything ready to continue analysis from back home?" Zura turned her attention to Johan now.

"Yes, of course. It's the same process I've done every year, my love," he smiled as he touched her shoulder gently.

"Uh huh, and the latest data is loaded for today's meeting already?" Zura asked absently as she decided to seek refuge in the ROC room.

"Yes, honey," he called after her as she walked away.

The goal of everyone she came across was simple – keep her from having any other reason to reach her peak fury. Even Johan with his quiet patience and Mave couldn't seem to bring her back to calm.

The mounting tension was getting to them all. Mave followed Zura into the ROC room with a cup of coffee.

"Coffee? It might help settle your nerves a little," Mave offered.

"Coffee isn't going to do a damn thing for my nerves, Mave. The only thing that's gonna help is if everyone here pulls their weight so this meeting goes like it's supposed to," Zura snapped as she looked up briefly from her work.

She was revising her talking points for the meeting. Mave just looked at her with a raised eyebrow and sat it down beside her before walking back out of the room.

"Whatever we do, we need to do it right today," Johan said when Mave came back into the science center.

"Yeah, we will already have the funders on us looking for any reason to discredit us. We don't need Zura on us too, not if we can help it," Rupert agreed with Johan.

"She'll be fine once we get started and she's in performance mode. Plus, we'll be there to back her," Mave said with certainty. They'd been in difficult meetings before, but none as difficult as the ones recently. She hoped she was right.

"My friends, we need to head down to the ROC room. Let's hope a few minutes to herself has helped," Johan said hesitantly.

Zura and her team now waited in the ROC room - ready. Zura had made them go over everything key to both the report and to the argument they planned to make again and again, ad nauseam. The notes that had been prepared now served only as a prop, no longer needed to state their case.

Mave looked at Zura, trying to send her some calming thoughts but Zura wasn't receiving anything. She was still on edge and needed to reserve every one of her emotions to get through this. She needed them to drive her past her nervousness and fear.

Zura thought about the kids and the pangs of guilt she'd become too familiar with, returned. She hadn't seen them today and didn't know if she would. The kids would be okay, she told herself. They were almost para-adults after all. After today she could finally plan their sixteenth birthday party. Last minute planning, but there was nothing new there. At least Mave had promised to help her.

The door from the lab opened, bringing Zura back from her thirty seconds away from the thoughts of the meeting that had consumed her entire being. It was one of the kitchen staff coming through the door rolling a double stacked cart filled with food. Johan directed him to set up the table on the side where coffee and juices were already waiting.

Zura stood up after the young man setting up the food left the room. She studied the layout, satisfied at her choices. Perhaps another cup of coffee, another one, would help settle her nerves or at least give her some momentary comfort. She grabbed her mug from her seat and poured herself a tall cup of coffee, rich with fragrance.

She looked at Mave and felt guilty for snapping about the coffee earlier, but now wasn't the time for apologies. She added cream and two cubes of sugar, stirring it slowly as she watched the crystals dissolve in the coffee that had turned a lighter shade of brown.

Mave took the pitcher of coffee and poured herself a cup of coffee, black, one scoop of sugar, before passing it to Rupert. Johan passed, one cup was good enough. He'd be jittery if he had another.

"I believe we are as ready as we'll be," Zura finally spoke to her team.

"Agreed," Johan said tapping his fingers on the tablet in front of him.

"What will be will be. We can only present what we know and try to convince them to do the right thing," Rupert said. He ran a hand over his hair before pulling it back into a low ponytail. "Johan, will you propose revisiting your solution again today?" he asked curiously.

"I'll have to see how the rest goes. If I think there is a window for it, I will. If they balk at the rest of this, well, I'll save it for another day. Don't worry though, at some point, we'll have to look at real options to solve the problem." Johan looked at his beautiful wife Zura and smiled. He thought he almost saw a small smile cross her face, but he wasn't sure. She was still only partially with them.

A sense of foreboding quiet permeated the remainder of the ARC. The core team was in the ROC room, waiting because after months of preparation, they'd gotten down to the meeting day. The prior weeks had been unusually intense and stressful and finally culminated in today. It was their one chance to impress upon their funders the importance of taking action immediately.

The representatives from UniCorps and the World Consensus would be arriving any moment. There were more people than usual this year because of what was in the report.

***

MOST OF THE other staff were preparing as well, in different ways, trying to get their work done so they could leave for home and the winter season. The family unit belonging to Zura and Johan was no different.

The light bounced off the walls in the living room and tried to find its way down the halls, but was blocked by the angles. There would be no one in there until hours from now. Everyone else's preparations to leave meant the twins finally had some space and time to do what they'd wanted to do for days.

CHAPTER TWENTY-EIGHT
Explorers

Antarctic Research Center

STEPHEN AND STELLA took advantage of the distractions to finally investigate some of the information, mostly blueprints, Marco sent them from the Noah folder. He and Alexis were able to open a few files which he sent in chunks – just bits and pieces of a larger puzzle.

Most of what they'd been able to open included the layout and design of the ARC. Having those files opened meant that they could feed their curiosity and explore. Stephen synced all the data he had from Marco to his tablet as he and Stella set out again.

Today was day two of Stephen and Stella's exploring the ARC using the blueprints. The first day hadn't shown them anything new or exciting. The level one details were mostly the areas Stephen and Stella had lived with and in since they could remember. It also had the special safe room their parents had shown them a few years before.

The fact that food and supplies were stored in those first areas made sense given the ARC's remote location. If for any reason no one could get to them, at least they wouldn't starve. None of this was new and it felt like a wasted day, except for the nature of the blueprints' requirements.

Today they were going to the next layer of the blueprints. The blueprint program required that certain locations be accessed in the building before being allowed to continue. It was like an additional level of security so that someone following it couldn't just go for the food or supplies or whatever else the mammoth ARC held.

Stella sent Zura a quick note saying they were fine and would stay out of the way since they had all the meetings.

Zura quickly shot a message back. "OK. Thanks." Stella knew her mom was under more stress than usual. She continually heard her thinking how happy she'd be when it was all over and they were packing up and getting on that transport carrier back home. Of all the years they'd spent here, this had been the hardest for her mom's team.

Stephen and Stella got their ARC issued emergency light caps and flashlights and headed through the living areas of their family unit to the main area of their honeycomb. The green light flashed on the blueprint as they walked. They'd covered a good part of the honeycomb structures and had skipped the science center section, for the most part.

Just the day before, as they started exploring, Stephen tucked the tablet in his pocket and walked in during the morning's activities to say hi and let it register that he'd met that location requirement. They would go the other way today. The ARC was much larger than either of them had imagined and the blueprint showed at least three levels just like they thought they saw before.

The three levels seemed to nearly mirror each other in size, but the sections varied with the second level having large sections that Stephen reasoned must be the warehouse and storage areas. Only exploration would tell.

"Here we go," said Stella as they went through a door leading, eventually to the warehouse area. She laughed nervously, "We would get in so much trouble if our parents found out what we were doing." She thought of how gutsy Alexis had been back at camp. She wished she had half of that courage.

The twins walked more than a hundred yards through a winding dark hallway too narrow to move shoulder to shoulder. Stephen took the lead. The only guidance they had was the blueprint, which they followed as they wove beyond their normal allowable range.

The only sounds were the faint humming of a motor or engine running and the occasional sound of gurgling water. The air felt strangely dry though the temperature seemed to be extremely well controlled. The temperature reading on Stephen's watch hadn't changed since leaving the main level. *Good insulation*, thought Stephen.

They continued walking slowly, allowing the light from their hats to go ahead of them. A few more turns and they finally made it to a door on the blueprint that simply read WS1. To the right of the door was a scanner. The door would require official identification to be opened.

Stephen held his hand up and Stella knocked it back down. "Are you crazy?" she said furiously. "If you scan yourself it's going to be recorded that you scanned in here. We'll have to try to get in another way, if we have time."

They continued down the hall passing more doors marked with WS and then numbers.

"I would say that WS is for warehouse storage?" Stephen reasoned.

"Makes sense to me. There are a lot of them. At least we won't go hungry," Stella shrugged. Of course, the idea of stored food wasn't really appealing. "Probably dehydrated everything. Yuck."

As they left the honeycomb section marked by WS doors they headed down a short hallway and entered into another section. This one had doors marked with an S and a number only.

"I wonder what these are?" Stephen wondered aloud to Stella.

"Maybe more storage?" Stella wasn't seeing anything exciting and boredom was beginning to creep in. "So we are just walking around storage and more storage. Maybe this is like a special storage center in case there is a major food crisis. They figure it won't get damaged down here in no man's land. Do you want to look at anything else? Something that's maybe actually interesting?" Stella said turning to Stephen with a look of boredom.

"Yes, we don't have much time before we go home and I know there is something here. Otherwise, why would anyone keep it all under such high security?" Stephen answered unwilling to stop.

The faint lighting cast shadows from their bodies along the ground as they walked. Her eyes followed the shadows for a moment, as she let herself get distracted by the distortion of their appearance from the overhead light. Their elongated legs and short torsos put her in mind of something alien. Then she thought of what Canson Pritchard had said about their being made. She didn't want to think about that now. Hopefully, they could ask Mave about that strange conversation soon and get answers.

Periodically, one of them would try a door, hoping that perhaps it would open. Every door was secure, as it should have been. Neither Stella nor Stephen would be able to get into anything useful or interesting down here. At least not without the right access, but that wouldn't stop Stephen.

Stella came to a sudden stop. "What was that?" she asked.

"What was what?" Stephen asked back. He hadn't heard anything.

"That sound. Come on - this way." Stella grabbed the tablet from him and was now leading them down the narrow hallway, slowly; listening for the strange noise she'd heard. "There it goes again," she whispered.

"I heard it but I think it's just the normal sound of something as big as this," Stephen said. Her ears had always been much better than his.

"I don't think so. It sounded like groaning," she said.

Stephen raised an eyebrow skeptically. "Let's keep moving." Stephen took the tablet back from her.

"I want to get to this section on the blueprint today before we go back so that tomorrow we can start on the next level. We've only hit two of the four required locations to gain access to the next level." They continued to walk but Stella was sure what she heard wasn't just the sounds of the ARC.

"What do you think we might find, Stephen?" she pondered. She needed to do whatever she could to stay interested.

"I don't know. I am hopeful that we'll find something to help us figure out what is really going on. Something to answer the question of why the World Consensus and UniCorps don't want to do everything possible to warn people," he said seriously.

"Even if we do find that, what are we going to do with it? We can't tell anyone. Everything here is top secret. Even we are sworn to secrecy. We could be tried for treason. Well, I guess if we find it now and say something we wouldn't be tried for treason but we'd be sent away for reconditioning. I don't really want to be sent away for my sixteenth birthday Stephen. I don't want to be sent away at all. Especially since they keep you until *they* think you are ready to rejoin society," she said worried.

"Why the sudden change in your behavior Stella?" Stephen stopped walking to ask her.

She looked at him. She was the big sister by a matter of just six minutes. "I don't want us to screw up our lives, okay? And for what? Something that won't make a difference anyway?" she answered.

She'd always been there to protect him and look out for him and now she was letting them do this, risking their freedom. She didn't want to wind up homeless. That's what happened to para-adults who didn't successfully receive reconditioning and the behavior modification programming by the time they reached adulthood at twenty-one. Their lives would be ruined.

"I think we should go back. Maybe the meeting will go better than we expected and there will be nothing to worry about. Maybe they'll agree to prepare for evacuation and warn people," she said grasping for her usual optimism. "Mom and Mave can be pretty persuasive," she said with hope, trying to convince Stephen and herself.

"Based on the past behaviors of the World Consensus and UniCorps, the probability of that happening is about .28. In case you are wondering, yes that is too low for comfort," he said smartly. "We have to continue." He added what little bit of bass he had to his voice.

Stella sighed with frustration. She was torn and confused, and he hadn't helped. She followed Stephen to the next location spot. It was in a section with doors marked RS. He allowed the geo-locator to mark that they'd made it to that location and then he kept moving.

"It's hard to judge from these blueprints, but we probably have another quarter mile to walk to get to the last location," he said.

Stella sighed heavily this time, trying to get his attention. He missed her cue, forcing her to be more direct.

"This is pointless Stephen. I hope that what Marco sends us next has some real clues that don't require walking in honeycomb circles for hours."

Stephen kept walking, ignoring her comments. Moments later he heard it. It was the unmistakable sound of groaning.

"You had to have heard that!" Stella said in an excited whisper.

"I did. What is it?" he asked her nervously, looking around for the source of the strange sound.

"Heck if I know! But that's what I want to find out. Let's check that out now, then we'll do the last location."

Stella started walking at a near gallop towards the direction of the strange sounds. The groaning faded in and out and sometimes sounded more like moaning. She barely looked back at Stephen to make sure he was keeping up with her pace. Something exciting was finally happening and she didn't want to miss it.

"Slow down, Stella. I'm trying to follow this blueprint and need to make sure we don't miss one of the required locations." At this point Stella didn't care about the blueprint. Her curiosity had been peaked and she was going to follow it before she got scared.

"Hurry up. We don't have much time and I'm starting to get hungry. It must be almost lunch. They'll probably take a break and someone will come to check on us. If we want to check it out, you need to put that thing away." Stella stopped to say the last part to his face, just so he'd understand the importance, before turning back around and continuing at the same pace.

"It's getting louder," Stephen said.

"Yeah. I think we must be close. I thought this thing was built just before we were born. It must have some old systems to make this much noise," Stella said as she listened to the odd sounds.

"I wonder if we are coming up on the central power source or something," Stephen said curiously. "That would be nice to see. I can't imagine what it must look like to keep something like this powered independently. It is its own power source for sure," Stephen added matter-of-factly.

As they approached another door marked RS11, Stella slowed down. The sounds seemed to be coming from there. It was another door with the security panel, just like all the others they'd come across. She gently pushed on the door, optimistically. *Maybe we'll get lucky and it'll open.* But there was no budging.

"I think it's in here. Remember this door, Stephen. When we get back down tomorrow, we're coming straight here."

She pressed her ear to the door and heard the groaning again and in the distance it sounded like something scraping against concrete.

"The whole system must be through here. It's strange to put it down here, but I guess they don't want people accidentally messing with it," she said.

Stephen looked at the door and at the blueprint. It didn't make sense that the central power system would be there.

"I think this may be a smaller secondary power source, if anything. Based on where we are on the ARC, it wouldn't make sense to have the central power here. We have to keep moving. I want to get to this last point before we go back," Stephen said, starting to walk again, his pace a little faster.

Stella gave the door one last look and then joined Stephen as they continued. She had the distinct sense that it held something other than power but even trying to tune in, she got nothing. Not a whisper of thought, not an image, or a sensation of taste or smell. It was like nothing was back there, but something definitely was.

They could still hear the strange groaning and moaning sounds. As they continued the sounds became fainter until Stephen couldn't hear them any longer and they were just a whisper to Stella. Then, they were gone.

"We have just a little bit further to go. For some strange and very disconcerting reason this blueprint presents no distances, no measurement - anywhere. Marco said there is another one that is a bigger file size. Maybe that one will be more complete. It would be helpful to know how far we've gone and how long we have before we get to this last location check," Stephen said pointing to a bubble floating on his screen. Stella looked at the bubble and then the green flashing dot that showed where they were.

"I could try to estimate based on the approximate size of the honeycombs and the average pace of our walking and," he stopped speaking as Stella cut him off.

"It's okay, Stephen. We are probably pretty close," she said, clearly irritated. This wasn't the kind of exploring she had in mind. She was hoping to unlock some doors, find some secrets, something more along the lines of what they'd done in Southern Allegiance. This was nothing like that.

They went around a few more turns and the flashing green light on the tablet moved slowly towards the location check.

"I can't believe all of these doors are locked," Stella said as she gently pushed against almost every door to test them. "I guess we really are part of some top secret project," she frowned. "What do you think it's all about? I think mom, dad, Mave, Rupert, and all those other people are trying to protect the ocean life as part of an indicator for overall environmental health. They are trying to make sure we don't damage the overall ecology of Earth any more than we have. I believe they are doing that," she stopped then and Stephen walked into her as he stared at the tablet. "Stephen!" she complained impatiently.

"Yes. I'm sorry. What were you saying?" he asked.

"Ugh! Stephen! Never mind. Anyways, I think that mom and dad are doing what we know they are doing as far as the environment and ocean and keeping on top of the emissions pumps. BUT, I think they are also doing something else. Something they aren't telling us. That's what I think," she said smugly. She started walking again.

As she walked Stella continued talking, letting her voice carry behind her, "Why else would there be a freaking maze down here with dozens of locked doors and that's just what we've seen so far. They know something and they are the ones who were here to build it. Dad designed it. We should just ask him about all of this. Have him take us on a real tour rather than us sneaking around finding nothing. Well except for some engine groaning and moaning," Stella finally stopped speaking.

"We're here, Stella," Stephen was finally able to say. This is the last location check we have to do for us to move on tomorrow.

"But I want to come back to RS11 first, then we can go to the next level," she said.

"Agreed. Give me just a second to let this register that we are here before we leave," Stephen said.

Stephen waited for the tablet to register the last location check and then looked down the other side of the honeycomb hall.

"We'll go back this way, just to see what's around that side. It should be about the same distance back to the top. Besides, there's something interesting ahead on the other side. It looks like it is just about opposite the other secondary power system behind door RS11. I want to walk by there and just see if maybe it's another smaller control room," he said.

"We can't tell anyways, Stephen. The door will be locked." The excitement was now gone for Stella. "It'll just be another door with moaning and groaning sounds coming through it that we can't enter."

She knew Stephen was just trying to get her back into this expedition the best way he could but she was ready to go back up, eat lunch, and relax, especially since they didn't have time right now to come back to RS11.

They'd be headed home in just a few days now. Then there would be all the unpacking and finishing the last weeks of school there, which meant she needed time to get her hair done and pick up some new accessories once they were back. She'd already moved on in her mind. Now all that was left was for them to get out of the grey building that reminded her of the old prisons they'd toured during history studies as a child. At least upstairs was more vibrant and lively.

Stephen moved quietly ahead of Stella. He wanted to see if another power system was on the other side. If so, he reasoned there might be more in order to produce enough power for the ARC to operate independent of any other outside power source.

He thought about how much energy it must use every day. As he heard the sounds he wondered if down here the widely used models initially discovered by Tesla were the source. Stephen imagined they would have to be enormous models given the size and that multiple devices must be located throughout the ARC.

They continued their silent trek in the shadows until Stella heard the faint but familiar sound of groaning. She slowed down. "Did you hear that?" she asked Stephen.

"No. What was it?" he asked.

"It sounds like the same thing we heard on the other side. I think you may have found another power system for the ARC. I bet there are more considering how big it is. We definitely need to ask Dad for a tour. Tell him it's for science class and promise him we'll keep everything top secret," Stella said, optimistically hoping their dad might consider it. Stephen would have a better chance convincing him.

"Let's head back up. I can't check the secure system Marco is using to send us the opened files from down here. Maybe he's sent something that might give us some better clues to what all these sections and room codes mean. Of course it would be nice to know how big the ARC is too," Stephen said with excitement.

CHAPTER TWENTY-NINE
Sooner

Antarctic Research Center

STELLA AND STEPHEN were on the same level as everyone in the ROC Room located across the ARC. They'd managed to cover the full area of the second level, despite having learned little about what was behind the locked doors.

Zura sat between Mave and Johan with Rupert beside Mave. The team's backs were towards the ocean and windows at the oval conference table. The stern faces of the men and women they'd been employed by for the past two decades looked at them from across the table. Her team was like family to her and the others had always been like good acquaintances.

In years past, the meetings had always been a bit celebratory - a check in on the work done and the facility. Talking about their children and plans for after the season on the ARC ended. This year, the tension could be felt from before they touched down in Antarctica and it had only gotten higher from there.

Her favorite pilot, Jonathan Adams, had brought them over and Johan had gone out to meet them and bring them back. They'd come back in near silence once they'd dispensed with the customary cordial greetings.

Johan had brought them into the ROC room and Zura could tell immediately that they were angling, considering their approach and how they would instill their opinions and ensure the desired objectives were met.

That year three representatives had made the trip from each of the funders. Representatives Magiro and Silver were joined by a high ranking official named Admiral General Mylar of the Combined Operations for Peace and Security. He was a regular attendee of the annual review meeting and often drove the discussions, despite Zura's attempt to maintain control.

From UniCorps they brought Chief Scientist Dr. Tomas Sporgsman from the emissions pumping side of the global organization as well as the Chief Scientist Dr. Cliven Phillips and Lead Researcher Dr. Sandy Ashby from the environmental, ecological, and impact side of what was formally known as the Technology, Science, and Development Division.

The beautiful ocean view in front of the guests seemed to barely make an impression on the temperaments. For this occasion they had coffee, hot cocoa, fresh squeezed juices and the chef's specialty breakfast. Zura always felt it was better to have difficult conversations over good food.

She'd instructed the ARC's cook to prepare a full brunch with eggs, bacon, sausage, tofu sausage, muffins, grits, pancakes, and French toast. Johan insisted she was overdoing it, but she argued that it was harder to be angry when sitting around a table filled with delicious food.

But the tense pleasantness had ended soon after everyone had enjoyed their brunch. The last bite had barely been chewed and swallowed before UniCorps set in.

For the past couple of hours they'd hammered into Zura and her team about the importance of the work they were doing. While the funders interrogated her team, they were, however, unwilling to share anything with the ARC team at all. Instead it was a barrage of questions to learn exactly what they'd found, how much they knew about what they'd found, and what each finding meant.

They were going around and around in circles and Mave recognized the tactic meant to confuse them and have them second guess themselves and their research. She, like her coworkers, was confident that their information was solid and since the transmission more than a week before, they'd gotten even better information from the Science Institute and other partners.

After this meeting, there was no doubt there would be several other meetings between the Science Divisions of the World Consensus and UniCorps with all of their partners and grantees. The others would be drilled just like they were and reminded of their allegiance to the World Consensus and of any non-disclosure agreements that might have been signed.

Rupert sat quietly, contemplating all that was said, done, and not said, as was his way. He didn't believe anything coming from their lips and was busy making mental notes of the path of their circular arguments.

Every person in that room could be personally affected by what they had found, yet neither UniCorps nor the World Consensus, particularly Mylar, were at all phased by that reality, which Rupert found odd. Instead, they were adamant about tying their hands. At the same time they were trying to make it seem okay to do nothing, just because it was legal to do nothing.

When time for the long overdue lunch break finally came Admiral General Mylar stood up. He immediately requested that Johan take them on the tour to see the storage areas on the lower level. Johan knew the ARC better than anyone and had given the tour every year since it was completed.

This year was different. Zura hadn't done a fancy lunch since they had a large brunch and wouldn't be meeting over lunch. They needed something they could walk with and had ordered the chef to prepare simple sandwiches. It wasn't fancy but after how the morning had gone she was glad she hadn't gone all out for the group for lunch as well.

As they grabbed sandwiches to eat during the break, Johan could feel the nausea build in his stomach. Once again, he would journey into the belly of the beast. He gave a weary glance to his wife before they headed out and hoped that the solution that had to be out there would be found, and fast.

Gregor Magiro had barely spoken to any of the members who'd come from UniCorps. The tension between their two main funding groups was as plain as the sandwiches they were eating. They weren't in agreement about what should be done. Though they rarely openly disagreed, he'd been around them long enough to know all wasn't well.

Representative Silver had barely spoken at all and although she didn't speak much, she usually offered some wise piece of advice or a new way of looking at the issue. On this day, she was quiet when it came to the main conversation. On more than one occasion, Representative Magiro had tried to follow UniCorps questions to the ARC team with another question aimed more at World Consensus or UniCorps. It hadn't gotten past Johan or the rest of the team. But even his questions went unanswered.

Johan wasn't sure where Admiral General Mylar stood on how the situation should eventually be resolved. He'd been the most vocal in his questions and the one person most against telling anyone outside of those already approved to know, and that concerned Johan.

Up until five years before, Mylar's visits to the ARC had only been every two to three years. Since then he'd come each year during the final reporting and his largest interest was always the tour and being updated on the progress of the programs Johan ran.

His interest was rarely what was happening in those science labs, but this year he'd shown more interest in what was happening on that side too. Johan hoped it meant he might be willing to do something about it. At the same time, he wondered if the original plan as he'd understood it had been changed and he just wasn't aware yet.

Everyone in that room had staked their reputations, sacrificed good parts of their lives, for the ARC and what it meant for all of their futures. In that regard, Johan was no different.

As the group headed down the honeycomb halls, winding and turning towards the door marked 'No Entry', the six visitors and Johan tried to chat casually about their homelands in between bites of their sandwiches. The conversation felt forced and fake. When the dead space of silence crawled into the conversation, no one broke it and Johan took it as a welcome relief. He couldn't wait to get back above ground and for this visit to end.

Johan opened the door and let his guests walk through ahead of him and down the stairs before allowing the door to close behind him. They walked down the ramp towards the first honeycomb chamber, taking the same steps Stella and Stephen had taken earlier.

"Progress is going well for the next phase of the ARC," Johan said. "We've had great success with growing food in our greenhouse. Johan opened a door to his left and they all filed in.

The group continued through another door and down a long hallway with the same lights. They stepped along the concrete floor triggering the light sensors which lit up the next twenty feet or so ahead of them, until they reached a small keeping room. They entered the small keeping room that kept the greenhouse sterile and secure. Looking through the glass they could see inside to an open area that was the size of a football stadium.

The room was bustling with activity. Men and women working inside moved about performing all sorts of activities. There were groups busied with checking the leaves, watering the soil, adjusting the artificial grow lights, pruning, or harvesting the fruits and vegetables that were ready.

"We've been successful in growing corn, tomatoes, a variety of lettuces, spinach, eggplant, lentils, a variety of legumes, apples, pears, strawberries, mangoes and bananas, in a special room, and more. We haven't been able to grow rice because of the requirements for significant amounts of water, which we are still working on, but we can grow potatoes and other substitutes. Within a year we should have a fully functioning, self-sustaining, fresh supply of fruits, vegetables, beans, legumes, and grains," Johan informed the ARC guests.

Before long a small group of staff had brought over trays for them to sample their produce. There were small white paper cups with fresh tomatoes cut up, spinach leaves, and cut apples for the group to sample.

"They all taste so normal," Representative Silver said, surprised after taking a bite from all three. She let the taste of the tomato linger on her tongue. It was one of her favorite foods. "It doesn't taste like it's engineered," she added. The others made similar remarks, pleased with the progress.

After leaving the produce farming section of the ARC, the group walked through another door with the same set up. There was a second inside door followed by another long hallway with the same lights. When they finally reached the small keeping room for this area Johan spoke.

"In here we have our dairy and poultry pasture. We recognize that the expense and resources required to maintain full size animals for eating is too great but we can still have dairy and eggs. This pasture is already supplying the dairy needs and enough eggs for everyone on the ARC who cares to partake, even now. Best of all, everything is fresh," Johan said with confidence.

"Excuse me," Johan called out to one of the workers in the pasture. "Can you give us samples of the milk?" Johan smiled.

He was proud with how the cows were producing and that the taste was on par with cows kept in fields, without them being kept in tiny pens. The cows were free to roam within a large area which appeared to be nearly the size of almost two football fields. The chickens had coops placed around the front section.

A few years earlier, the engineers had brought in natural grass and laid it on top of a surface made to absorb excess water. The water would be recycled back into the ARC's water system for purification and watering of plants in the garden. There were at least two hundred hens in the pasture. In separate smaller pens were three dozen or so cocks.

The pasture keeper handed Johan and his guests each a small cup of milk and waited for their reaction.

"Wow. It's better than it was even just last year," Representative Magiro remarked. "What did you do differently?" he asked.

Johan looked at him and the others. "We had to modify a few things in their diet and over the past nine or ten years we have begun replacing the bulls with those originating in areas that were less affected by the pollution and commercialization process of food. They were more 'pure' so to speak, so what they produce as far as their offspring is concerned has been better too. It took a few years for us to find a good balance of the diet since we have to provide a diet that will be sustainable in the long-term."

"Great job on the food so far, Johan. You should be very pleased with the work your team is doing," Magiro complimented Johan. "This research and your success has the potential to bring sustainable and reliable food to areas that are hard served now," he said, pleased at how well that initiative was going.

"Have we been as successful with the other project?" The Admiral General asked Johan.

Johan looked at the Admiral General with confidence, "Yes, sir. We have. Things are going according to the design and nearly everything is in place for the last phase."

"And if we needed to expedite all of this to happen within the next year; would it be possible?" the Admiral General said turning to look Johan in the eye.

Johan took a deep breath. "It would be extremely challenging, maybe even improbable given that the rest of us are leaving soon and the amount of time that is required for the bonding to take place. That alone isn't something we have been able to force to happen any sooner. And the only people remaining are those working on these levels on these projects. For us to be ready in a year, would mean the team staying and figuring out how to speed up the process. The science just isn't there yet and it isn't something we've been trying to do since we were fine with our timeline. Has something changed?" Johan asked.

"I see," Admiral General Mylar said, looking around at the others standing and waiting in front of a door. He chose to ignore Johan's question. "Would that be a problem? The team staying? You all working on a solution to the rate and timing of bonding?" he then asked Johan.

Johan was taken back by the question. This Admiral General was the reason they had missed the chance to leave Antarctica nearly sixteen years ago when the twins were born. He'd pressured them into staying because of how important it was to complete everything by a certain time. Nothing had changed.

"Stay? In Antarctica, over Winter, with my kids?" Johan asked with surprise.

"Well, you have some family and Zura does too. Can't they stay with her grandparents or your sister?" he asked with no concern.

Johan couldn't deal with his complete lack of sensitivity right now. He looked at Admiral General Mylar in the eyes and mustered up a tight light lipped smile. He was furious that Mylar had the nerve to ask him to leave his kids somewhere for six months so he could make a timeline that hadn't been discussed before that moment.

"We'll have to see. I'm not an island and don't make those decisions by myself. Let's continue walking. It's getting late." Johan turned and kept moving before he said or did something he might regret.

A year was really pushing it whether they stayed through the Winter or not. What Mylar was asking would turn their twelve to fourteen hour days into sixteen hour days and even that might not be enough. They would need more staff than what was on the ARC. They would even miss Stephen and Stella's sixteenth birthday celebration, unless they didn't send them back until afterwards, which wouldn't be fair.

Johan broke the uncomfortable silence. "We still have a lot more to discuss and the rest of my team will be looking for us. Besides, we have a tele-transmission with the Science Institute very soon. I don't think we have time to stop long in the next section."

"Well, let me go in and check it out," Admiral General Mylar said.

Johan opened the door for him and he stepped in. This project was a UniCorps funded initiative and they had given Mylar oversight, as a proxy for the World Consensus. The only people with clearance to go into those sections were Chief Scientist Phillips from UniCorps and Admiral General Mylar. Phillips followed Mylar through the door and Mylar held the door and waved his hand for Johan to come in.

"No thanks," Johan said with a sickening look on his face. "I don't need to see it today," he added.

"You don't really have a choice. If we have questions, you're the man to answer them. Come on, Johan. We need to get on with this." Mylar pushed the door open wider as Johan walked in.

In the hallway leading back to the door where the others waited, Admiral General Mylar stopped walking and faced Johan with a frown. "I'm concerned about the age of our specimens. I want to talk to you about that very soon. Not today. There's enough other business today. That could be an issue for our timeline and will likely be the cause of having to stay through the winter," he said as they turned to walk back the way they came.

Mylar stopped again before leaving through the door to join those who didn't have the clearance. He turned to speak to Johan and Phillips, but the message was intended for Johan's benefit. "Before we go back up to the main room, I need something to be clearly understood. The World Consensus and UniCorps have recently developed a new and very detailed plan and part of its success relies on those specimens being ready in time."

"I don't understand Admiral General. We've always been working to get them ready in time. I wasn't aware that the timeline had changed until just a few minutes ago," Johan responded with irritation.

"Yes, I know," Mylar said as he glanced back. "We cannot have a repeat of past failures with similar efforts. UniCorps has been around, under other names and has had to operate in secret for longer than I'd like to discuss before we were finally able to birth the government and world we and our predecessors envisioned. You understand this, Johan. Things have changed, and I'll need you to adjust as well."

"We've been doing everything according to the plan that was outlined. I've been operating from those orders. We haven't missed any deadlines," Johan said as he began to feel defensive about his work.

"Yeah. Well, now it's time for the next step. We must be able to move on to the next phase, and rest assured, if for any reason we," Mylar said moving his hand to point to Johan and Phillips before continuing, "can't do it, they will find people who can. This is our duty. It's for our survival." Mylar finished speaking and turned to walk back towards the exit.

The three men joined the small group waiting in the hall. As they began to walk, their hard shoes clacking on the solid floors on the left side of the lower level, they didn't hear the quiet footsteps of Stephen and Stella on the right side. The twins headed back through the winding twists and turns to the main level and through the door marked on the other side with 'No Entry'.

As they quietly walked towards their living quarters they heard a voice that seemed to come from nowhere. "There you two are. I was looking for you. We are taking a lunch break and I just wanted to check in on you," said Mave with a curious look on her face. "Have you two enjoyed your morning away from all of this boring grown up stuff?" she smiled and Stella wondered if she knew.

Stella and Stephen didn't know how to answer her. They weren't sure if she'd noticed anything or heard anything.

"Yes, thanks." Stella jumped in.

Stephen looked down for a moment before Mave asked him, "Have you enjoyed your morning Stephen? You get to be away from these intense meetings. It's pretty tough in there right now."

Stephen looked up at Mave, guilt clouding his eyes as it twitched ever so slightly. "Yes. It's been nice hanging out with Stella," he answered.

Stephen wanted to get back to his room to check what Marco had sent. He wanted to find out if it was a clue, a new map, or something else helpful. "I hope the rest of the meeting goes better than the morning, Mave," he added.

"Yeah, if you see mom and dad, let them know we're fine. We'll probably be in Stephen's room for a while or in the lounge area," Stella said, sounding calm and relaxed.

"Okay. I guess I'll talk to you later. I'm just avoiding going back in there a minute before I have to," Mave smiled. "I guess I better head back. The big heads will be back from their tour soon and we will have yet another *important* meeting," she said with a slight eye roll.

Mave had a way of being ridiculously smart and calming and real all at the same time. Something both Stella and Stephen usually liked about her, but right now they were in too much of a hurry to appreciate.

"We'll see you soon. We're trying to catch up with a friend so we're gonna head to Stephen's room," Stella said as they began to scurry off. Mave looked after them. She could only wonder, and hope.

They could feel Mave watching them but willed themselves not to turn back around and look. Instead they walked quickly away from her gaze. When they turned the corner to their hallway, they each took a deep breath. Until that moment, they hadn't even realized they'd been holding it.

Stephen opened his door and they both scurried inside and closed it behind them. Stephen immediately sat down at his desk to pull up the message he'd gotten notice of while they were still on the lower level. Now, he was back at his system where he could retrieve it safely and without risk of exposing it to the ARC's general system. From down there he couldn't tell anything about what the message might have said or whether it had a file. He logged in and accessed their secure system.

Flashing at the top of his screen was the message from Marco. A file was also sitting there. Stella watched from her cozy spot on the bed behind Stephen and smiled to see something there.

"Hurry up and tap it, Stephen," she urged impatiently.

Stephen's finger tapped on the file first to see what else Marco and Alexis might have been able to crack. It was just what he'd been hoping for, the detailed blueprints. He started looking through the different layers and noticed some areas were unmarked. It was as if they had been left unmarked from the beginning. Stephen couldn't find a rationale for why someone would do that.

Stephen looked at the section of the blueprints where he and Stella had heard the noises. The door was there but there wasn't any drawing of what was behind that door. No size or measurements or shape to go by. No name, just the same door number RS11 with a second notation N3 on it.

"What do you think it means?" Stella asked Stephen looking at the blueprint's layers near his wall.

"I don't know. It's not complete and that room where we heard the unusual noises shows here as just a door with another notation of N3 on it," Stephen said rubbing his head.

"It would definitely help if we knew what N1 and N2 were." Stella said smartly. "Can we look for other Ns?"

Stephen did a search for N1 and it only showed up as a part of the file name of the first blueprint they'd followed. "That's interesting," he said to himself. He then searched for N2. The current file he and Stella were looking at had N2 embedded as part of the file name in the same place.

"This isn't random or coincidental," Stella said, "is it?"

Stephen had already moved to searching for N3 in the filenames of the other files they hadn't been able to access yet.

"There it is, Stella. No this is not random or a coincidence. These files are all blueprints. If I would guess, I would think each provides another level of detail," Stephen said.

"What I don't get is why they need to have so many files of just the blueprint. What is so important that it needs to be kept under such tight security? It's blueprints of a place that does research on Antarctic sea life, emissions and environment," Stella questioned.

"I'm going to message Marco to have him try to open this file next. I want to see what is in the N3 file."

"What about tomorrow? Do you think what he sent today will help us find any other cool discoveries or what's behind that door RS11? If not, I suggest we take a day to sleep in and then ask Dad about getting a real tour, when they are done with their meetings. After all he should know, right?" Stella reasoned.

"I'll look at the blueprints more carefully and see what I find. I want to go down to the next level tomorrow and hopefully these blueprints have information on that level," Stephen said before looking around nervously as if someone might suddenly appear. "I'd rather not ask Dad before it's necessary. Don't you want to explore some first, Stella?"

CHAPTER THIRTY
Stay

Antarctic Research Center

THE PACING WAS beginning to wear on Stephen's senses. Stella had walked back and forth between the bed and the window more than twenty times already as he synced, moved, and organized files.

"If we are going to do it, we should go back today," Stella said, surprising Stephen.

He couldn't tell if she was being serious or messing with him. "What do you mean?" he asked.

"Stephen, we should go back out when they go back into their meeting. They'll be in there for hours and tomorrow who knows what will happen. They may shut this whole place down and then we won't be able to get back in. I just have a feeling - a knowing that I can't shake."

Stephen looked at Stella. "I want to go down to the next level. We can do that with what we have, but we don't have any more information on what anything is. So all we will be able to do is look at closed doors."

"Maybe all the doors won't be closed. Maybe we'll have some good luck and something will be open for us," Stella said optimistically.

"I'd like to grab lunch like we discussed before coming up here. I am starving. Not literally starving, but I am very hungry," Stephen said.

"Good idea. I'm starving too," echoed Stella.

As the two were about to leave for the kitchen, a message came through from Marco. "It'll be tomorrow before I can get to N3. Have full day of training and can't get away."

"Does that mean that he won't even be able to look until tomorrow or that he'll send it tomorrow?" Stella asked with concern.

"I don't know. It sounds like he won't be able to look at it until tomorrow and then who knows how long it will take. They've done two so I guess they are getting the hang of what is required. If that is the case it probably won't take them very long to do N3 for us. We just don't know if we can get down there tomorrow. They won't be in their meetings so we won't be able to move so freely," Stephen answered Stella trying to borrow some of her optimism but regressing.

"I would really rather not ask dad, so I agree with you. We should take the chance today, when they return to their meeting." He didn't want to risk that Stella's intuition was right and they couldn't do anymore exploring after today.

"I'm going to record it this time, Stephen. In case there is anything strange, maybe we can capture it and figure it out later."

"Good idea. But first, we need to get lunch," Stephen reminded her.

They snuck back out of Stephen's room and walked silently towards the kitchen, checking for anyone from the ARC team or any of the visitors. Seeing it was all clear, they scurried like mice into the kitchen and made sandwiches as fast as they could.

"We should put this away," Stephen said pointing to the mess they'd made.

"Put the mayonnaise and turkey away. The rest will be fine," Stella said heading out of the kitchen.

Stella checked the living area and waved Stephen to hurry up. They snuck back the way they'd come after the prior expedition and soon arrived at the door marked 'No Entry'.

Years earlier, Johan had told the twins that if there was ever a serious emergency on the ARC that they were to go through that door and to the first room they saw. The door would remain unlocked and they could close it from the inside.

The large room had food, water, medical supplies, and beds. It was a small self-sustaining apartment that would take a bomb or other detonation to break into. The room was the only reason the 'No Entry' door was not locked and the panic room looked just like all the other doors from the outside once closed.

If under attack the attackers couldn't tell the difference. The twins had always wondered who would want to attack a research center in Antarctica, but their dad just said, "You never know. Better to be safe than to be sorry."

"Let's get past this level and down to the next. Where is that staircase again? We saw it on the blueprint and I think I remember seeing a strange marking earlier. It didn't say 'Stairs'. It looked more like the face of a stepped pyramid. I thought it meant Danger or something," Stella said, looking at the tablet with Stephen.

"There it is," he said. "Ahead on the right. Come on." He walked while looking for the symbol along the walls and doors.

"I see it!" Stella said excitedly as they turned a corner and passed a dull marking at the top of the hall with the pyramid symbol. The symbol appeared to have been hand etched into the plastic sign that hung loosely by the door.

Stella walked to the door under the symbol. It had a security panel on the side, but the lights on the panel were out.

"If it's not locked, must mean we're allowed in, right?" she said without waiting for an answer.

She gently pushed on it like she'd done with so many other doors, expecting it to be locked. What neither twin could see was that the keypad had a short and wasn't communicating with the main security system for the lower levels.

Stella pushed at the door and it clicked and opened. A faint white light flickered unpredictably as the door swung in. They found themselves standing at the top of a wide landing, on either side of which were steps. Both sets of steps lead into darkness.

Stephen tapped on his tablet and recorded the location. It wasn't a check but he wanted to precisely identify where it was, given the lack of detail on the blueprints.

Stella tapped several buttons on her watch. She could hear something coming from down below. She wasn't going any closer, but she could record the sounds. She grabbed the hand rail and leaned her other hand over the center of the stairwell to get it closer to the sound. What was under her hand felt odd, scratchy.

It should've been smooth metal but when Stella let her light shine on the rail, she could see it was anything but smooth. Long scratches crossed the rail going from right to left before fading. She shined the light along the rest of the rail and could see the same type of scratches start again right where the staircase began to wind down.

"Stephen, shine your light on your side. Do you have long scratches there too?" Stella asked. She traced the scratches with her fingertips. They could be fingernails but that would require very sharp, strong nails.

"Yes, they're on this side too. What do you think they are?" he asked, tracing his fingers along the path, and taking a step down the stairs.

"Don't go down there. We don't know what's down there, Stephen!" Stella said grabbing his shirt.

"It's a staircase on the ARC. It's probably a boring science lab."

"With those sounds? I doubt it, Stephen," she said, not letting go of his shirt until he turned and stepped back up to the landing.

"I'm still recording, so be quiet for a minute."

Stephen stood quietly, his fingers still tracing the scratches in the rail. He ran his fingernails across them. They weren't evenly spaced or sized. They weren't always straight. They were at different angles, almost as if some metal had been dragged along them for short bursts before lifting up.

***

THE SCIENCE INSTITUTE was wrapping up their time with the group. "We are confident that if we don't take action now, we will not have time to properly evacuate the at risk areas and there will be significant loss of life. If we act immediately, there is still the possibility of a high number of casualties given the amount of activity and the magnitude of both earthquakes and volcanoes that will likely be triggered. Ladies and gentlemen, we are literally sitting on a ticking time bomb. We don't know what the timer is set to, but sooner rather than later, it is going to blow," Dr. Hudson said to the group.

"We have sent you all the data we have been able to pull together and it is conclusive. If I may, I would recommend," Dr. Hudson began before being abruptly interrupted by both Tomas and Phillips.

"Thank you, Dr. Hudson," The two said in unison.

"That'll be all for now," Phillips nodded, ending Dr. Hudson's attempts to persuade them.

"Yes," the Admiral General chimed in, "If we need anything else we will be in touch. Until then, just remember your confidentiality agreements and that on all matters related to this project and the research associated with it, you are sworn to withhold that confidentiality. Any breach of information, Dr. Hudson, could be considered treasonous," Mylar paused. "Do you understand, Dr. Hudson? And I need to know that those people behind you also understand. You are all held to that same standard."

"Yes, sir. I understand." She looked back at her team.

"We understand," they said in unison.

"Thank you. That is all." Mylar cut the transmission and clasped his hands in front of him.

Mylar sat forward in his chair and when he opened his mouth his words came out in a whisper, forcing everyone to lean in towards him. "Just for the record, no one outside of official World Consensus government leadership may inform the public of any concerns regarding this matter. It becomes a matter of security and I am second in command for that area. If we deem it is necessary to inform people of any possible issues, we will do so; on the terms we decide are best for the continuation of the World Consensus and what is in the best interest of the majority."

"Please excuse me for just a moment," Zura said, pushing back from the table.

"What do you mean? This is a very important meeting and you need to be here," Mylar said to Zura.

"I will be back in just a moment. I need to use the restroom. While the rest of you had a break and a tour, I remained in here to finish a few things and make sure that transmission happened. Now, I will be back in five minutes," she said, giving Mylar a look that dared him to stop her as she left the room.

Zura's heart was beating so fast she thought they might see it thumping beneath her uniform. She walked at a quick clip trying to keep her steps sure and confident as she moved away from the table and towards the ROC room exit. When she got through the doors to the lab she ran up the stairs to the decontamination chamber. She anxiously waited for it to finish its process.

The moment the door on the other side opened, she took off her footies and began running. Zura ran up the stairs to the work room and then right on through. In seconds she was out the door into the corridors leading towards their living quarters, proving why she'd deserved the track scholarship during her undergraduate years.

She ran into Stephen's room. Empty. She then turned and left to check Stella's room. They were both empty. Then she stopped, turned, and ran back towards the living areas and kitchen. Bread and knives were out on the counter but her kids weren't there.

Zura paused for a moment and closed her eyes. *Where are they?* She took off running again. She was at a full on sprint now, only slowed by the angles of the ARC. She ran down the same hall the twins had walked through not that long before and only hesitated momentarily as she stood in front of the door marked 'No Entry'.

She pushed through it and ran down the steps to the next level. Zura darted down the hall, knowing which way to go.

"Stella?! Stephen?!" she said in a loud whisper. Yelling would trigger the sound decibel alarm. There was no answer. "Stella!? Stephen!?" she said slightly louder. Then she saw a faint glow coming from down the hall. There shouldn't be any lights on down there unless someone had triggered them.

Zura took off again in a dash towards the light. She reached the place where the pyramid front was above her and the doorway still had light coming from underneath. She pushed the door gently, startling Stella and Stephen.

"Mom!" Stella said dropping her camera. She fumbled to pick it up. "What are? I. We. Um…" Stella stumbled over her words, stuttering nervously.

"Come out of there. Now!" she yelled in a whisper. Her eyes becoming wide with fear. A look they rarely saw except when they were about to be in trouble for almost getting themselves hurt.

From below they heard the faint sound of clanging. It was what Stella and Stephen had heard earlier, but it was louder, as if trying to get their attention. "What's that sound?" Stephen asked leaning over the rail trying to get a glimpse into the dark.

"I said now," Zura repeated, ignoring the question and holding the door open for Stella and Stephen. The twins knew they were in trouble and wondered how their mother had found them. She was supposed to be in that meeting.

"Mom, we were just bored and wanted to check out the ARC before we left," Stephen said.

"I'm sorry," Stella said.

"I don't want to hear it," Zura said, quieting any conversation before it could start.

Zura remained silent as the three of them walked back through the door. She looked at the keypad on the side of the door. She pushed the door shut and punched in a code to make it relock. She wasn't sure how that panel hadn't been locked but the technicians would have to fix that immediately. The code she entered was only a temporary fix.

Zura didn't speak a word until they had reached the Exit side of the 'No Entry' door. The three walked through and Zura closed the door behind them.

"We will not speak of any of this until we are back home. Just in case you are wondering, Stella, yes, you two are in big trouble. You know the rules and you both can read. It clearly says 'No Entry'. Right here – plainly. There's a damn good reason for it saying that and the two of you decided you were just going to stroll down to where you had no business going because you were bored. Go to your rooms. Separate rooms. Find a good read, do some homework, study ahead, solve world hunger but you won't be coming back out until dinner." Zura was furious.

Her stomach still churned with the fear of what might have happened. They had no idea. She didn't have a real idea, only enough to know there was something down there that was worthy of her fear.

Zura marched them back to their individual rooms and then put her watch up to their security panels, pressing in a code at each door. She would know if they left their rooms and for how long. They'd managed to get themselves on lockdown, but they'd also managed to discover another door with a cool staircase and what felt and looked like intentional scratches or carvings on the handrails. The twins had been taking pictures of them and recording the clanging sounds they heard when Zura had found them.

Zura stopped at her room and went into the restroom. She looked in the mirror and wiped away the beads of sweat that had formed on her forehead. Her hair had fallen out of its bun. She tried to recompose herself as she put her hair back in place. She did actually need to use the restroom and might as well do it since she said that's where she was going.

When Zura arrived back in the ROC room, she was met with a glare from the Admiral General. She smiled graciously, first at him, then at everyone else before taking her seat.

"Thank you for waiting as I was away. I understand we have a lot more to discuss and it sounded like you had more to say Admiral General Mylar. You may continue."

Mylar looked at her dumbfounded. Most people didn't speak to him like that. He recognized that though he was the Admiral General she thought she owned the room.

"As I was saying while you were gone, I will be writing up an action report to be followed by all parties. This will be the official course of action and anything else will be considered unsanctioned. I understand all the concerns that have been expressed by your team, Zura, by the Science Institute, and even by Representatives Magiro and Silver. I will take those concerns into consideration. However, we cannot risk our long term plans by diverting resources, time, and attention away from what is necessary."

"Diverting them to save the lives of our citizens?" Zura asked, pushing the issue.

"Diverting them away from the vital work being done here and elsewhere to ensure the continuity of life, even if it means there are some casualties," the Admiral General said to Zura, unwilling to waver from his mission.

"So you are saying that even if it means hundreds of thousands, millions, or possibly even billions of casualties, that is acceptable? At what amount of loss of life is it acceptable to divert resources?" she pushed again.

"That's enough, Dr. Zura Bello. You have your job and I have mine. My job is to ensure continuity. Yours is to provide research and information so that everyone else can do their jobs. Do you understand that?" he said with his eyes turning into slits.

Zura took a moment and looked at him. "I thought your job was peace and security, but I understand - perfectly," she said.

Changing her tone, she glanced around the room. "I think we've done enough for today. Since there is nothing that my team can do to help prevent the death of millions or billions of people, we might as well dismiss and begin preparations to leave in the next few days. You all can get back home a day early." She gave a tight lipped smile, aimed at Admiral General Mylar. Every word she said dripped with sarcasm.

"There is still the matter of the other work being done on the ARC," Phillips said.

"We talked to Johan about it while we were checking on the progress. The farming is going very well. We can see a lot of progress being made there and it seems it will be able to self-sustain soon. The other project with the specimens has given us some concern. We have an updated plan and that plan requires us to advance the timeline," Phillips continued.

Zura shuddered inside with the term specimens. She'd never liked that term and she'd only been given enough information to keep it operational. They had placed Johan over that project and she only had clearance to a certain point.

"What's the concern, Dr. Phillips?" she asked him.

"Well, those of us from UniCorps and Admiral General Mylar are all concerned about the age of the samples and that they may be too young. We are hopeful we can fast track this program to be ready in the next year. I know that moves the timeline up a bit, but everything else will be ready in that time, and the need will be greater," he said calmly, as if he hadn't just asked her to shave almost two years off of a project that they'd been cultivating for more than twenty years, with an ambiguous justification.

They still wouldn't be clear about it and although she wasn't one hundred percent sure how the specimens would be used and why they needed to be ready in a year, she knew what it meant for her team. She couldn't refuse and she didn't want to agree. She sat there silently for a moment looking at Phillips, Tomas, Ashby, and Mylar.

They were all so smug and self-assured. It was only an order and directive to them. For her team, for her, it was giving up their freedom and personal life for a whole year. It was her kids either being isolated on Antarctica for a year or being separated from them just as they were turning into para-adults.

"What happens if we don't finish in a year?" Zura asked.

"That isn't an option, Zura," Dr. Ashby now spoke.

"I don't think you understand, Zura. We have people we have to answer to as well. They demand that all phases of the program be ready before the Winter comes here in Antarctica next year. As I told Johan, if you can't do it or if you think it is too much for you, we'll find someone who can," Admiral General Mylar said.

"Now, I don't expect that you all will need to be packing up completely for home since this is going to be home for a while longer. I will grant you a leave of four weeks to get your affairs in order back in Northern Allegiance and make sure your kids get settled, wherever you choose. This isn't a vacation though. I expect an initial report in two weeks on how we can meet the adjusted timeline and then a detailed programmatic plan by the time you return here in four weeks.

"My children's sixteenth birthday is June seventeenth, sir. Four weeks from our departure date would have us back here before their birthday celebration. This is an important milestone for them," she said, looking to Johan for support.

"Can we come back after the celebration Admiral General? It's just a day or two," Johan asked.

"I'm sorry but we have a very strict timeline and need you back here four weeks from your departure date. I will be meeting you back here at that time. Arrangements are already being made for the transport of new, more appropriately aged specimens so that they can be prepared over the next year. We recognize it takes time for preparation to occur. We are trying to do our part too. We must be finished with all phases and be ready by the World Memorial Celebration the last week of May next year. There is no wiggle room around that. I apologize for the inconvenience, Johan and Zura, but certainly your children are old enough that they should understand," Mylar said

"How could you possibly know Admiral General Mylar? You never had children," Zura said, as she stood and pushed away from the table. "I assume we are done then."

Admiral General Mylar stood up with his back straight. "Yes, we are done. We will see ourselves out. Johan, can you arrange for our transport to come after dinner this evening?" Mylar asked him casually.

"Yes, sir. You all will be dining in the main dining hall. The chef has prepared a special course for you," Johan told their guests.

"Won't you be joining us?" Silver asked.

"No, Representative Silver. Not tonight. I'm sorry but we have a great deal to do before we leave and we need to wrap up a few things," Zura answered. She couldn't even fake a smile. She felt like her insides were boiling and could feel the heat rising. If it weren't for her deep brown skin she was certain they'd see the blood under it, coloring her cheeks.

She stood near one of the windows and watched the guests walk out, followed by Rupert who would lead them back to their quarters. Johan and Mave stayed behind with her in the beautiful room that felt like it was suffocating her.

"Aaaaaarrrrgggghhhh!" Zura exploded before mumbling a string of curse words under her breath. Even those failed to diminish the anger she felt at the moment. "Who the heck do they think they are? It's not right. It just isn't. They want to force us to stay on this blasted frozen block of ice for a whole fricking year! Want us to just let our babies have their sixteenth birthday celebration without us? Want to have us keep them here isolated or with my parents for six months until the Spring comes back? My parents aren't that young anymore, Johan. They can't keep up with two para-adults and Stephen has barely even hit puberty! I'll be damned if I'm playing these stupid games this time. They are the reason our kids had to be born here, with all those risks." Zura ranted, her voice rising along with the heat under her constricting uniform collar. She adjusted the collar and unbuttoned the top button before falling into her seat and spinning towards the ocean.

"I know, Zura. It's not fair. But it's not all bad," Johan said as he tried to comfort her.

She shot him a withering look. "Not all bad? Tell me, please, Johan Anders, what is the good part?" she demanded.

Johan looked at Mave for help and Mave just shrugged. She was already thinking about what this all meant for the mission.

Johan knew Zura was impossible when she was like this.

"I don't really know. I just know we may be done with this project sooner and then get on with living a normal life for once," he answered her, giving the smile Zura had fallen in love with. He pulled her into his chest to hold her. She hugged him back trying to muster a little smile as she spoke.

"I'm still pissed off. I guess I'll ask the kids what they want to do. And you'll have to ask your sister if she can keep them in case they don't want to stay," Zura said, trying to build a plan so she didn't feel so out of control.

"I just feel like we don't have much more time with them and them being gone for six months is a lot of time to miss at this point," she said with tears welling up in her eyes.

CHAPTER THIRTY-ONE
Departure

Antarctic Research Center

STEPHEN WAITED OUTSIDE of Stella's door. They were finally going home, but this time would be different. When they came back to the ARC they'd be para-adults. If they got caught by the wrong people in the 'No Entry' areas, they could be in much more serious trouble.

After the pyramid stair incident the twins had been put on near lockdown. Their time of exploring beneath the main level had quickly ended and the new files from Marco hadn't done them any good. They needed some kind of key to make sense of what all the letters and codes meant. This key file wasn't even a part of the Noah folder.

Stephen had been wondering why his mother had wanted the pilot to get a copy but since the representatives from World Consensus and UniCorps had left, no one had much to say. Even Mave was in her own world. Their parents had never done so much to prepare to leave before. Johan was spending countless hours on the lower levels and Zura was locked up either in the ROC room, working alone, or in the science center.

They'd talked to them a few days before about what was happening, but there were never any details. Everything was classified, top-secret, or required confidentiality agreements which they were too young to legally sign for two more years. Stephen felt confused. Things were out of order and it made him uncomfortable. He wanted to feel a sense of control and normalcy again.

Johan's sister Edela agreed to come stay with Stephen and Stella for the Winter months. Her own children were grown and in University and her very busy partner had reluctantly agreed to come visit her in New South City between work trips.

As a top ranked consultant on social systems development she was always traveling to work with the established regions and the smaller local systems. It was a lucrative career for Leif, and it allowed Edela the flexibility to raise their two children and pursue her own career as a successful author and illustrator of children's books.

When they got the news, Stella jumped at the chance to stay in New South City with her favorite Aunt and be back home where there were other people her age. Neither of them was happy that their parents would be stuck working all winter, and Stephen had been reluctant to stay in New South City but Stella wasn't going to stay on the ARC. He didn't mind the ARC as much - and he had projects to work on there. He could actually be helpful to the team, but Zura didn't want him to stay.

Mave had better plans for them, at least that's what she'd promised. Spending their break on the ARC wasn't fair to them. Aside from that, things were going to be intense and she wouldn't be able to give either of them much attention.

Stephen and Stella left their unit to meet everyone else in the great hall and then they would all fly out according to regions. Mave had decided to go back to Northern Allegiance with them and Rupert was going back to his home on one of the islands off the northeastern coast of the Southern Allegiance Region. He needed the break since they'd be on duty for the next year and he'd already been told by Mylar that he would be taking on the expanded responsibility of scientific data analysis for the new specimens and comparing them to the old.

It was a role he didn't look forward to, in a job that was becoming more and more uncomfortable. He was a peaceful and honest man and the idea of not speaking up troubled him as much as it did the rest of the team. With the specimens, he wasn't sure what he was getting into.

Mylar wasn't forthcoming with exactly what Rupert would be doing. It required new confidentiality agreements and at the same time he was being processed for a higher clearance level. Rupert could only assume the lack of information was because Mylar knew Rupert might not willingly go along. Rupert prided himself with always being one to think freely and though he wasn't one to speak just to hear himself, he also wasn't one to be kept quiet.

Rupert stood in his room and packed a couple of uniforms and then the digital frame that only showed one picture – him with Mave at the gala. She looked so beautiful that night. If only she would have been his life partner, he'd be the happiest man alive. For them it wasn't an option, she always had other plans.

Rupert looked around at the room he'd occupied for six months out of each of the last eighteen years. His room was rather sparse and there wasn't much to take with him that was sentimental or very valuable.

He took a picture Stephen had drawn for him years before and the knitted hat that Stella had gotten for his fiftieth birthday. It held all of his hair back and he always wore it when he was back at home. *That's it.* There wasn't much else there to take, especially since they were expected back in just four weeks.

Dozens of people milled about the great hall; all waiting for the various transports to take them back to their regions. Rupert walked in, his normal limp slightly more pronounced. He'd spent so much time over the years with the people in that room.

There were too many goodbyes he needed to say before he left for Southern Allegiance. Some staff had to return in four weeks for the extended assignment while others would have the luxury of staying away until Spring returned.

There were unanswered questions and grumbling permeated the room at a low steady volume. Zura's hands were tied and her voice was silenced. Just like her, her team couldn't say anything either. She knew some of them were returning to the same areas they'd labeled as hot zones and she couldn't even give them a warning.

UniCorps had sent someone along with SEP Agents to supervise the departures. They wanted to make sure no one was smuggling any sensitive or confidential data, materials, or specimens off the ARC. There were body scanners set up at the doors leading from the dining hall to the corridor to the outside. SEP Agents manned the body scanners and another was stationed at the exit door. He sent back anyone who hadn't been registered as cleared by the body scanner.

Johan, Mave, Zura, Rupert, and the twins stood against the back wall, near the corner. They would be the last to go. Mave was nervous, as was everyone else. They didn't want any trouble and the departure needed to go smoothly. Rupert moved to stand beside Mave, resting again on the wall. He'd miss her and hadn't really had the chance to tell her goodbye. In a couple of hours they'd be headed out on different transporters.

"Is your leg okay, Rupert? You seem to be walking with more of a limp today," Mave asked, looking at his knee.

"Yeah, it's fine. It's just the weather getting cooler and you know how that bothers where it is connected."

"I don't know why you don't just upgrade it and let them fuse it so you don't have that problem anymore. They've been doing it for years now."

"Because, this one works fine," Rupert argued with a knowing smile.

"Except when it's too cold or when it's too hot," Mave laughed at him.

"Hey, I get around fine with it. It does everything yours does, except a little better and it's stronger," Rupert said.

He had his reasons for not upgrading and when the doctors had offered him the upgraded prosthetic he'd turned it down. Instead, he chose to donate to an organization that provided children with prosthetics. Without the upgrade he wouldn't have to pay for the additional medical maintenance. It may not have seemed like much to some, but every year since he'd been on the ARC he'd donated the cost of a prosthetic limb to a para-adult.

By the time they reached para-adult status most of those in need of a prosthetic were into their full sized limbs and there was less chance of outgrowing it too fast. It was also the age when he'd lost his leg and a generous gift from a donor was how he'd gotten his first prosthetic leg. He'd since upgraded but couldn't justify a new one now and this one served another purpose.

The room was slowly thinning out as people passed through the security scanners. They were going by Regions but Rupert was waiting as long as he could before leaving. The rest were all going to the same place and so the Northern Allegiance Transporter would be the last to load.

He heard them call Southern Liberty Region and he sighed. He wanted so badly to hug and kiss Mave right there.

"Will you walk with me over to the scanner, Mave?" he asked her.

"Yeah, come on," she said before taking his arm.

Rupert gave a half open smile to Mave and said, "I'm really going to miss you, Mave."

"I know. On the bright side, at least it's only four weeks this time. Usually, we are away from this place for six months," she said to him in an almost whisper.

"Right. Four weeks will be gone in no time," he said in a distant sounding voice.

The line was going too fast and he wished he had more time. He let others leaving for Southern Allegiance go ahead of him. He lingered near the back so he could spend just a few more moments with Mave.

"You act like you don't want to leave, Rupert," Mave teased. "You could just stay here for the four weeks and skip this whole process."

"I don't want to go, but I also don't want to stay. We all have to do what we have to do, right?" he said.

Mave looked at him from the side of her eye. She couldn't tell whether the odd response was because he was going to miss her. She was going to miss him too. She couldn't imagine spending as much time as she did on the ARC without his quiet strength, his laughter, his smile, and the way he could piece together a picture that made sense from seemingly senseless pieces. Mave loved him even if she could never really let him know.

After all this time and as far as she'd come on her mission, it would be worse if he knew just how much she loved him and yet still refused to be with him. She thought about how many times she felt like telling the Council and Dr. Lima to just screw it. So many times she'd wanted to walk away and have a normal life; only to have to step back and remember why she had chosen the life she had. Unfortunately, this was as normal as it would get for her.

It was finally just Rupert and Mave in the line. There was no one else to let go ahead of them.

Rupert turned to her. "I have to go now, Mave. But before I do, I have to say something to you. I know you don't want to hear it but if I don't say it, then I might regret it." Mave tried to stop him but Rupert wouldn't let her, this time.

"No, Mave. Don't stop me. I have to tell you that I love you. I have loved you since the day I met you. I have never stopped loving you and I never will. What I do, I do because I feel it is right. One day, when I leave this existence and am held accountable for my life, I don't want it said that I didn't live an honest life. I must be honest now and going forward, and that includes with you. Mave, I honestly love you."

Mave's eyes were beginning show the first signs of tears forming in the corners as Rupert leaned in to give her a kiss. He then hugged her and in those stretching seconds he never wanted to let her go. After holding her for far too little time, the SEP Agent cleared his throat to get their attention.

"Are you ready, sir? The transport will be departing soon," the agent said.

"Yes. Yes. Thank you," Rupert slowly let his arms drop from the embrace and stepped away from Mave onto the body scanner system. The lights shined all over his body, showing a skeletal image except where his prosthetic limb was. There, the metal blocked much of the light but you could see the wires and connections. Once the scan was completed the agent waved Rupert through.

"I'll see you the next go round, Mave," Rupert said.

"Goodbye, Rupert. Take care," Mave said with a curious look on her face.

Mave walked back slowly towards Zura, Johan and the twins. She wished she'd said something back to Rupert, but she didn't know what to say, and instead chose to say nothing.

"Are you okay, Mave?" Zura asked her.

"I really don't know," Mave answered, deep in her own thoughts as she found a spot to lean against the wall and wait in silence.

The announcements for Northern Allegiance were being made and the remaining people were lining up. Zura's team moved slowly forward as they began making the last calls for

Northern Allegiance. It was time for them to leave, but they all waited for everyone else to get in line. The only people who'd be staying behind were the annual crew who lived on the ARC year round to maintain it.

For the next year they'd experience the same thing, being on the ARC year round, and none of them looked forward to the forced change.

CHAPTER THIRTY-TWO
Home

New South City, Northern Allegiance

THE HUMIDITY HUNG thick in the Spring air outside of the aircraft as it pulled into the old private air field. The suffocating heat was a sharp contrast to the cool dry air of Antarctica. It had already descended over the historic city and summer was still more than a full month away. The transporter slowly coasted into the private station in New South City in the southern part of Northern Allegiance.

Most of the passengers had managed to get a few hours of sleep and now, finally in New South City, they were the last ones leaving the transporter in Northern Allegiance.

The plane had barely come to a still hover when Zura stood up, feeling antsy after the trip. She'd stayed up and watched her people get off at the different stops, knowing many of them would have to leave their homes and families and return before even the Festival of Fireworks in July.

At least they'd get the World Memorial Holiday at home with the kids but the Festival of Fireworks was one of the biggest celebrations around the world. This year they would be on the ARC and aside from possibly holding a small party inside, there would be no celebrating this year.

Zura loved the holiday. The concept had originated in what was then the United States of America a few hundred years before. The story that had been officially sanctioned was that the people in that country had lit up the sky in celebration of having an overabundance of tea, which represented prosperity, and being able to share the outpouring of that gift with what was then Britain who helped found The United States.

Every year on the anniversary of the founding of the World Consensus on July fifteenth the world was lit up in honor of the abundance that would come from a united world where everyone worked together.

People would gather in large groups in all the regions and the party of the year would happen. *They would miss the celebration this year.* Zura looked over at her twins. Stella was starting to wake but Stephen was still snoring. He hadn't even stirred since they'd stopped. How Stella had slept beside him, she had no idea.

"Hey, mom. Are we finally here?" Stella asked, gently opening the shade to look out. Zura nodded. She was clearly still deep in thought. Zura had been like this since the UniCorps and the World Consensus representatives left.

Outside the craft, blackness stole the sky. The hour was late and Stella couldn't wait to get home and into her bed. She looked forward to seeing her Aunt Edela who would be arriving in two weeks. Stella wondered if her older cousins and Aunt Leif would make the trip too, at least for their birthday party. Stella turned her thoughts to the party and poked Stephen. She needed someone to talk to and everyone else was preoccupied with work.

Stephen moaned and turned his head. It was obvious he was tired. He hadn't slept the night before at all, trying to get everything he could from the isolated ARC system. She nudged him again. He would have to wake up anyway since it was time to get off the aircraft. She could see the lights from hovehicles in the distance. Usually their family needed a large one but this year her parents had only brought back the bare minimum and a regular van would be enough.

"Stephen. Stephen. We're here." Stella said again, almost shoving him to get him awake.

He finally opened his eyes. He looked over at Stella, then around the craft. His eyes swam as he tried to focus. He'd slept hard through the long ride back. He looked over at his parents who were both up and trying to get ready to get off the craft. Neither of them could sit still for very long. They were always like this by the time they got to this point in the trip.

Stella was ready to talk but she could tell Stephen wasn't quite ready to listen. She hadn't been able to sleep much since their visit to the staircase. There was something about the clanging and scratches that would wake her up out of sleep, afraid. The clanging would begin and then the sound of metal scraping against metal would pierce her dreams, driving her awake. She hadn't told anyone about it but hadn't been able to get past it either. She was glad to be going home and away from the ARC, if only for six months.

Stephen rubbed his eyes and let out a big yawn with his arms stretching over Stella's head.

"You know you snore like a race horse, don't you?" Mave said, coming up from behind Stephen as he twisted in his seat to get out of his seat belt.

"I was wondering where you were. I was afraid I slept through your getting off," Stephen said through a yawn while at the same time ignoring her comment.

"I wouldn't do that to you two. Besides, don't you remember, my surprise for your birthday? I'll be in New South City with you all, at least for a while and I'll be staying at your place tonight. My temporary residence won't be ready until tomorrow. We get one more night together, in the same building," Mave said with a bright smile. And the special surprise for both of you – I want to do that a few days before your party. It'll be really special."

Just the mention of the upcoming party turned back on her talkative side.

"Oh, I am so excited. All of my friends are going to be there and of course yours too Stephen. Who did you invite?" she said more to herself than to him. She then turned to Mave. "Did mom already order the cake, it's gotta be special. I don't want a regular store bought cake this year, please. This year is super important and even though I know I have to share a cake with Stephen, I want to have half of it decorated just for me," Stella said feeling suddenly giddy.

"Or even better, we can get two smaller cakes so that I can finally have my own and it can be super amazing and he can have his and it can be…well it can be whatever it is he wants. What do you think about that, Stephen? Finally having your own cake?" Stella paused just long enough to catch her breath.

He opened his mouth to answer but she'd already started talking again. "Oh, and we haven't even talked about the decorations and the entertainment," she said worried. She called out to her mom, "Mom, what are we doing for decorations and entertainment for our birthday? Please tell me we can have something good. We only turn sixteen once."

She actually stopped talking so Zura could answer. She waited silently for a few seconds while Zura looked at her with a blank look on her face hoping she'd do what she typically did, and keep talking. Stella let the void of silence linger as she waited for Zura's answer.

"Oh my goodness, Stella. I am so sorry. I haven't booked anything yet. I will tomorrow. I promise," Zura said looking tired and guilty.

The past few weeks had thoroughly worn her out mentally and physically and even coming home she wasn't going to get any relief.

Stella sighed. "I'll find what we want and then give you the information to schedule them. We only have a month and our birthday happens to be at the same time as graduations and unity ceremonies so we are already behind."

The look of disappointment that Stella shot Zura and Johan wrenched Zura's heart. Every year their birthday turned out to be an afterthought. After they got back from Antarctica, usually with just a couple weeks to spare, they would frantically try to pull something off. It generally wound up being just barely okay but she didn't want barely okay this year.

At least they'd been able to leave a little earlier than usual, even if it was only so that everyone could return before the weather got worse in Antarctica. Stella now hoped that those two weeks might make the difference this year.

Zura stood by her seat, trying to avoid looking at Stella and Stephen. She already felt guilty enough that they hadn't done any planning ahead of time, again, but the twins didn't know that she was going to miss their actual sixteenth birthday. The most important for any teen. They would be para-adults.

"We may need to move up the date a week," she tried to say casually.

"But we won't be sixteen a week earlier," Stephen said with his no-nonsense voice. "Usually, you move it back so that you are actually sixteen at the time of the celebration, otherwise it would be anticlimactic," Stephen added.

"Yeah, besides, everyone is always busy the two weeks around the World Memorial Holiday," Stella said with an attitude of, 'why would you even suggest such a thing?'.

Zura wasn't going to tell them the bad news tonight. There was nothing she could do about it and she was too mentally fatigued to deal with Stella.

"Mom, what's going on? You aren't telling us something about that day, are you?" Stella asked, picking up on Zura's thoughts.

Dangit, thought Zura. She needed to change her thoughts quickly to something else so that Stella wouldn't pick up on any more of her thoughts about their birthday. She knew if she opened that can of worms now, there would be no rest for any of them.

"Stella, honey, I'm just really tired. Let's talk about the birthday party tomorrow, okay?" Zura tried to say sweetly.

Stella looked at her mother, then at Mave and immediately knew something was wrong. No one was being honest with them. All the secrets were getting to her. Stella rose to her feet, and walked to the door. She didn't want to talk to them about it tonight or tomorrow. If they weren't going to be there, why bother talking about it at all?

"Liars," she muttered under her breath as she stared out the window next to her.

Stephen got up to stand by Stella. "Stella, what's going on?" he whispered.

She just looked at him then back at her parents and Mave. "They're lying," she said.

"Oh," he said with a confused look. "You don't think they are going to throw us a party?" he asked innocently.

"I'll tell you later. I don't feel like talking now," she said turning back to look out the window of the exit door.

The pilot spoke to the remaining passengers. "We should be ready to exit the craft very soon. Since this is the final stop for the night, we will be parking over there in the hangar and then letting you out. It's almost ready for us. It's a shorter walk to the hovehicle lot but it means we'll be moving again. I'll need everyone to take their seats again so we can taxi in. Thank you," she said turning off the speaker.

Feeling defeated, Stella stomped back to the seats where she and Stephen were. She squeezed past him to take the seat by the window so she'd have more space between her and everyone else. She couldn't wait to get off the transporter, but then realized it would only be to get into the hovehicle which would be cramped with all of them inside, along with their luggage.

The aircraft began to slowly lift up and glide towards the hangar. The lights of the hovehicles in the lot got closer and closer and dim lights now felt like high beams as Stella looked out of her window. She didn't want to be mad but she didn't ask for much from any of them.

Her parents knew this was the one thing she'd wanted since she was about ten. By the time she'd turned thirteen she'd already started talking about what her sixteenth would be like. Now, a month out, nothing had been done. *Nothing.* She felt crushed and betrayed.

Stella waited for her parents to get up and go to the door first. She didn't want to be near them any sooner than she had to be. Stephen watched his sister, searching for the right words to make her feel better, but he was never very good at having the right words so decided that sitting beside her, even without speaking, was the best idea. Besides, he had other things on his mind as well.

Those other things had kept him up all night. He needed to figure out what he'd been looking at in in the Noah files and the specimen. He couldn't figure out what they were specimen of and what it was related to. Stephen hoped his grandfather, who'd been a highly successful geneticist before retiring, might be able to help; if he could convince him. He wouldn't have much time since they'd only be coming in town for two weeks.

His grandfather, Wilson, had been a key player in advancing some of the human genome work and had found great success at the Science Division of UniCorps, helping to found the department before taking a less demanding role the year Zura had the twins.

Wilson still dabbled in his work although he was now at a much smaller private company that was still under one of the UniCorps organizations. He'd been in the phase down years of his career for the past six years and soon he'd reach retirement at eighty-three.

He maintained a lab back in his homeland to continue work on a very small but specific project. No one knew, even his wife Priscilla, what it was about since he never talked about it. Wilson was sharp as a tack with a no nonsense attitude, but with a sense of adventure that rivaled men a third his age.

They would be in New South City, visiting from Hankura in Southern Liberty in less than two weeks. Then he'd have to try to sell his granddad on helping him do something his granddad would likely frown on. Stephen knew he would have to appeal to his sense of adventure.

The voice coming over the intercom felt like it surrounded Stephen as it sliced into his thoughts.

"Okay, everyone, the doors will be opening. Please exit the craft in a straight line. Watch the steps and use the handrail. We've made it this far, and don't need any accidents," the pilot said before switching off.

She and her co-pilot had been switching back and forth and it was now time for both of them to rest. The sooner they got the craft emptied out, the better. As the remaining ten people or so walked down the steps, Captain Patawa walked back to the rear of the aircraft. She informed the crew to use the rear door and unload as quickly as possible.

She then walked back to the departing passengers to catch up with Zura.

"Dr. Zura, can I speak with you for a moment before you leave?" Patawa asked.

Zura stepped back. "Yes, what's going on?" Zura asked looking worried.

"Nothing is wrong. I just need to give you something from a pilot friend we have in common. He said it took a while, but he did his best and he'll keep the other secure. I suppose you know what that means," Patawa smiled at Zura.

"Yes, I do. Thanks Captain and thank you for getting us home safely. Will you be with us on the return trip?" Zura stopped to ask.

"I think so, we'll know in a week or so. If not, good luck," Patawa said, waving her off the craft.

Zura clasped the tiny package Captain Patawa had given her. She stepped quickly back onto the aircraft and walked past the two crew members before slipping into the small restroom. She needed to stash it somewhere safe before the SEP Agents checked them again. She unzipped her uniform slightly then placed the thin microdot concealed in a small piece of candy wrapper into her bra, along the center wire frame. Zura zipped up her uniform, checking that it wasn't visible and headed back to the exit door.

"Have a good night," Zura called out to Captain Patawa as she passed her on her way off the craft. She trotted to catch up with her family and Mave. She noticed Mave was walking behind Stella, but Johan and Stephen weren't with them. She slowed down trying to give Stella her space and scanned the hangar looking for them.

Johan waited at the craft with Stephen and the attendants to collect the luggage. They used a rolling cart to push it towards the hovehicle where their driver helped load the luggage into the van. The five passengers, in various stages of exhaustion and frustration, claimed seats. Stella jumped into the front seat next to the driver, surprising her. She'd rather sit next to a stranger tonight.

They rode in uneasy silence back to their home in the city. Stella loved the building. It was a historic landmark, built almost two hundred years before but it still held its beauty. The glass exterior and its round shape were her favorite features.

The top overlooked the city and was still one of the most recognized parts of the busy skyline. It had stood up beautifully to the changing designs over time and when she walked into the lobby of their building, the pictures of the building at different times over the years seemed to tell the story, a quiet history of New South City.

She and Stephen had often speculated about what the people who lived there at the turn of the century were like. She imagined they were at least not stuck wearing the boring uniforms everyone now wore on a daily basis.

She'd read in the building's history that it had once been a hotel. It was a strange idea to her to have a hotel that large in the middle of the city. All those empty rooms when people needed places to live. They still had hotels but most of the larger places were converted into permanent residences to house the burgeoning population. Smaller places that were once private homes or small apartment buildings were more often hotels.

Stella's thoughts of home had only partially dampened the noise. She cradled her head in her hands and took a deep breath. She wanted everyone to just shut-up, but she couldn't say that since no one was talking. At least not with their mouths. Despite the outward silence, everyone's minds were so busy. She hadn't meant to tune in but she had gotten emotional, and in trying to get answers, she'd turned it on. Now she couldn't get it off or them out of her head.

She needed to calm down and just focus on herself, which is exactly what she was going to do once they got to the twenty-seventh floor. When the elevator doors opened she practically ran out and down the hall. She held her hand up to the pad and let herself in, not caring that the door closed behind her. They wouldn't be seeing her again that night. She was over it - over them.

Zura looked at Johan and Mave and shook her head. Stella had every reason to be upset. She knew that Stella knew and she'd just have to deal with that in the morning.

They'd gotten themselves into this situation and Zura had to accept that this moment was years in the making. Every decision and choice. Every time she said yes to them – UniCorps and the World Consensus, when she should have said no. Every time they'd decided to move forward on the entire ARC program, they were building to this, and now it happened that their sins would be visited on their children. Their children would once again have to pay for their choices and it might not end with just a poorly planned birthday party.

Zura needed a drink. A glass of red wine while sitting in her favorite cozy chair in their bedroom sounded nice right now. She felt guilty and although Johan hadn't said much, he probably felt even more guilt. The only bit of solace was in knowing that what they were doing would help their children and many more.

Johan and Stephen dropped the luggage in the middle of the living room floor, and Mave came in and sat on the sofa. Over the years, she'd stayed many nights at their home. She'd make her way to the guest bedroom soon enough, but first, she needed to talk to Johan and Zura.

She knew Zura well enough to know she'd be back out soon, in cozy bedtime clothes, to get her welcome home drink. Stella wasn't coming back out of her room and Stephen was still dragging from multiple days on too little sleep. Mave was sure she wouldn't hear from either of them that night. She'd talk to them when she could get them both together and when they were rested and preferably, in better moods.

"What are you going to do Mave? Turn in for the night? It's been a long day," Johan asked, as he got ready to walk back to the bedroom and change too.

"I need to talk to you and Zura, Johan," she said seriously. "When you get changed can you both come out here? We can all share a much deserved glass of wine," she added.

Minutes later, the three sat around the living room on the soft sofa and chairs Zura had picked out a few years before. When the twins turned thirteen, she thought it was safe to replace the furniture they'd destroyed as children. Wine glasses on the table were already nearly drained and a bottle of Cabernet sat in a wine holder on the counter.

"I need to talk about what is supposed to happen here, Johan and Zura," she said and gave both of them a look to make sure they knew what this was about.

"The twins will be sixteen and that's already a big deal, but they are also supposed to have their ceremony. We've talked about doing it soon, but we hadn't said how soon. In light of everything else going on we need to make sure it happens before their birthday - it can't wait. If we wait, we may be back on the ARC and we can't miss it if we are going to make good on the other mission. There are a lot of people depending on us."

"If I'd known we were going to be so pushed for time this year, I would have tried to do it sometime last year, any time, for that matter. That's neither here nor there – it's done. We are all sacrificing so much with the ARC but we cannot sacrifice these two kids. They are critical to the mission being successful. Besides that, I love them," she paused again looking Zura in the eyes and then Johan.

Mave could make you feel like you were under a microscope at times. For this mission, she was the leader of their small group. They hadn't had time to discuss it before leaving the ARC with all of the extra commotion.

Mave waited a moment and then she continued in a firm and deliberate tone. "The twins and the others need to have their Awakening Ceremony within the week leading up to the twins' sixteenth birthday. It's the only way to do it before we are gone. There are things that will be happening here and in other places while we are stuck in Antarctica and those things have a better chance of being successful if they have their Awakening Ceremony."

"Yes, I understand," Zura said in a tired voice with the hint of just a little too much wine.

"Do you remember the two girls I told you about in Southern Liberty? Then there is the other girl and boy, both with connections in Southern Allegiance? And then there is Ren, who we will bring in. You remember Ren?"

"Yeah, of course. His mom is Kim. They used to come around but stopped a few years ago. I think he had some adverse reaction to the serum. He was the first Dr. Lima injected," Johan said, nodding as he remembered Ren.

"That's him. He's been through a lot but we need him. He's in New South City already for his regular treatments and will be participating with Stephen and Stella. They all need to do the same thing and soon so our timeline doesn't get blown to hell. With the new demands from UniCorps we don't have time to waste, we have to move things forward." Mave took a deep breath. There was still more. Zura saw her about to speak again and jumped in.

"Wait, Mave. This is a lot and very fast. I know we agreed to this concept but please slow down just a little. It's been a very long day," Zura said.

"Okay. I get it, Zura. You're tired. We're all tired, but bear with me. The Awakening Ceremony needs to happen on the night of the ninth. It is the first day of the full moon, one of the most ideal times. We'll be gone by the solstice so that is not an option The other Keepers are making arrangements with the help of the Council for all of this to line up. We've had to work really hard to pull this off and to coordinate everything. Screwing up the planning of your kids' most important birthday party cannot be what unravels the entire plan," Mave chastised them and then stopped for a moment to let it all sink in.

"Their party is after the ceremony but we need to make this party special and having their friends here and Ren will make it seem like you have worked hard planning this. They haven't seen Ren in years and he'll be here for the Awakening so they might as well get reacquainted by having him at the party. With that said, tomorrow you must figure out a way to be here for their birthday. Piss off that dictator Mylar. Don't miss this moment in your kids' lives. You won't get over it and neither will they," Mave warned them. "I know this and I don't even have kids."

Mave could see the exhaustion in their bodies and in their eyes, but that didn't matter. She had to say what she needed to say just as they needed to do what they needed to do.

"Johan, have you sent for the Awakening Ceremony materials? Please tell me you have," Mave asked, looking less than optimistic.

"I'm sorry, Mave. We have been so busy, buried with work, and-," Johan tried to finish when Mave cut him off.

"Never mind. I'll send the order off for them but you will need to pick them up. You'll also need to work on the entertainment first thing tomorrow. Zura, you make sure their friends are coming and that we have a place and a theme for this party. They want separate cakes so Johan, you take Stephen out to pick his and Zura, you take Stella out. It'll give you two some time to make this right."

"Are you really sure about all of this, Mave? So much is happening right now," Zura asked as she rubbed her temples. They were still her babies.

"If you still want this mission to work, it has to happen and we don't have much time. Besides, this is more than the Awakening Ceremony. They are turning sixteen. They'll be para-adults and that by itself is momentous."

Johan took a deep breath in. He couldn't help but feel the same reservations that Zura did, but he knew they had to make their own marks. They couldn't protect them from their future.

"I'll pull together a plan for those specimens on the ARC. Mylar is concerned about their age suddenly, so there must be a reason we don't know about," Johan said trying to get his head around what lay ahead.

"The Council is concerned about this new timeline crunch as well. It puts pressure on our plan. The Council needs to be assured that whatever happens, we'll be ready to handle it," Mave said and then stood up.

Zura and Johan both looked at Mave, their eyes glossing over. Mave downed her last couple of ounces of red wine and put the glass on the counter in the kitchen. "Good night. I'll talk to you in the morning."

CHAPTER THIRTY-THREE
Rationed

The Capital City, Northern Liberty

PRESTON ROCHESTER DAVENPORT, II didn't want another meeting with one of the founding partners, Sontamon Foods. He already knew what they were going to say.

However, they were one of the original organizations and their President had one of the purest bloodlines aside from Preston.

"Preston speaking," he finally answered before missing the call.

"Preston? Grapper Bellarde from Sontamon Foods."

"Hello Grapper. How are you today?"

"I'll be honest, Preston. I'd be doing much better if my distribution channels weren't from here to the ends of the earth. I've been telling you, we can't move food that far affordably. Then there is the issue of safety. Those damn homeless are robbing our transports. Compounding the logistics issue and outright thievery, is the fact that people aren't moving themselves fast enough. Do you hear what I'm saying?

"Of course, I hear you Grapper. We're already using trained SEP Agents to handle the transports. I really do understand the issue beyond that and I do hear you," he said sitting down, one hand on his head.

"It's a basic supply and demand problem, Preston. Basic economics. We have the food, nearer to the cities yet the people are spread out. We can't continue to try to feed twenty billion people like we are, especially when we have less land that can grow food and each year the crops are worse. We have more people needing the food and each year more babies are born. I don't need to spell it out any more for you. We need to get the World Consensus to agree to our population plans."

"Like I said, I hear your problem Grapper but relocating that many people is a nightmare. It would bankrupt the World Consensus and probably us too. I understand it's a logistical problem, but unless there are fewer people to move, it's not going to be feasible."

"Well, hell. How long is that gonna take? Our grandparents didn't take care of it, not like they should have when they had a chance and now here we are. Preston, I think we need to push a lot harder on this. We've been sending fewer rations to the outlying areas hoping people would eventually move. Those people are barely budging. What do you think about us reducing it to the bare minimum? To the point that they realize that unless they move, they'll starve.

Preston listened to Grapper with veiled impatience. Sontamon Foods wasn't the only one calling with the issue. All of his major corporate partners were arguing for more central distribution. On more than one occasion, he'd looked at the option with the Population and Relocation Management Division. The timeline was at least ten years to have the housing supply to handle them, let alone the general logistics of moving billions of people, wasn't going to help any plan they had now.

"Grapper, let's table this conversation again. You know the long plan. This isn't it. Just be patient and your stockholders' demands won't even matter anymore.

"Preston, I'm tired of tabling it. Our partners want action. I want action, Preston! Are you willing to do what's best for your people?"

"Don't I always look out for us, Grapper?"

Preston hung up with Grapper, and called Mirkal 'The Stache' Dempstead

"Dempstead? You let those closings get pushed through and now production is down. I need you to make sure something else gets through. Consider it a way for you to make it up to us, since you've let us get into a bad situation."

Preston could hear movement in the background and then the sound of a door opening and closing.

"What do you need, Mr. Davenport?" The Stache finally responded. He never talked business in front of his mother. No matter who it might be.

"I need you to get your friend Magiro to back down about getting information out. I don't want people moving. I don't want people leaving their homes."

"People are moving already, sir. People are starting to move because of the earthquakes and because of the issues with food. They are moving to the areas with higher populations. That's what you and your partners want, right? Better for logistics and management?"

"Yes, that's right. We don't want those in the cities to leave because of the perceived threat of earthquakes, understand? That becomes counter-productive to our plan, Mirkal," Preston said, his voice tired.

"I understand," Mirkal responded.

Preston ended the call abruptly before he began coughing violently into his handkerchief.

"Is everything alright, sir?" a well-dressed woman with her hair in a neat bun asked, as she entered Preston's lavish office. She carried with her a small gold-plated tray with a matching tea set made of white porcelain with golden inlays. On the side of the saucer were a tea bag and two lemon wedges. A small spoon rested on a white napkin. She set the tray down beside Preston as she poured hot water from the side table.

Preston's coughing spell ended and he looked at the woman, his eyes teary and cheeks red. "Please close the door." He couldn't allow his regular staff to see him like this. "I will be fine, Mel. Did Mylar's report from his ARC visit come in yet? Are we going to be able to move forward with the shorter timeline?"

Mel sat down and put the tea bag inside his cup before pouring the hot water over it. "The report did come in. It seems there are several on the ARC who don't view your decision to not report the findings, favorably. However, Mylar has reported that the core staff and leadership will be returning after a four week break, which they've already begun. He cannot promise that with the specimen they have and even with the new ones they are gathering that one year will be enough. I'm sorry," she said whispering. She touched his hand and squeezed it before kissing his forehead.

"Will you still be going home for the World Memorial Holiday?" he asked her.

He hated when she left. It was all the way to the far eastern side of Northern Liberty, and whenever she was gone he missed her. He could never marry her but she'd been by his side for fifteen years.

Now she was in the unenviable position of watching him slowly deteriorate and there was no medicine to stop it. They had managed to slow down the degenerative blood disease, but stopping it would take a miracle of science.

"I will. Just remember, I'm only a flight away. If you need anything, Preston, I'm here for you. Before I forget, Rochester called. He wants to know if you will be home this evening for dinner?" Mel asked already prepared for his response.

Preston looked at his watch. It was 6:45 and he still had calls to return from the leaders over several of the other key members of UniCorps. For the most part, he knew what they were calling about but the conversations wouldn't be easy, or brief.

"I'm sorry. Please let him know that I will have to miss dinner. Tell him I'm sorry again and that," Preston's voice trailed off. He didn't want to make any more promises to anyone that he might not be able to keep. "And tell him, I'll call him this evening if I don't make it in before eleven or so. Thanks Mel."

Mel nodded. She kissed him once more on his cheek this time, now that the flushing and wetness were gone. *Sixteen years.* A tear, barely visible, crept from the inside of her eye but was nearly gone by the time it reached her cheek. She wasn't born of the right blood and if Preston accidentally sired a child with her and it became public, it would compromise his legacy, Rochester's legacy, and both of their positions.

She walked out of the office and called Rochester to give him Preston's message. She could hear the disappointment in Rochester's voice, like so many times before. It was not as pronounced as it had been when he was a child, but it was still there, she could tell.

Tonight she couldn't spend time trying to comfort him or reassure him of anything. Not that he needed it anymore. He'd stopped asking questions years before but she always felt guilty, being the one to deliver the bad news each time. Tonight she couldn't worry about that, she had a flight to catch.

CHAPTER THIRTY-FOUR
Familiar

In the Skies Heading to Southern AllegianceSantoria, Southern Allegiance

RUPERT LOOKED OUT the window at the clouds that gathered beneath. Puffy and white with just the slightest hint of silver; they gave an illusion of pillow-like softness but in reality they were just wisps of moisture that would never catch you should you fall. *But we all fall, sometimes,* he thought. He was surrounded by men and women he'd worked with for years, some of them for the entire time he'd been on the ARC.

Rupert's mind drifted as he reclined his seat and stretched his right leg into the aisle. She hadn't said anything. He'd told her how much he loved her and she'd said nothing back. He had hoped that she would say something.

Just once, she could have given him hope. He sighed. Rupert knew Mave. She had her priorities and had always made that clear, leaving no room for any uncertainty about what she needed to do and how nothing would get in her way. He still loved her and he'd wait for her. He'd wait his whole life for her if it came to that.

He rubbed just below his right knee. His leg was beginning to ache now but he couldn't risk removing the source of the pain. The SEP Agent would check all ARC passengers one more time before clearing them to leave. No one in the crew working the flight was familiar to him. He'd hoped one of the pilots he trusted would be on this flight because what he had was too sensitive to entrust to someone new. He would have to bear it for at least six more hours as they made the remaining four local stops before his.

If he were on the island it would be much harder to get the information out to the mainland subsytems. He couldn't just connect to the old lines since he didn't know anyone with access. He considered his options for getting access back in Southern Allegiance. He could think of one possibility, but it already felt uncomfortable and discomfited.

He would need to call on someone he hadn't spoken to in fifteen years because she was unfortunate enough to have access to two things he needed.

He needed Marco. When he'd seen the location of the communication transfers between Stephen and someone in Southern Allegiance it made him curious. He'd gone to school with a man from that same city, Santoria, east of the Amazon.

Zura asked him to check on what the kids were doing and so he continued to dig, until he found the class they'd logged into and the names who'd logged in. It had taken a full week of searching, but Rupert had finally figured out that Marco was who he thought he was. The last time he'd spoken to his mother Teresa it was after his friend and college roommate Sandro Garcia disappeared.

Rupert never found out exactly what happened to Sandro and Teresa didn't want to talk about it. Despite knowing very little of the truth, she tried to keep her boys much closer and out of trouble. Something that seemed impossible given they had their dad's adventurous and indestructible spirit.

The only time he heard from them was a periodic holiday greeting during the Winter Solstice. Over the years they'd become more and more sporadic. The last one was after Marco had turned sixteen and had a picture of him and his brother Locan, who'd become a pilot after serving as an SEP Officer.

Sandro's disappearance was much harder on Locan who was almost nine when it happened. Rupert had gone to see Teresa Garcia after Sandro's disappearance and he still remembered how hysterical she'd been. She'd finished her training and become a nurse only a year before Marco had been born, and then dealt with the stresses of his constant illnesses that first year.

She hadn't reported them but she knew it was the serum. After the first year he hadn't been sick more than a day in his life, but it had taken a toll on her. He was barely through those challenging days when their lives were turned upside down. Locan tried to be strong but his eyes told a different story as he looked on at his changed world in silence.

Marco was barely more than a toddler and just wandered around the room touching everything he could get his hands on while his mother was distracted. He was indifferent to the fact that their lives would never be the same.

Even then, the photos on the walls and in the displayer hadn't been changed since Marco was a baby, still crawling. There were pictures of Sandro, Teresa, and Locan together before Marco was born. Then the photos seemed to stop, and after Marco there were only a few pictures of his father at all and even fewer of Marco with his father.

Sandro's disappearance had shaken Rupert too. Whatever the cause, it didn't happen overnight. It had been going on for years until one day he didn't come back, leaving behind a wife and two sons. Rupert had felt so guilty sitting in her living room, eating her homemade fajitas and sipping on guava juice. He always felt guilty. He still carried secrets with him that in the dark of the night seemed to steal a piece of his soul, leaving him with less of who he was when the dawn broke again.

He couldn't continue like this and he couldn't tell Teresa, Locan, or even Marco what little he did know about Sandro. Though it wasn't much, it was more than his family knew. He had to keep that to himself, at least for now, but he still needed his old friend's sons. The pilot and the tech wiz could do something he couldn't do on his own.

Rupert hoped that the agents would understand his desire to stop on the mainland before heading home. As he sat looking out the window, he cooked up a plan to use the excuse of buying food and supplies. He honestly had nothing back home and things took longer to get to the island.

If he could get Marco to load the info into the subsystem, he would find a way to get Locan to take him home. It had to work and if he could do it, that meant Zura wouldn't have to and no one else he loved would have to risk their freedom and their lives to get the information out.

* * *

TERESA'S MIND HAD been racing all day since she got the message that Rupert wanted to come by while on an overlay. She had been trying to figure out what was behind the sudden contact. Fifteen years had passed since she'd last seen him.

It felt like a lifetime and she wasn't' sure she wanted to resurrect the past. He said he wanted to see the boys too, but Locan rarely came home anymore. If she saw him twice a year she felt lucky, but Marco was home and he wouldn't have any idea who Rupert was.

She didn't talk much to Marco about Sandro. When he was younger she tried to tell him stories of his father, but as time passed it felt useless and only caused her more pain and anger. The few memories Marco held of his father came in flashes, like damaged photographs. He could never place the scene or what was happening in the brief images he got. A look on his dad's face, a smile, a slight movement captured with no frame of reference.

He didn't miss him like Locan who'd gotten him for eight years. He missed him in other ways though. He never had a father and Teresa could see the difference in how it affected Marco who never even knew what he was missing.

Marco heard the unfamiliar voice through their entry system and ran to the door. His mother looked at him as she opened the door to greet Rupert. She wore her hair pulled back and away from her face, barely any different than she'd worn it the last time he'd seen her. Marie's eyes were tired and it looked like she'd just gotten home from work.

When Rupert arrived at her door, she knew him immediately. His face hadn't changed much but his hair had grown and there was now grey in it. They'd both changed, mostly in ways that didn't show on their faces. Time and circumstances had given some age to their appearance, hers more than his. She'd been busy working and raising two boys while he had the easy life of being single with no kids. That's how she saw it.

"Who's this?" Marco asked sticking his chest out and trying to make his voice sound deeper.

"I'm Rupert Charms. Your father and I went to school together. Sandro and I were actually roommates and good friends. You wouldn't remember me though, you were only knee high the last time I saw you."

"You knew my dad?" Marco asked curiously, as he took a step back to let Rupert in the door. His knee still ached but he was now safe.

"I did. Good man," Rupert said eyeing Teresa for her reaction.

He never knew what she thought about Sandro's vanishing. She didn't know if he'd left them, been killed, or something else. She never got answers from anyone. Instead, she was left to her own overly active imagination. That imagination had gone through every scenario from him running away to the southern tip of Southern Allegiance with another woman, to him being kidnapped and tortured, to him being killed and dumped in the ocean.

If she ever found him alive, he'd better hope he'd been through hell already because otherwise she'd send him straight there.

"Do you mind if I use your restroom? The ride over here was long," Rupert asked. Teresa pointed him down the hall to the restroom and watched him, her eyes unwavering until he was in, door closed.

"I don't know why he's here. Fifteen years and suddenly he wants to see us?" She rubbed the back of her hand over her head.

"Us? He said he wanted to see me too?"

"Sí. You too." Teresa sat down on the chaise by the window.

The window was open, showing a screen in need of cleaning, but it served the purpose of keeping the bugs out. It was almost too warm outside already but she liked to wait as long as possible to close up the house for the artificial cooling. It cost money that could be used for Marco's school when he finally went to university.

Marco looked at his mother. He wanted to know who this Rupert was and decided it would be easy enough to find out. Within seconds he found an old profile of him. Same man but the picture must have been from at least ten years before. He was a scientist and data analyst and the profile said he was in Antarctica at the time. Antarctica.

There was only one real reason for scientists to work in Antarctica. Marco stood, his back against the wall as he waited for Rupert to come out. He had an idea what this might be about and wondered if Stephen and Stella had put him up to it.

"Why do you have that silly look on your face?" Teresa asked Marco just as Rupert came out of the restroom. He was walking with less of a limp now and his leg was already feeling better.

"Do you know Stephen and Stella?" Marco asked once Rupert was almost back to the living room.

"Yes. I've known them pretty much all their lives," Rupert answered with a smile. *This is a smart kid. I like him already,* he said to himself.

"What is this about? Who are Stephen and Stella?" Teresa asked walking over to where Marco had stopped Rupert in the hall.

"Nothing, Mom. Rupert works on the ARC and knows one of my classmates who lives there half the year. It's a small world, that's all. Hey, can I show you something?" Marco asked. He grabbed Rupert's shirtsleeve and pulled him away from his mother's view before Rupert could answer or Teresa could protest.

From down the hall she heard them whispering, Rupert talking more than Marco, both barely audible. After several seconds of trying unsuccessfully to eavesdrop, she decided she would just go and ask what this was about - as was her right. *Her son. Her house. Her business.* She marched down the hall towards the two men. The moment they saw her Rupert stopped talking. He smiled and began walking towards Teresa.

"Teresa, I know it hasn't been easy, but you seem to be doing a fine job with them. How's your oldest boy Locan? Is he still flying?" Rupert asked trying to shift her attention away from his business with Marco.

"He's still flying for both the World Consensus military and private charter but he never visits me. What is going on here?" she asked waving her hand back and forth between Rupert and Marco.

"Oh, he just wanted to talk to me. I guess he doesn't meet many people who actually knew his father," Rupert answered with a genuine smile on his face. Teresa pursed her lips together and let her eyes go back and forth between Rupert and Marco, before walking off into the living room.

Marco didn't meet many people who knew his father. Besides giving him the data and instructions for what needed to happen, Marco had taken the rare chance to ask about the man he barely remembered. Was he alive? The only thing Rupert could say was that they'd never had any confirmation otherwise.

When Rupert finally left the house, Marco contacted Locan and told him what happened. He'd met someone who personally knew his father and who was willing to say something about him. He also let Locan know that Rupert needed his help - a flight to his island.

CHAPTER THIRTY-FIVE
Open

Santoria, Southern Allegiance

MARCO WATCHED RUPERT walk out of the door and followed him with his eyes as he headed down the sidewalk. He looked worried. Marco felt his pocket for the small microdot that had wedged itself into the corner. He would have to take his pants off and turn the pockets inside out to get it.

"What was that about?" Teresa said sitting down on the sofa that had seen better days. The seams frayed on the arms, where her sons had spent too many hours sitting even after she'd told them not to. The once vibrant red was now faded and the wooden feet and trim were scratched and banged. She cocked her head to the side waiting for Marco to answer this time with more than 'nothing'.

"It wasn't' anything you need to worry about. He told me some things about dad, I never knew. I didn't know how high ranking he was, Mom, in Southern Allegiance's COPS program. Teresa shook her head and stood up. She'd never talked much about Sandro's life to Marco after he'd disappeared. It was pointless then and still was.

"Was that it?"

"No. He needed my help and Locan's with a flight. I guess since he was asking for a flight he felt he could at least tell me something about my dad. No one else seems to want to,"

Marco added for effect. He needed his mother to stop asking questions and bringing up his dad usually worked.

"Fine. Dinner's in the kitchen. I'm not feeling up to eating right now, so go ahead and eat if you're hungry. I'm going to go lie down." Teresa took the apron off and hung it on the kitchen door before sauntering to her bedroom, her body looking tired.

Marco felt guilty. It wasn't her fault that things were like they were. Either his father had been killed or he'd abandoned them. Marco preferred to think he'd been killed in action to the alternative. After his conversation with Rupert, his visions of his dad's death were no longer as a regular officer or agent but as someone who had more rank and power. He had new questions, *"Did he die? If he did, how? And why did no one ever found his body?"*

Marco made a plate of rice, beans, and grabbed a protein packet. He picked at it half-heartedly as he considered what Rupert had told him about Sandro, and what Rupert had asked him to do with the data he'd given him. There wasn't much he could do with the information about his dad, but he could do something with the microdot.

Marco scraped the rest of the food into a small container and put it in the refrigerator. If Teresa came out and saw it in the trash, she'd ring his ear. He pulled out a slice of pizza wrapped up in a paper towel and left the kitchen.

The stairs to his loft bedroom seemed to creak more than usual. He attempted to move quietly and not disturb his mother as she escaped to her room. She had to have heard him, but wasn't calling out. *Perhaps she'd had enough of him tonight.*

He closed his bedroom door and pulled his pants off. He turned the pocket inside out and pushed the small microdot out of where it was lodged. He needed to know what was on it as much as Rupert needed him to get it out to those it could help.

He pulled his wooden chair over to the matching desk and slid his reader out from behind his keyboard. He put the microdot in and waited for whatever was on it to come up. A single file appeared that read 'To Send'. Marco touched it and it opened two documents.

The first one read 'Science Report' and the second 'Science Data'. He touched the file and a ten page report appeared in front of him. As he scrolled through the pages reading the headings, his breathing changed. Summary, History, Current Issues, Future Issues, Possible Solutions, Actions Taken, Cover Ups.

He jumped back up to read the section on current issues and saw that the earthquakes in Southern Allegiance were just an example of what was happening in all the areas with tectonic plates. The future issues section didn't look better. Things would only get worse at the rate they were going.

He needed to know if there was information being withheld from the citizens in Southern Allegiance. He skipped to the end of the report to read the section on cover-ups. Marco read about the restrictions placed on every person who had any legal information of the issue. The non-disclosure agreements were meant to be enforced. Anyone with information had been reminded of this and threatened with treatment as traitors and criminals if they violated the agreements.

He thought about what he and Alexis had gathered and wasn't surprised. What he'd done with Alexis was minor compared to this. This was more than just his region. It dealt with all the regions from the World Consensus level. UniCorps and the World Consensus had no intention of telling the truth. He wondered what their end game was, if they were willing to risk millions of lives to avoid the costs of relocating people. He felt the knot form in his stomach as the feeling crept in that he was missing something important.

***

RUPERT PLANNED TO spend a few days on the mainland before heading home. Unfortunately, Teresa said it might be a week before Locan could make a special trip home, but she would still ask. It would give her an excuse to get her son home, even if it was just for a few hours.

A week was longer than he'd planned. He had to get his affairs in order back home and this whole break was only scheduled to last four weeks. At this point, he had no other way back that didn't leave him traceable. He'd intentionally made the request midflight to get off on the mainland in the hopes that no one had updated the passenger list.

Unfortunately, he wouldn't know for sure unless someone called to check on him and ask why he hadn't gotten off at his scheduled stop. He given his excuse and would use it again if necessary. He preferred not to use it again and hazard leaving a longer trail.

Rupert checked into a small hotel that accepted lubles as payment. It was one of the few around, located at the edge of Marco's town, where dust swirled in the Spring air, carrying with it pollen and bugs. The paint peeled from where it tried to cling over stacked stones. The windows looked as if they hadn't been replaced in more than fifty years, and the smell of dampness wafted through the air and into his nostrils, causing him to sneeze.

The worn carpet under his boots was stained and ragged around the edges from having more than its fair share of weary travelers. When he'd stayed in this hotel fifteen years before it was nice and comfortable, but time and circumstance had taken its toll on this old place too. He'd been in worse places and his stay here would only be a few days. He was grateful it was even an option.

Rupert hoped that Marco was as good as he thought he might be, based on the communications he'd found. Rupert had carefully and thoroughly scrubbed those same communications off the system before leaving the ARC. No one else needed to be sullied by seeing them, not even Zura, Johan, and Mave. If all the hands were dirty, there would be no one left to clean them.

Tomorrow he would get food, water, and a few other supplies. When he got back home, he would take care of his business there and prepare to leave again. He looked in the mirror as it warped his image, making his face stretch long and accentuating his nose.

He had to do this. There was no choice. Everyone has their moment. Mave would understand - she had to. There were some things he could try to make right. There were some things that all the trying in the world wouldn't change. He knew the difference. Looking at the reflection of his face, he accepted that this was something he could try to make right, despite the costs.

He couldn't control the dual powers of the World Consensus and UniCorps. They had chosen not to act, and by their inaction, they had forced his hand. He would not have blood like that on his hands. He'd done enough in his life he had to make amends for already.

The data was in Marco's hands now, and he had to trust him. It was all he could do and now Marco had to get the information out and warn the people of Southern Allegiance. He'd made Marco promise not to send it until he was back on the island and not to mention it to Stephen.

"The less any one person knows about what is happening, the better." It was what Rupert told Marco before leaving. He believed more people would be kept safe that way.

Besides, Rupert was confident that when Stephen made it home he would be busy with investigating the ARC. He hoped Stephen would find whatever he was looking for. Stephen was also doing predictive modeling of the earthquakes, which might not help for the one coming to Southern Liberty, but Southern Liberty was just the beginning. The data was clear on that.

Rupert waited a couple of days before trying to call Mave. As the call tried to connect, he thought about her reaction to what he'd said. He wouldn't take it back even if it made her uncomfortable. It was the truth. He did love her, but maybe she needed space or time to think.

The light on his watch blinked as it tried to connect unsuccessfully. He wondered if his phone function was still working since he'd talked to Marco the day before. He attempted the call to Mave once more, and again it didn't go through – this time the attempt to connect suddenly ended. He couldn't imagine she was sending his calls away, but he had no other explanation.

***

TWO DAYS BEFORE Rupert thought he'd be able to head home Marco called again. "Locan is on his way. He's coming a day early because there is danger coming, Rupert."

"I know. It's why I gave you the report, to get the warning out," Rupert responded.

"I think it's worse than you might think. I started looking at the data you gave me Rupert and comparing it with some that I got hold of from Southern Liberty. They don't match Rupert. What you gave me isn't all the data. It's like someone randomly plucked out maybe ten to fifteen percent of the activity in the fault lines and took it out of your data set. So what I have looks even worse than what you have," Marco said reluctantly.

Rupert looked at his watch. Even they at the ARC had been lied to. He wondered how much more data they were missing and just how serious the problem was.

"To make things worse, Rupert, based on what you show and what I show, I think we've got two fault lines, both active and converging. It wouldn't look so bad with just one fault line, but the second one isn't showing up in your data. I hadn't gone in really to look at the stuff I had until you sent your report. Honestly, it just wasn't that interesting until now."

"So something changed?" Rupert asked wondering what Marco knew.

"Yeah, between these two reports, we are looking at a major disaster on the northern coast and it looks like it could happen anytime within the next month. If I had to guess, I'd bet it's going to be as bad as or possibly worse than Southern Liberty. Rupert, you can't go back home. You need to stay here, inland, where it's safe." The sound of concern was sincere in Marco's voice as he waited for Rupert to respond.

Rupert was silent for a moment. Staying in Santoria was dangerous in other ways, given he was presumed to be home and the air transport would expect to pick him up there. If there were no earthquake he would have no excuse for not being there. If there were an earthquake, he'd be trapped on his small island home with little chance of survival without evacuation. He already knew there were no plans for warnings or evacuations.

"Are you there?" Marco asked into the silence on the other end.

"Yes, Marco. I'm here. I'm just thinking. Neither leaving nor staying is favorable at this time. Did you already send out the report?"

"No, you said to wait until you were gone. I figured I'd check with you since you may not be going. Do you still want me to wait to send it out? The longer we wait, the less chance our folks here have to save themselves. The danger in the Rift Valley seems on part with what's happening right here. From the data we both have, it's likely to wrap right around to your home in Trinabago. We have to do something, fast."

Rupert thought about his little island. At one time the risk was considered low or very moderate but since they'd put pumps in the northeastern parts of Southern Allegiance the whole area was experiencing more activity. More activity than had been reported to him and the others on the ARC.

Rupert was a scientist and could see the data, but he reasoned that anyone who was paying any attention had to know that the tremors and minor earthquakes weren't normal and the excuses and rationale given to the public weren't realistic. Now they had more information that put the region at risk and no one was telling anyone anything.

At that very moment, they were evacuating the Rift Valley, and though no full reports of how it was going left Southern Liberty, he was pretty confident it wasn't going well. The same could happen in his home but this time there was information – facts and data – that could be used to convince people to get out of the danger zones.

"Send it Marco. We do what we must," Rupert said and clicked off the call.

The tremors and small earthquakes were the rumblings of a giant slowly waking, with its moaning, groaning, and stretching. They needed to know that over the centuries, they had managed to awaken a sleeping giant.

Marco pulled the reports and data he'd gotten from Rupert together and then added what he and Alexis had taken from their local government's science division. He worked them both into a secure file and encrypted them before sending them the same way he and Stephen had sent files just a couple weeks before. It had to work. The subsystem was the only way to get the information out and he hoped someone was paying attention to it.

He would know soon enough if the message made it into the right hands. He and Alexis didn't think they would get to use the information they'd taken so soon, but now he didn't feel guilty at all for hacking into the system to find out the truth.

CHAPTER THIRTY-SIX
Shift

Santoria, Southern Allegiance

MARCO WAS STARTLED by the sound of buzzing by his head. It was Alexis. He wasn't expecting any calls to come through.

"Hello?" Marco said anxiously.

"Marco! Are you okay? Where've you been? I've called you three times? I heard what happened. Are you and your mom alright? Where are you?" Alexis asked without taking a breath.

Slow down, Alexis. This is the first of your calls that has come through. We've been pretty much in the dark here. But I'm alright."

"How are you so calm? Haven't you heard? There was an earthquake on the coast. It's about a hundred miles from you. Didn't you feel the aftershocks?"

"Yes, I know about it. This one wasn't nearly as bad as we thought it might be. I'll save my panicking for when I really need it. My mom was called out to help. She left a couple of hours ago. I've felt a few aftershocks but nothing major." Marco moved away from where he peered out the windows.

It wasn't long after the earthquake hit early in the morning that Teresa had gotten a call on her emergency communication device. There was a shortage of emergency aid workers and medical providers in Valencia Major and anyone who could go was requested to come. She'd woken him up to tell him she was leaving and wouldn't listen to his attempts to make her stay.

Now, with the sun well over the tree line it looked like an ordinary day outside. He sat down at his desk to turn on his system. He didn't want the regular news. He wanted the reports coming through the subsystem.

"How bad did they say it was? We didn't have much news here about it. They told my mom it was around a 5 or 5.5," Marco spoke into his watch.

"The news is saying it was a 6.0 but no one is seeing anything. They said the earthquake knocked certain data feeds out, so there are no pictures or video - only voice. I think that's a little suspicious. Don't you?" Alexis asked skeptically.

"Yeah - very, but wait. What I'm reading now says it was a 7.7 on the Richter Scale but the news is saying it was a 6.0? And they told my mom it might be just a 5? " Marco questioned, trying to wrap his mind around the thought that they'd flat out lied about how severe the earthquake had been.

"Can you reach Stephen and Stella?" Marco asked. He'd been trying but the calls would not connect. "How'd you get through to me?" Marco asked curiously, since she was back home in Australia and not at her dad's.

"Cloning and masking and a few other tricks up my sleeve, but most people can't get through. My dad says its only voice within Southern Allegiance. Since he deals with people from across the region so he would know."

Marco scratched his head and rubbed his eyes as the reality of what happened began to settle in. He'd sent the information out just three days before. There was no way for most people to move out of danger that quick, even if they listened to the report and believed it.

Marco sat in his old wooden chair, careful not to rub his hands along the sides. He didn't need splinters. He wanted to see what had happened and he needed to know how bad it was.

He tried to pull up the reports from the subsystem, but it was painfully slow. Users not able to access the regular network had overloaded the old system and the only data that could come through was text. Videos and images weren't available. Marco was getting the feeling that someone was making sure no one saw images of the truth.

He didn't need to see much more than what he saw in front of him, typed up under the heading, 'Truth about S.A. Earthquake'.

TRANSMITTED REPORT START

Today at 7:26 a.m. Eastern Allegiance Time (EAT), an earthquake hit along the northern coast of Southern Allegiance. The earthquake, reported to measure at a between a 5.7 and 6.0 on the Richter Scale was measured by our local scientists at between a 7.6 and a 7.8.

Loss of Life: At this time, actual numbers of lives lost are not available. The area affected is highly populated by regional citizens and many visitors from other regions. It is estimated that at the time of the earthquake there were seven hundred and fifty million to one billion people in the metropolitan area of Valencia Major. Based on the reports of missing persons, devastation, building collapses, and the collapses of roads and bridges we expect that the number of lives lost may number as many as a half of the people in the region.

There was no public warning of the earthquake though data surfaced a few days ago of information that an earthquake was imminent.

The source stated that warnings could have been given weeks to months prior to the incident.

No photos or video feeds can be sent at this time. Once those capabilities are restored, images will be available.

**Next Update Scheduled for 12:30 P.M. EAT
TRANSMITTED REPORT END**

CHAPTER THIRTY-SEVEN
Giants

The Capital City, Northern Liberty Region

GREGOR MAGIRO ADJUSTED his shirt and tucked it into the back of his waistband. The sun was beginning to set and he'd already missed dinner with his wife, again. They'd been going around in circles like they were windmills being blown by multiple storms. Presently, that storm came in the form of the towering figure of the man who appeared to be crossed with a titan, The Stache.

Magiro counted eight times in less than two weeks that The Stache had been by to see either him or Silver. He'd come to Magiro's office clopping his big black boots and casting shadows over everything within six feet of him, as he stood menacingly in the door way. Magiro could only step back out of the darkness and let The Stache in for another one of his unrelenting debates about the merits of UniCorps's position.

Each time he'd come, it was with the same argument. The same one that Mylar had made on the ARC just weeks before and the one Magiro and Silver had yet to give them the satisfaction of their full agreement on. They were feeling threatened -threatened by Magiro and Silver's noncompliance. Threatened by the possibility that the two troublemakers might convince others to share the information that was still legally considered confidential.

Magiro looked at The Stache, with his dodgy eyes in a murky shade of brown, and knew he and Silver weren't the only ones he'd been visiting. The Stache had been up and down the tower and across the halls, visiting every major Representative so he could pressure them into staying silent and not allowing the bill Silver and Magiro had sponsored on environmental reporting transparency to go through.

Magiro was fairly certain any conversation also included a clear reminder of the costs of desertion, which in their world meant not going with the program that UniCorps designed. What he didn't know was how successful The Stache had been. Nearly all of the Representatives had fallen in line, not wanting to jeopardize their future political careers and the guaranteed lifestyle once their years of public service were over.

However, Magiro and Silver had promised each other that neither would agree to anything The Stache asked, no matter how tempting. They now had the information they previously needed and burying it was no longer an option either of them could consider.

Magiro sat down at the end of his oval table, his back towards the large window. The Stache stood with his fists leaning on the table. Magiro rested his elbows on his side, attempting to counteract the weight as he thought The Stache's sheer size might tip it before he stood back up.

"Do you know who I work for, Gregor Magiro? I mean who I really work for?" The Stache's expression changed from the menacing bully. Magiro got the sense that his tough guy act was just that, an act, but one he'd mastered well.

"You work for UniCorps and probably always will," Magiro said, folding his arms over his chest and leaning back.

The shimmery fabric of his special Representative uniform caught in the falling sun. He didn't want to be here. As he looked at the mountain of a man in front of him, he could see that neither of them did. The Stache wasn't any freer than he was; he'd just gotten a higher fee for his freedom.

"You know you can't beat them. No one can. They have lasted as long as they have because they will defend their position at all costs. I sat down with your friend Silver today and I told her the same thing. You two are okay and I know you mean well, but you are roaches getting in the way of a steamroller. You can't win."

"Who knows? Roaches are pretty tough to kill. Trust me, we tried," Magiro said back to Mirkal in an easy conversational tone.

This was something new, a different angle from The Stache. He actually seemed concerned for them, but Magiro had known him long enough to know that he'd say just about anything to get what he wanted and right now he wanted Magiro's agreement to pull in Silver. He wanted to know neither of them would talk, and more importantly, that they'd pull their proposed bill off the table to ensure it never received any press and that the public never heard of it.

Magiro looked at the time and stood up, putting himself back into the shadow The Stache cast. It was late, it was Friday, and the last day before the two week break.

"I have plans for the break and I hope you do too. I know why you are here. I know why you've been here nearly every workday for the past two weeks. I can't give you what you want, Mirkal. I can't tell you what you want to hear. Let me show you out because right now I'm going home to enjoy my family."

Magiro walked past The Stache and opened the door. "Have a good break, Mirkal." Magiro handed him the tablet he'd placed on the table by the door.

"You can't go against UniCorps; not if you're expecting to win. They're like Goliath and you're like David, only without the rock," The Stache said filling the doorframe.

Magiro wondered what had been set into motion. He could feel the rumblings everywhere he turned. The attention of the two-headed Goliath had been peaked. The planet, with the problems that had been pushed beneath the surface, was now finally stirring itself awake, uncomfortable in the mess in which it slumbered.

"I've known you a long time, Magiro. You get in their way and they will crush you. I wouldn't want anything to happen to you or your friend Silver."

With those last words echoing in Magiro's ear, Mirkal 'The Stache' Dempstead walked out of Magiro's office, taking his shadow with him.

As the dark mass vanished down the hall, Magiro felt his wrist buzzing. He considered that he shouldn't be hearing from anyone now. It was time for vacation. He looked at the number, which showed Preston Rochester Davenport II. He didn't want to answer this call but not answering would mean even more trouble.

"Magiro speaking," he said after taking a deep breath.

"Magiro, this is Preston. Preston Davenport."

"Yes, sir. Of course. What can I do for you this evening? I was just heading out for the break."

"I'm sure. It's why I wanted to catch you before you left. I wanted to make sure we were going to have a smooth break and wouldn't have any surprises. You understand?"

"No, I'm not sure I understand that there would be any surprises."

"Gregor Magiro, I'm certain I don't need to explain myself. You are a smart man and you've been in this position a long time. I'm sure you value that privilege of being able to serve. Am I right?"

Magiro pressed his lips together for a moment as he looked around his office. The sun had faded in the time he'd spent with Mirkal and the skyline now showed. It was nothing like the pictures he'd remembered seeing in his history studies. He could see the lights from the UniCorps Headquarters tower.

They weren't leaving for the break and he was certain it was where Preston was calling from, with a room full of people.

"Look, Preston. I know what you are saying. I've gotta get going. I have people waiting on me. Perhaps we can talk after the break?"

"I don't think you understand Magiro. I need to know that you understand. I need to be sure that we won't have any trouble from you," Preston said, his voice becoming more somber. The threatening tone was now unmistakable.

Magiro thought of his wife at home, waiting for him and the security he'd personally hired for both inside and outside.

"I plan on having a nice quiet break with family and friends. You don't have to worry about me working over it, if that's what you are asking, Preston. I am taking a vacation," Magiro replied, giving Preston as much as he could and nothing more.

CHAPTER THIRTY-EIGHT
Lies

Santoria and Valencia Major, Southern Allegiance

MARCO PICKED AT the leftovers from the night before. His mother had to be almost to the coast by now. Shortly after Marco had learned of the earthquake, she was in the hovehicle Sandro had bought her when they'd learned they were expecting Marco.

She was going right into the hot zone. Even before trying to convince her not to go, he knew it was pointless. She wasn't going to stay put if there were people who needed help. It wasn't her way and wasn't how she'd raised her sons. She had to go.

Marco connected to the subsystem again. He saw the red blinking indicator for his chats. Stephen had sent him a message.

"Marco – are you okay?"

Marco typed back, "Yes, the quake was near the coast. We just have a few aftershocks. What are you hearing about it?" He wasn't sure Stephen was still on, but after a minute the words appeared on his screen.

"There is almost nothing being officially reported Marco. What I have found says it was not too bad. A 6.0. But, our reporting equipment here shows something different. I show it was about a 7.7. I checked repeatedly and even had my dad check too."

"The reports coming through the sub-system said the same as you. Do you show any other earthquakes around here that I need to watch out for?"

"You are in a pretty safe location. Keep inland, away from the west and north coasts. You should only have aftershocks. Our reports show the aftershocks near the coast are still in the five to six range."

Marco swallowed hard. His mother was nearly there.

"My mom is headed to the coast. I have to go Stephen."

"Get her out of there. I've got a bad feeling, Marco!" the message read. "Can you call her?"

Marco looked at it. "Stephen?"

"No. It's Stella. Just trust me. You need to warn her and get her out of there."

Valencia Major had become one of the largest coastal cities in the northern area of Southern Allegiance. The metropolitan area had swelled to more than seven hundred million people and in the medium cities and smaller towns that bordered Valencia Major to the west, south, and east, were another two hundred million within fifty miles.

The idea of her driving in or out alone in her old hovehicle made Marco cringe. She'd been a nurse for nineteen years and an aid worker for seven years before that. If she were called to serve, she would never say no. She wasn't going to come back just because he asked. She'd have to pretty much be carried out.

"Thanks Stella. I gotta go guys."

Marco clicked off the chat with the twins and sent a message to Locan. Calls still weren't going through to anyone outside of Southern Allegiance and Marco wasn't sure if Locan had made it to their home region yet.

An aftershock of a five or six on the Richter scale could kill his mother if she got trapped in the city or even nearby. Marco rubbed his forehead, sending his dark hair back over the top of his head. Locan needed to find her and bring her back. After their mother was safe, then he could get Rupert. There was no way Teresa knew how bad it really was and what she was driving into.

"Locan? Emergency here."

Moments later Locan responded.

"On way. Fast as I can. Had to check in with border agents. Be to Santoria in less than an hour."

"Mom is headed to Valencia Major. She'll be in the area in the next hour. Once you are officially in our air space can you pull up her registration and location and go get her?"

"Yes. It'll mean cutting it close for Rupert," Locan responded. "Never mind. He can't go there anyways."

Marco looked at his watch. 12:31 p.m. "Locan keep me updated with when you get mom."

"Definitely."

Marco's watch buzzed with an incoming call from Alexis again.

"Did you see the last report?" she asked hurriedly.

"No. I was on with my brother. I'm pulling it up now."

"It's bad, Marco. I talked to Mr. Pritchard too. He called me this morning. I guess there was something that is supposed to happen. Some ceremony with us and he says it's important that it happens next month. They can't delay it anymore," Alexis reported to him.

"I don't know if I can think about that now Alexis. I've got more important things to deal with," Marco said as he searched for the newest update.

"Do you have the latest report pulled up yet?" she asked again impatiently.

"You forget I don't have the same fancy systems as you. Yes. Got it. Give me a minute to read it."

TRANSMITTED REPORT START

The earthquake that hit the northern coast of Southern Allegiance today at 7:26 a.m. EAT is confirmed to have been a 7.7 on the Richter Scale and not the 6.0 officially reported. Aid workers have been called in from everywhere within a four hour commute with workers assigned to the areas of worst devastation.

Loss of Life: Nearly seven hours after the earthquake there remain no official numbers of lives lost or numbers of persons missing. There remain no official reports of any kind regarding this earthquake. We do have unofficial local reports that, aggregated, put the current estimate of missing people or those killed in the earthquake at 350 million. This is a conservative estimate given the number of people en route or already at work in this heavy tourist area.

Again, there was no public warning of the earthquake though data surfaced three days ago that the information warning of an imminent earthquake was available weeks to months prior to the incident.

We expect that our ability to transmit photos and video will continue to be hampered, just as the truth has been.

###

Next Update Scheduled for 4:30 P.M. EAT
TRANSMITTED REPORT END

MARCO'S FIST MET the top of his desk, causing a small cup of microdots to fall off and splatter on the floor.

"You still there, Marco?" Alexis's voice broke through the cloudiness. He'd forgotten all about her."

"Yes, still here," he said, nearly speechless.

"I told you it was bad. What are we gonna do?"

"We're gonna do whatever we have to for the truth to get out. They won't get away with this, Alexis."

***

LOCAN HAD LOCKED in on Teresa and was just twenty minutes from where her communicator showed her. She was almost in the city of Valencia Major. His charter aircraft began to fly over the area affected by the earthquake. It didn't look like any 6.0 he'd ever seen. He radioed in to the checkpoint where he'd entered.

"Eastern Border Control- Southern Allegiance," the man said into the radio.

"Yes, this is Captain Locan. I am heading into Valencia Major. I need to report that the damage appears worse than the 6.0 reported. Perhaps I can help. Where is air support currently? I can work a different area. Land support may have been called but there is no way anyone is driving in and a normal hovehicle would have a hard time clearing this much debris."

Locan looked out of his window at the scene below. He'd been trained for combat and peace keeping but this would require something else. There was no way that nurses, medics, and doctors on the ground would reach the people in need.

"Copy?" he called into the radio after several seconds without a response.

"Captain Locan?" a different voice came in. "I was told that you were heading to Santoria. Is there a reason you are headed to Valencia Major instead?" the voice asked.

"Sir, my mother is there. I have to get her before heading home."

"I see. I advise that you hurry and do only that. That is an order. We have everything under control. Air support will also be dispatched. Carry on with your immediate business and head to Santoria. I'll expect you to check in upon your arrival. Over."

"Over," Locan answered back after hesitating a moment.

He looked down to the streets and ruined buildings, with smoke still coming out of the windows. Small fires still burned in some. Between the standing buildings, there were others crumbled in heaps and others with sides lost. He could see people waving scarves and sheets out of the windows.

Air support will be dispatched? It had been more than six and a half hours since the earthquake and no air support was on the scene. They'd called in the local support of people who would come in regular hovehicles, knowing they would never get through the debris.

"Marco? Marco?" The interference in the call was worse than usual.

"Locan? Where are you?" Marco answered choppily.

"Almost in Valencia Major. Mom is here. I need you do to do something. Check for a local airfield. I need a light hover aircraft."

"What? I thought you were getting mom and coming back!" Marco said surprised.

"I am, but they haven't dispatched any air support, Marco. None. I'm not coming all the way here and doing nothing."

"Okay. Let me search. Hold on." Marco went back to his system and began searching for airfields where pilots could land

and that had the aircraft Locan needed. The light hover aircraft was named accordingly because it could hover as low as fifteen feet above ground and as high as fifty feet above ground but could also land in place like the hovering plane Locan usually flew.

"Locan, there is a field twenty miles east of Valencia Major City. It's called Valencia Eastport."

Locan entered it into his navigation and studied the route in detail before turning his aircraft east. Looking at the devastation, his mother would never forgive him if he just came in without trying to help. It would be nearly impossible in the craft he was flying, given its bulk and inability to hover at low levels for more than a few seconds. He sped up and flew off. There had to be another option and he hoped it was where he was headed.

***

TERESA'S HOVEHICLE CAME to a standstill amidst a sea of rubble dotted with broken down and crushed hovehicles. She took a deep breath at the sight of the bodies strewn in odd places, trapped by large cement blocks or pinned under the fallen debris. The buildings in the distance, hotels, businesses, and the casinos were crumbled, some lay waste along the road in front of the coast.

There was no way she could reach the place she was supposed to be meeting the other aid workers, not by car at least. Looking at what remained of the city she wasn't sure the meeting place would be standing or stable. She would have to go by foot.

As she looked around at the damage, far beyond any description she'd gotten; she was startled by the face of a child whose bloodied hand slapped against her window. The girl looked to be ten or eleven despite her height. Debris was in her hair and drops of blood ran down her face. Dirt and dust covered her as she stared through the window, a look on her face that Teresa quickly recognized as shock.

Teresa tried to open the door but the girl didn't move. She tried again but the girl simply stood there staring blankly into the hovehicle at Teresa. Teresa couldn't get the girl to respond in her current state and she had to get out of the car to help her. She climbed into the backseat, snagging her leg on the grey faded and torn fabric of her rear seats before opening the back door.

The girl followed with her eyes, without any other expression, to watch Teresa as she crawled out the back seat into a pile of loose detritus blocking the street.

"It's okay. It's okay. Te voy a ayudar. I'm gonna help you," Teresa said to the girl whose eyes glazed over. She fell to the ground, from where she'd been standing on her knees, the rest of her legs missing somewhere in the crumbling city.

CHAPTER THIRTY-NINE
Sorrow

MASTER KEANE BOWED his head and placed one thin hand over his darkened eyes. A single tear escaped, finding freedom from the pain.

Your Review Is Appreciated

I hope you enjoyed reading **Chosen: A Paranormal, Sci-Fi, Dystopian Novel.**

Would you **please leave a brief review** to help others find it? Word of mouth is one of the best ways for an author's works to be discovered and it won't take but a minute. Here's the link: **www.Amazon.com/db/B01H7TAQXW**

Thank you so much and I hope you enjoy my other works. A sample of book 2 in the Chosen series follows.

PREVIEW OF BOOK 2 - AWAKEN
Chapter One
Valencia Major

THE SMALL HOVERING plane circled the debris looking for a place to come in low enough. Locan could see his mother's hovehicle at the edge of the rubble. She was crouched down against the car, a child in her arms. The trunk was open and her red medical bag lay on top of a cement block.

He would have to try to hover over one of the larger box-truck hovehicles now turned on its side and hope the natural magnetic pull from the earth would be enough. He brought the small craft down and let it rest all the way. He planned to get his mother and then search for other survivors.

Locan crawled down the side of the truck by the passenger side door and looked in the open back. He thought he'd seen it from the air but now he was sure. A ladder was thrown against the side, beaten up but it would work. He placed it against the side of the truck he'd come out of and then ran over the broken buildings to where his mother sat just twenty yards away.

"Locan! Over here! Get her to the plane. I have to go help others, but I couldn't leave her," Teresa said as she loosened her hold on the panicked girl. Her legs were bandaged at the knee but she needed a hospital.

"Mom, you have to come with me. I'll go find anyone else I can but you have to get on the plane. You stay with her." Locan tried to order his mother but she just steeled her eyes.

"Locan, what did I just say?"

"Mom, I know what I'm doing, too. I'll find them and bring them back for you to help, how about that?"

Teresa looked at Locan. He was stronger and younger than she was. It was only more efficient and logical that he use that strength to bring them back where she could treat them.

"Fine. Hurry. They haven't had any help. No one can get in except on foot. Many of the aid workers who came didn't stay. The few who have can't get out. We have to help them, Locan. When is the rest of the help coming?" she looked up to him and asked as he took the girl with thick white bandages on her knees. She was weak, in and out of consciousness.

"They said they were sending air support. I don't know when. I'm here because Marco told me you came here and we have to bring you home."

"Home is no place to be when there is this much work to do, Locan, you know that," she said standing to her feet, grabbing her supplies, and following him to the turned truck and his plane.

Once he had the little girl settled into the plane, he left again. His little plane couldn't do much justice out there. At most, it could hold thirty people. Two hours passed as he brought injured men, women, and children to the plane. His body was fatigued and Marie's supplies were running low along with space for any more passengers.

In the hours they'd been in Valencia Major, no other air support had come through.

Locan would have to get them somewhere safe and then come back for his own plane, stationed at the small airfield Marco had found for him.

His wrist was blinking again. This time it wasn't Eastern Border Control in Southern Allegiance. Marco was calling to check in again.

"Hey, Marco," Locan answered out of breath.

"Are you two okay, man? When are you and mom heading back?" Marco asked. He could hear the sounds of pain in the background.

"We're about to pull out in a few minutes. I just have to make sure everyone is settled," Locan answered irritably.

"Did the other help come yet? How many did you get?"

"No. No one else came, Marco. Not a single craft of any kind. Nothing. I can only carry so many. They are back there like sardines, but I can't hold anymore and Border Control is on me to get to Santoria."

"Locan, you did everything you could. It's not your fault they let this happen," Marco said, steaming on his end. They let it happen and didn't bother to send any help that could actually be of help. They couldn't be allowed to get away with this.

"I'll see you when we get back home and then I have to come back up to Valencia Major to get my charter plane."

"Okay. I'll see you soon." Marco clicked off the call. He didn't know if he wanted to talk to Stephen or Alexis more. They were the only ones he trusted and that got what was going on. He sent Alexis a message through the subsystem and while waiting, he sent Stephen another about the nonexistent air support and rescue.

"They are leaving them to die. We have to make sure that next time there is real warning. They can't deny knowing. They can't act like they didn't have time." He hit send and sat back in his chair fuming.

Two messages popped up at nearly the same time on his screen. Stephen's was simple and to the point. "We need a better way to get this information out. Something much worse is happening in the Rift Valley than is being communicated."

Alexis's message came through in all caps. "THOSE MURDERERS!!!" she screamed into her system. "They won't get away with this. They can't bury everything. Marco, I'm so sorry. It's not fair. Those are our people they are just throwing away like nothing. I wish I was there right now. We're gonna do something about this, believe me."

"You better believe it," Marco wrote back to Alexis. He reread Stephen's message. The Rift Valley was next and he was certain they didn't know the real danger. They were evacuating Southern Liberty but from what he'd seen it was probably too late and they were sitting ducks as much as the people in Valencia Major had been, regardless of the evacuation.

"Stephen, can you put something together that shows what's happening in the Rift Valley? We can send it out through the subsystem and try to warn anyone who is paying attention to it."

"I can, but my mom is watching everything I do closely. She is afraid I will do something like this. If I pull it together, can you send it?" Stephen asked. He was already looking towards the door in case Zura came by as Stella stood over his shoulder.

"I'll send it. Or Alexis. Or maybe both of us. We'll make sure it goes out. They sent my mom on what amounts to a suicide mission after thinking it was okay to wipe out millions of us in Southern Allegiance. Bastards!" Marco typed angrily.

On the other end, Stephen read what he wrote. He wasn't sure what to say back. They were bastards. Stella's hands reached over him. 'I'm sorry Marco. We're gonna make this right," she typed and sent.

Stella looked at her brother. "We have to do what we have to do Stephen. There isn't a choice and it doesn't matter if we are fifteen or sixteen. At least not to me. We know something worse than the people are expecting is about to happen in the Rift Valley. That means maybe we can warn someone. We have to at least try," she said in a whisper in his ear.

OTHER WORKS BY A. BERNETTE

Chosen: A Paranormal, Sci-Fi, Dystopian Novel –
http://www.amazon.com/dp/**B01H7TAQXW**
Crossed: The Karma Crusades -
www.amazon.com/db/**B01DOAN7AW**

Awaken - Book 2 of the Chosen Trilogy (Coming
February/March 2017)
Origin – Book 3 of the Chosen Trilogy (Coming 2017)

ABOUT THE AUTHOR

Author A. Bernette is a multi-genre writer of paranormal-science fiction, fantasy, children's stories, poetry, and inspiration. She creates worlds that include diverse characters and ideas. In between writing, thinking about writing, and pondering life's big questions she is actively mothering two amazing kids and enjoying her wonderful husband. Bernette has lived in the metro Atlanta, Georgia area for more than twenty years and graduated from Georgia State University with her Bachelors in Business Management and her Masters in Public Administration. She is also a metaphysician, certified life coach, and energy healer. She doesn't believe in limiting or boxing in herself or others which is reflected in her writing and other work.

Stay Connected
Website: www.Bernette.net
Chosen Series: www.ChosenSeries.com
Facebook: www.Facebook.com/AuthorBernette
Chosen on Facebook: www.Facebook.com/ChosenBookSeries
Twitter: www.Twitter.com/AuthorBernette
Amazon: www.Amazon.com/Author/Bernette
On Goodreads and Wattpad as bernewrites

Made in the USA
Middletown, DE
20 July 2016